THE RECLAMATION

IVY ASHER

Edited by Polished Perfection

Cover by Rainy Day Artwork

For Sunny. You stepped up so I could live the dream, and I fucking love you so much for it. You still can't have a motorcycle though.

PROLOGUE

Warm metal touches my neck. I don't even have time to process that it's a blade before Loa slices across my throat with it.

Pain explodes across my neck, and then I can feel warmth gushing out of me. I try to gasp, but the sound is a sick gurgling that hammers home the reality of what just happened. I press my palms to my slit throat, terrified by how quickly they're covered in blood. I press at the wound and watch as Treno falls to his knees, his large hands clutching his own neck.

The realization that he's experiencing some fucked up echo of what I am flashes through my mind as I press at my wound and wonder how the fuck I'm going to survive this. I blink slowly, and it's as if the world around me has exploded. It's hard to focus, because my mind seems to only want to be aware of the fact that I'm bleeding to death. I feel like I'm moving underwater as I try to comprehend what's happening.

Panes and shards of shattered crystal come raining down from above me, and I fall to my knees, unsure if they are too weak to hold me up anymore or if the strong burst of wind in the room shoved me down. I feel pieces of things fall on me, but all I can really focus on is trying to press the escaping blood from my throat back into my body. I fumble for the skirt of my dress and shakily bring a wad of the fabric up to my throat and press it there.

I'm having trouble breathing, but I can tell some oxygen is getting into my lungs and brain because neither is screaming for air, or maybe my brain is no longer working right because of the blood.

A roar fills the air, but I can't focus on the rage and retribution billowing out and surrounding me. All I can focus on is clumsily pulling more of my dress up and pressing it as hard as I can against my neck. I taste blood in my mouth, and for some reason, it sparks a flash of panic. I try to rein it in, knowing instinctively that keeping my heart rate down is better right now, but it takes root despite my efforts to crush it down.

I don't want to die.

Black talons and skin drop down in my line of sight. They step closer to me, and I can just make out a black paw impossibly far behind the ebony forelegs of what has to be a gargantuan gryphon. I blink lazily, and my vision blurs. Something sniffs at me and nudges me gently, and I can feel strength draining out of my hands. A keening purr kind of a sound reaches out to me, and I want to go to it. More roars and crashes suddenly fill my ears as if someone just unmuted a battle scene in a movie.

I go weightless.

I know I'm dying. I can feel myself rising in the air, like my soul is finally leaving my body. I'm surrounded by warmth and surprisingly...pissed. I've never thought about what it would be like to die, but there's no loved one to greet me. No calm or peace for my soul to float on as I make my way wherever souls go. There's not even a light. There's just pain and guilt and sorrow. All I can think, over and over again, is that I'm sorry any of this happened.

I know my death will pull the others with me, and it feels horrible.

I'm jostled, and my hazy vision blinks out altogether. I grumble internally about how the road to the afterlife shouldn't have potholes. This shit should be gentle and easy; why does it hurt? Something wraps around me, and then the sensation of flying fills the last of my working senses. Peace finally trickles through me, but so does panic because this must be it.

I don't want to die!

Everything around me grows quiet, and in spite of the cool wind I feel caressing my body, I'm warm all over. A flash of Ryn, then Treno, and finally Zeph streaks by the last of my consciousness before I can feel it finally start to shut down. I whimper, and death squeezes me tighter.

"Don't worry, little sparrow, I have you," it growls deeply into my ear, and then everything...goes...black.

1

I'm floating, but not in a soothing, calm kind of way. I feel like I'm floating in a vat of pain. It burns, and the sensation is draining. I would feel like a popsicle being dipped into hellfire, except the burning is cold. Instead of a searing sensation, I feel like a million needles are all trying to stab me at once. I get the distinct impression that something's trying to settle in the cells of my skin, but for some reason it can't, and now it's angry and punishing me painfully for it.

I wait for the torture to ebb. For some reason, I know that it will, and that alone is keeping me from giving up and just saying fuck it. *Am I dead?* Because if I am, it sure does hurt, and it's noisy as hell too. I focus on the angry voices swimming around me and try to make sense of everything going on.

"Why did you bring him here?" a deep menacing voice snarls.

"I had no choice, he's her mate now too," the other, normally smooth voice bites back.

"And how did you let that happen?"

"How did I let that happen? How did *I* let that happen!"

Ryn roars. "I should rip you apart right now. How I ever listened to anything you had to say is beyond my understanding. You forced her to leave. You knew she wouldn't be safe, and you did it anyway! I didn't *let* this happen. You did!"

"Watch yourself. I am still your Syta!" Zeph barks.

The laugh that fills the void all around me sounds manic and angry. If every inch of me wasn't currently frostbitten and hurting, that laugh would give me the chills.

"My Syta? You're Syta of nothing. You were so busy looking for outside threats that neither one of us saw the one sitting right beneath our noses. We have no idea what damage my sister did to the Hidden. We don't have the slightest clue what she told Lazza, but if it was one word shy of everything, I'd be surprised. We have no chance against the Avowed now. They'll know the entirety of what we've been planning. Lazza will be ready for every move we ever thought to make."

"So we'll start over," Zeph states simply.

"Not with me, you won't," Ryn declares evenly.

"What does that mean? You'd walk away from everything we've worked for...for some female?" Zeph demands, his tone seething.

"Not for some female, for my mate. I listened to you and your poisonous thoughts about who she was and who she might be. I let your issues cloud the truth."

"And what truth is that?" Zeph bites back.

"That it doesn't matter who she is, was, or what she could be, she's mine. I'm not going to waste another breath pretending otherwise."

"She could be the solution to all of this. Are you saying you won't do what needs to be done if the time comes?"

"I'm saying it's more complicated than that," Ryn growls.

6

"We called, she answered. I'm not going to pretend it doesn't matter, that she doesn't matter."

I blink and suddenly, instead of blackness all around me, I can picture Ryn and Zeph perfectly. We're in some kind of cave. It's huge, and there's a massive fire in the middle of it. I can see the legs of a body on the far side of the fire, and my heart slams in my chest as Treno's name pounds in my head.

Zeph stands, his massive wings folded against his back, blood dripping steadily from a gash on his side. His honey eyes watch Ryn like he's still deciding if he wants to rip *him* apart. His demeanor doesn't shock me. The sky shadow pretty much always looks like that, but there's an undercurrent of defeat and rage that normally isn't there.

Ryn on the other hand looks downright terrifying. The normally easygoing and snarky gryphon wears a solid mask of betrayal and rage. I've never seen him look this pissed, and I just watched him find out that his sister sold him out. Not even *that* induced this level of anger. I can feel the phantom of a wall against my back, and I realize that I'm watching all of this from the deep shadows of whatever cave we're in.

I question for a moment if this is real. I shouldn't be up and spying given what just happened to me, but then I remember the weird dreams I've been having with Zeph. This feels like one of those. Just as that thought flickers through my mind, Zeph's honey gaze snaps to my shadow shrouded hiding place.

"She's here," he announces quietly, his tone vacillating between shock and confusion.

Ryn steps more into the light and follows Zeph's focused gaze. He looks like shit. Half his face is swollen, tight and shiny and mottled with black and purple bruises. He's bleeding from a cut on his head, and small rivers of blood break up the black and purple landscape of his face. His hair is matted and dirty, his clothes torn, tattered, and stained with red streaks and splotches. I can't tell if it's his blood or someone else's. It's probably a combination of both, but I'm completely shocked by the state he's in. How is he up and walking?

I notice he's holding one arm close to his chest as he looks from the shadows I'm standing in to Zeph. And he has a pink line across his throat like something scratched him there. I look over to Zeph to see the same mark on his neck.

"Who's here?" Ryn asks warily, like he's not sure he wants the answer.

"Our little sparrow."

Zeph's nickname for me drips off his full lips, and confusion flickers through Ryn's battered face. His head snaps to a place on the other side of the fire that I can't see.

"She's still out," he observes, his gray gaze moving back to Zeph and then once again to me in the corner where Zeph's still staring.

Can Ryn not see me?

I step out of the darkness, and Ryn's widening panic-filled eyes answer that question.

"What is going on?" he demands, looking from me to the other me that I'm assuming is lying on the other side of the fire. Terror floods Ryn's features, and he scrambles toward my body. "No no no no no no no," he chants. "She can't be dead. Falon, you are not allowed to die," he yells at me, and if his tone wasn't so heart-wrenching, it would be funny and irritating that even in death, he's trying to order me around.

A keening sound pours out of his throat, and I clutch at my chest. The sound feels like it's ripping me apart. I've never heard anything like it, and the lamentation sinks into my soul and settles there, promising to be something I never forget for the rest of my life.

"She's still breathing," he exclaims, shocked, his head snapping back up to where I'm standing, and he scrambles back over to where Zeph is still just watching me.

I can't decipher what the sky shadow's face and eyes are communicating.

"You're not dead...we're not dead?" Ryn announces, like somehow saying it out loud will help him wrap his brain around what's happening.

"So those dreams?" I ask Zeph, needing to confirm what I already suspect.

I'm here, and yet I'm not here at the same time.

"Not dreams, it seems," he answers, his demeanor still oddly calm.

"What happened?" I ask, trying to make sense of what's going on.

"You almost...died," Ryn replies, his tone devastated and confused.

"Treno?" I ask, my chest hurting. I move to go check on him where he's lying unmoving by the fire, but Zeph steps in my way.

"He's still breathing too," Ryn explains, stealing my attention back to him.

I'm confused, and everything feels muffled as I slowly try to make sense of what's happening.

"I think since he was the last to bond with you, the connection was stronger. When you were dying, you pulled at our force to help replenish yours," Ryn goes on, tapping his open palm to his chest. "Treno was more affected."

I move to sidestep Zeph, and once again he blocks my path. The bewilderment I'm swimming in becomes an afterthought as irritation prickles through me.

"What are you doing?" I demand as my eyes move up Zeph's massive body and settle on his honey-dipped gaze. He looks...unsettled. The unfamiliar look in his eyes swirls with the usual pissed off gleam that I find in his golden stare. I don't know what he's doing here. Fuck, I don't even know where here is or why I seem to be split in two right now. The things I saw and did with Zeph while I was in Kestrel City obviously weren't a dream, and I'm not sure what the hell to think about the sides of him I spied when he thought no one was looking.

"Keeping you from repeating your mistakes," Zeph states. His tone feels like a quiet earthquake, both threatening and making it hard to keep my footing.

His meaning crawls over me like the rays of a slowly rising sun, and I heat with rage. "Mistakes...repeat *my* mistakes?" I growl. "That's super funny coming from you...*mate*," I snarl at him, stepping into his space until we're chest to chest.

He doesn't move, and his eyes heat at the challenge in my tone and radiating out of every tense muscle in my body. I want to rip him apart. Eviscerate him for everything he's done and tried to hide from me.

"The only mistake I see around here is you, you arrogant piece of shit."

A growl crawls up Zeph's throat, but I'm done being intimidated by him. I'm done feeling sorry for him. I'm fucking done with it all.

"You mated an Avowed. Lazza's brother, of all the rutting marked filth!" he yells at me, like he still doesn't see the level of fucked up that he achieved by not telling me about our connection.

I shove at him, and satisfaction blooms in my chest when he has to drop a foot back to keep his balance. "You mated *me* and didn't even fucking tell me. You forced a bond between us and didn't even bother to explain what the fuck was happening."

"I didn't force you into anything," he snarls back. "You

cried my name and begged for more all on your own."

My entire world flashes red. My fist smashes into Zeph's cheek in less time than it takes to blink. Pain screams up my arm, but I don't care. I pounce on him like a rabid beast, ready to break every bone in my body if it means he hurts too. Zeph does nothing other than try to protect his face from my wild hits. Arms wrap around me from behind and pull me off of him. The noises slipping out of my lips as I'm yanked away are feral bellows demanding retribution and promising pain.

I'm drowning in my need to hurt him the way he so carelessly hurts me. I'm not sure what Ryn is saying to me, but it's clearly meant to talk me down. All I can focus on though is that Ryn is just as deserving of my wrath, and I turn on him. Pigeon surges inside of me. She wants in on the action, but I slam a vault door on her, wrap it in chains, and chuck the key as far into the recesses of my mind as I can. They've all betrayed me, and they can all rot in fucking hell.

"You knew!" I screech at Ryn as I twist and try to get my feet under me so I can wound him too. "You fucking knew after what happened in the woods. That's what you were keeping from me when I woke up. Side effects of a Trammel magicked rope, my ass!" I yell at him. I get one arm out from under his hold and claw down the side of his face. He hisses and shoves me away from him.

I land on my feet and charge. He backs away, hands up, like that's going to keep me from trying to rip the asshole apart.

"We had to know who you were once and for all. That's why I came back to Kestrel to see what information had been recorded about your parents. To figure out if there was anything that would tell us where you'd come from and what you might be doing here now," Ryn defends.

"I fucking told you who I was and what I was doing here,

you stupid assholes." Zeph growls, and my head snaps in his direction. "Oh, fuck off with that shit. You screwed up, not me. Maybe if you had clued me in, I would have known the warning signs of a mating and none of us would be in this situation now. *You* are to blame for all of this, so go growl at yourself."

Ryn and Zeph both step closer, clearly not liking my point, and I ready myself to go full feral bitch in my efforts to mar them both. Pain explodes in my chest, and suddenly my neck feels like it's on fire. I gasp and grab for my throat. I feel warmth there, and a flash of what happened to me in Kestrel fills my mind. I can feel the blade again as it slices across my neck. The shock and panic crawl back up my esophagus to bleed out of the open wound in my throat. Clawing fear ices through my veins, and my eyes land on Zeph's. He looks just as panicked, and then everything blurs and I feel myself falling.

Was this all a dream? Am I still back with Lazza, hallucinating and dying? Something catches me, and booming yells bounce all around me as I pant through the pain and try to comprehend what's happening to me. I hear the faint sound of laughter as I lose all my strength, and my hands fall, powerless, from my throat.

I can't breathe.

I struggle silently to pull air into my lungs, but it's useless. The shouting all around me fades to white noise, and just when I'm about to give in to whatever is happening to me, a blinding light flashes, and I'm suddenly being sucked out of the arms of whoever has me and thrown into a never-ending darkness that sets every nerve ending inside of me alight with pain. A silhouette of a man's body, somehow bathed in both shadows and light, burns itself into my mind, and then as quick as a sharp inhale, everything in and around me just...stops.

2

My heart beats steadily in my chest, and my breaths are even and quiet. I lie breathing in and out, worried that one wrong move will invite back the pain. I know I passed out again, because the light teasing the other side of my closed eyelids is bright. I can tell it's daytime instead of nighttime like it was the last time I came to, and that means, once again, that my body called it quits and shut down.

If I never pass out again for the rest of my life, I'll be a happy fucking camper. I'm starting to be really not cool with taking involuntary little naps and waking up in strange places. It has not worked out well for me so far, and my body needs to get on board with staying awake and alert. It's time to toughen up.

I peel my lids back and immediately regret it. Fuck, it's bright. I thought we were in a cave; why the hell is it so damn sunny in here? I try again, slower this time. A headache is already starting to pound steadily at my temples, and I feel like the living embodiment of a dust-filled mummy. Minus the cozy wrapped bandages though, because it seems I'm once again sans clothing. I'm getting pretty sick of that happening too.

The blanket covering me is gray and a little scratchy. It looks worn, and I hold it to my chest as I work to sit up. I'm weak as shit, and it makes me wonder even more how long I've been out. I'm lying on another blanket that isn't providing any cushion between my ass and the rocky floor of the cave it appears I'm still in. My whole body is stiff and sore, but I'll take that any day of the week over the pain I felt before.

A fire that's on its last leg is barely smoking next to me, and I look up to find a large hole in the top of the cave that's to blame for the painful brightness going on all around me. I have no clue where I am right now. I can't tell if this is the same cave I woke up in to find Ryn and Zeph arguing—at least I think that happened and isn't just a figment of my imagination.

I look around, but no winged assholes are here to greet me. I freeze when my search lands on a prone figure lying on the ground.

Treno.

I try to stand up, but my body doesn't seem overly interested in cooperating with me. I end up seal crawling toward him instead, and thank fuck he's less than a handful of feet away from me, because by the time I get to him, I feel like I just jogged a lap around the globe. What the hell is wrong with me? I lean my forehead against Treno's blanket clad body and work to pull oxygen into my lungs. I can feel his chest rise and fall steadily, and a flicker of relief moves through me.

I get my shit together and lift my head to take him in. The first thing I see is a pink line across his throat. I reach out to touch it, but it's smooth, like it's an echo of a wound. I pull my hand back and run my fingers over my own neck. There's a raised line across my throat in exactly the same place. Goose bumps rise on my arms, and I jerkily pull my hand away, not ready to deal with the reminder of what happened to me.

I focus back on Treno, his long white hair matted and tangled, and a sheen of sweat layers his skin. He looks sick. I reach out my palm to his forehead, expecting to find his skin burning beneath my touch, but he's cool and clammy instead. I scoot up closer to his head and run my fingers down his cheek. He doesn't respond to my touch at all.

My first instinct is to try and wake him up, but I stop myself. I'm not sure what's wrong with him, and if he needs the sleep, I'll feel like a dick for stealing him away from it. The other issue is that I'm terrified if he does open his eyes to find me, I won't see relief or happiness in his two-toned gaze, but betrayal and anger instead. I'm not ready for that.

I go full Little Mermaid and just stare at him, while occasionally smoothing some hair back from his face as an excuse to touch him. I fight the urge to start singing "Part of Your World" and instead start monologuing in my head about what the fuck I'm going to say to him when he wakes up.

I have a shit ton of explaining to do. I try not to think about what will happen if he refuses to listen to me, or worse, pulls a Loa and tries to take me out. I hope he'll give me a chance to try and make my omissions right with him. I go round and round in my mind with all the different ways I can explain it all to him, but it all feels flat.

How do you make betrayal right?

Somehow, *"Sorry I lied to you. If I had known you were going to end up my mate, maybe I...would have done the exact same thing because you were Avowed and I didn't want to end up in a dungeon or dead,"* isn't exactly the begging for forgiveness Treno will probably expect.

The air pressure above me changes, and I immediately move to cover Treno from whatever is about to swoop down from above. I can feel Pigeon slamming against the walls of steel I encaged her in, and I try to ignore the broken pieces rattling around inside of me because of it. Like a missile, tan skin and black wings slam to the ground fifteen feet away. Dust plumes up to make the landing even more dramatic, and Zeph walks arrogantly through the cloud, his gaze landing immediately on mine. He takes in my protective positioning around Treno and growls his disapproval. He looks good. Healed. There's no blood weeping down his side, or bruises. And the line on his neck that was there before is gone.

Another missile, this one tan-skinned with white and gray wings, slams down to the dirt and rock cave floor. Ryn straightens up, some kind of animal that looks to be a mix between a teenage mutant ninja goat and a llama slung over his strong shoulder. He drops it to the ground as soon as he sees me and comes right for me.

I cringe back, trying to protect Treno and also myself, and Ryn freezes mere feet away from me. I watch as the relief I didn't notice before bleeds from his gray eyes to be replaced with hurt. He's healed too. There are hints of bruises still on his face, but he doesn't look a sixth as bad as he did before. He shoots a look at Zeph, and I'm surprised to see fury flash through his eyes as he does. When his stare lands back on me, the anger is gone, and all that's left is an aching uncertainty.

"I wouldn't hurt you, Falon," he states evenly. "I wouldn't hurt your mate either," he adds when my shaky arms continue to cage Treno in protectively.

"Wouldn't you?" I state simply, my voice cracking from disuse. I'm not sure if I'm asking or challenging.

Fuck, I feel tired.

Ryn takes a deep breath and crouches. The sigh he releases as he gets closer to eye level with me sounds sorrowful and resigned. It tugs at the tatters of my trust, reminding me of how their omissions and lies shredded me like I was nothing.

"I was wrong, Falon. I don't expect this statement to earn me an immediate pardon; I just need you to know that I'm aware of how badly this all went. I should have trusted my instincts and been straight with you. I will never let anything come between our bond again, I vow it."

Ryn puts his fist over his heart and bows his head, and I'm not sure how to respond. His words call to the part of me that knows anger will get me nowhere. I can see and feel his sincerity, and yet I'm still so fucking pissed. I can't help thinking about what it felt like to watch Lazza torture him. I thought he was going to die, and it pummeled everything inside of me to stand helplessly by and watch it.

But all of this is so complicated. I have the painful perspective of what it felt like to possibly lose him, and I also acutely feel the damage of what his secrets and exclusions have done to me; I don't know what to do with either. We stare at each other for a moment, I suspect neither one of us having the slightest clue about what to do or say now. Luckily, the raging asshole in Zeph rears its head and saves us from having to figure it out.

"We did what we had to do. No point apologizing for it," Zeph grumbles as he sets a pouch that looks like it's filled with berries on the floor of the cave. He pulls off another larger bag that has round watermelon looking things in it, but they just so happen to be pink instead of the green I'm used to.

I want to get up and slug him across his dour face, but I'm too tired to move. "Totally," I snark. "You were clearly just in the mood to redecorate that day you threw a tantrum and destroyed everything in my room. You didn't stare at my clothes longingly and realize that just maybe you'd made a massive mistake. I must have been imagining that though, because you were just doing what you had to do, right? No biggie?"

Zeph glares at me, but I don't buy that his cream-filled center is comprised of only heartless asshole. I've seen things that prove otherwise. He's still annoying as fuck though, and I don't have the energy to engage right now. My arms give out, and my efforts to protect Treno result in me just half lying on him and listening to him breathe. It's comforting in a weird way, which is good because I can't move.

"You need to eat," Ryn declares, and he stands up and moves over to the llama-goat.

He pulls out a long knife and starts doing things that turn the animal from dead carcass into future dinner. Surprisingly, I'm not revolted by the sight of him skinning, draining, and removing and cleaning things. He moves fluidly and with purpose, and I can't help but recognize almost a soothing poetry to his sure actions. Or maybe I'm just so hungry that I couldn't take my eyes off of the meat even if I wanted to.

A massive hand places a pile of what look like black berries in front of me, and I look over to see Zeph moving away. I watch him for a beat as he pulls out a long sharp-looking dagger thing and starts peeling the pink not-water-melons. I pop a blackberry in my mouth as I watch him, wishing I could peel back his gruff exterior the same way he's peeling the fruit in his hands.

Juice fills my mouth as I start to chew the berry, and I

quickly realize that these couldn't be further from the black-berries I know and love. I spit out the rancid fruit and simultaneously gag and try to wipe my tongue with the blanket still around me.

"What the fuck?" I demand as Ryn comes striding over, a concerned look on his face. Zeph just looks offended by my reaction to his offering, but what else is new? "That tastes like raw rotten fish!" I declare, looking at them and the pile of fish berries like they've each betrayed me.

Fucking nasty!

"They're grot fruit. They'll help you heal faster and get back on your wings quicker," Ryn explains, as if somehow knowing the name of the nasty, treacherous berries will make them more palatable.

I try and fail not to flinch at the mention of wings. What I'm going to do about Pigeon is filed nicely in the *I have no fucking clue* cabinet in my brain. It's right next to *what to do about three mates* and *how to recover when you find out your entire life is a lie.*

I shove the pile of berries away from me with a shiver and warily eye the fruit Zeph's peeling. With my luck, it will taste like rotten meat or, worse—grapefruit.

"So are we just going to not talk about what happened?" I ask, hoping the change in subject will make Ryn stop looking at me like he's trying to figure out how to shove the grot berries down my throat. Where's a duda fruit when a girl needs one?

Zeph's and Ryn's features both close off, and it's like watching the curtain shut on a movie theater screen. They both clamp down so fast. Zeph suddenly gets real interested in peeling not-watermelons, and Ryn puts all his attention into starting a fire and building a spit. I push away from Treno so I can position myself closer to the growing fire and its warmth. I didn't realize I was so cold until right now.

"Don't think that avoiding the subject is going to change the fact that your spying sister betrayed you and your people and then slit my throat." I rub my neck but immediately stop when it hurts. I feel like I'm bruised, and I picture a black patchwork of bruises surrounding the new scar accessorizing my neck. Maybe my voice isn't fucked up solely from sleep. Did she do damage? I try to palpate my neck again, suddenly feeling like I need to know just how bad it is, but it feels swollen and too tender. The scratchy material of the blanket I'm wearing suddenly feels like sandpaper against my skin when I move, and I want it off of me.

"Any extra clothes hidden in some well-placed wooden chest inside this cave?" I ask, recalling the well-stocked cave Zeph and I holed up in after our lake tour and subsequent crash landing. I don't see one around, but they got these blankets from somewhere.

Zeph puts his peeled fruit on some kind of wooden looking plate and rinses his hands with a skin of water. He reaches behind his head and pulls off the gray tunic he's wearing. He chucks it at me, and it smacks right into my face and falls uncaught to my blanket covered lap. I shake away the image of his well-muscled body and ignore what it does to me.

Apparently, my body is too tired to move much, but not too tired to appreciate my asshole mate's muscles. The word *mate* snaps me all the way out of my daze, and I pick up the shirt and sniff it. I'm totally checking to see if it's clean and not at all going for a nose full of his rich masculine scent. Nope. I don't care if he smells like Bvlgari and bitterness, and I can do laundry on his abs. He's a bad fucking dude.

I pull the gray shirt over my head and then try to reposition the scratchy blanket under my now cotton clad ass, using as little energy as possible. Pieces of meat are placed so they can start cooking over the fire, and I try to keep my eyes off the other pieces of meat walking around this massive cave, being all surly and shit.

"So you guys treat me like crap, lie to me, and keep vital information from me all because you thought I was a spy. Meanwhile, neither of you detected the *actual* spy in your midst. I take it you and your sister weren't close?" I ask Ryn, watching as he tenses while putting more meat on sticks to cook. "She was pretty adamant that I stay away from you," I go on. "I thought it was because she wanted to fuck you; guess I read that all wrong."

Ryn doesn't say anything.

My stare moves from Ryn to Zeph. "You should have let me kill her when I had the chance," I tell him, anger and unmasked accusation leaking into my tone. "If you hadn't stepped in and saved her, maybe all of this could have been avoided." I gesture—or at least try to gesture—at the cave all around us, but my weak muscles don't want to cooperate with the level of drama I'm trying to achieve. It's all I can do just to sit here...sitting up. I glance over at the grot berries and contemplate plugging my nose and just going for it. My weak state is really starting to worry me.

"What are you talking about?" Ryn breaks his silence and asks.

"Your sister tried to kill me while pretending it was a training exercise. I'm pretty sure Zeph purposely kept Sutton away from me, because he's a petty little shit, and put Loa the Betrayer in charge of training the kiddies," I explain.

"He had his hands all over you," Zeph snarls from the other side of the fire. The flame's shadows dance over his skin and muscles, and a flash of him underneath me as I use his solid chest for leverage and fuck him hard and fast pops up unbidden in my mind.

"Oh right, and you didn't have your hand shoved in the top of some female practically fucking you in front of everybody?" I counter, reminding him of the lap trophy he was playing with that night of the festival. "The difference between you and me that night, is that I didn't know you were my mate...you did."

"Is nothing sacred to you?" Ryn snarls at Zeph.

"It was just Neece. I didn't do anything with her, but I had to keep up some level of pretense while I was waiting for *you* to bring back answers," Zeph defends. "Sutton crossed a line. I could smell his want from a league away, for rut's sake. Neece knows her place."

"Oh, I'm sure she's very good on her knees," I snap at him. "Loa fucking challenged me, and then you stepped in to save her ass when she lost! Stop pretending like Sutton was the problem, and not you and your bullshit issues with trust!"

"My issues with trust?" Zeph growls. "I have to be careful. You've been in our world for less than half a sun cycle and you think you know the dangers we face? You have no idea what we've been through."

"I know enough to get why you'd be cautious. But I was your mate. Where was the trust in that? That should have meant *something* to you. It should have allowed for some benefit of the doubt. You threw me out," I scream at him, my voice and soul suddenly feeling raw and painful. My throat throbs, begging me to stop talking and abusing it even further.

"You tried to Ouphe bend me!" he shouts back.

"Are you fucking crazy?" I demand, furious. "I didn't do anything to you other than attempt to make you stop trying to fuck me after I said no. It was just an instinctual reaction to what you were doing!"

In a flash of movement, Ryn is over the fire and attacking Zeph before my eyes can even focus on what's happening. I'm so shocked by the burst of action and the violence of it all that it takes me several heartbeats to react. They're a blur of fists and movement, and the sound of punches landing and threats being spewed fill the entire cave until I'm drowning in them. They're brutal in their attacks against each other, and I can feel the promise of blood and death in the air.

I try to stand up and then curse my useless, uncooperative body. I crawl over to the pile of grot fruit and shove handfuls into my mouth in hopes that it will help me get up and try to stop this. Pained bellows and enraged growls bounce off the cave walls, and panic surges through me so potently that it steals my breath. I swallow down as much grot as I can between dry heaves and terror-laced tears. I hate Ryn and Zeph right now, but I don't want either dead.

I'm on the verge of doing the last thing I want to do right now, which is letting Pigeon out and hoping she can somehow stop them, when Ryn and Zeph both explode into their gryphons. Instantaneously the massive cave seems tiny as the two gargantuan beasts circle and snap at each other. The setting sun fills the cave with oranges and purples, and it makes Ryn's huge white and gray gryphon look like it's splattered with watercolor. Zeph's all black sky shadow soaks up all the different hues like they were never there in the first place, and if I didn't know better, I'd think I was watching the night and the sunset themselves fighting.

I search for the steel vault I trapped Pigeon in at my center, but before I can do anything else, both gryphons leap up and take off one by one through the hole in the cave roof, like cyclones of rage and torment. I stare at the open ceiling and surrounding cave, an imprint of fury and pain now seemingly stamped over every surface. I feel like I'm choking on the hate both of them just expelled, and I hold my chest and try to get up.

I scream when a hand clutches my wrist, stopping me

from moving. My head snaps over to find Treno staring at me with concern. Fuck. I forgot he was here for a moment. Fear and relief slam into me as his blue and purple gaze settles on mine.

"Let them go. You'd just get hurt trying to stop them. They'll sort it out."

I can practically hear the unspoken *one way or another* in his statement.

"They can't kill each other without hurting you," he adds, answering my unvoiced worry about how far the fight can go. The flash of hurt in his eyes as he relays this information bitch-slaps me back into the cold reality of betrayal and lies, and I hate that in this case, *I'm* the perpetrator of Treno's pain.

My eyes flick back and forth between his mismatched stare. I'm suddenly so fucking sorry and so fucking happy to see him that it's like the two overwhelming emotions crash together inside of me and explode out in a sob that opens the dam, and I have no choice but to come flooding out. I wrap my arms around his neck, and shakily he sits up and pulls me into his lap. My guilt and sorrow pour out of me, and I hate that after what I've done to him, he's still willing to hold me while I leak weakness all over him.

I know that he's hurting. I can feel it in our connection, and yet here he is, holding me, reassuring me silently with just his mere presence that I'll be okay. I hate my frailty more in this moment than I have in any other. I've floated through this world, delusional and purposefully naive. I've refused to open my eyes, to trust my instincts, to see what was right in front of me, and now everyone all around me is hurting and fighting.

I allow myself this last moment to break, and vow that *I* will put myself back together in a way that will never let this happen again. No more blinders. No more poor helpless me.

No more ignoring my instincts and second-guessing every-thing. It's time to become the woman I need to be to survive in this world. It's time to own my shit and find my way. It's time to accept that this is my life now, and I better get fucking used to it.

3
_____

The cave is silent. The smell of campfire and rage stings my nostrils, and I try to subtly chase the smells away by inhaling deeply while my cheek is pressed against Treno's chest. I suspect he hasn't showered for a bit, because he's a tad ripe, and I squirm a little with the fact that I probably smell like ass too.

He looks tired, his long white hair tangled and dirty, and I feel a slight tremor in his hold. I don't see any injuries, but he was out as long as I was, so something must have happened to him. I want to ask, but I bite the questions back. I need to talk to him first. Explain what happened before I do anything else.

I need to start putting the pieces together and fixing things after all the shit that's happened to lead to all of us hiding out in some random cave, but I have no idea how to go about trying to repair anything. Treno releases steady breaths, and I take that as a sign that he's ready to talk, either that or he's ready for me to get the fuck out of his lap.

I steel myself and scoot back away from him. He lets me go, and I try and fail to read the look in his eyes as we separate. We both just stare at each other for a moment, taking each other in, breathing through the uncertainty and hurt.

"I'm sorry," I finally say at the same time he says, "You lied."

I can hear my heart hammer in my ears for three beats before he speaks again. "Are you?" he asks.

I shoo away the defensiveness that automatically springs up inside of me and truly think about his question for a moment. "Yes, and also no. I'm not sorry that I lied. I didn't want to die or to be tortured in a dungeon. Stating half-truths was the only way to keep either of those things from happening. But I *am* sorry for hurting you."

As the last words exit my mouth, I see a flash of devastation in Treno's mismatched gaze, and it feels like a punch to the gut. I hate that I put that there, and I hate that if I had all of this to do over again, I would do exactly what I had done before.

"So were you spying?" Treno demands, more bite to his tone and hardness in his eyes than was there before.

"No," I defend. I want to snap that he should know better than that, but what do either of us really know about the other at all... Nothing. "I was telling the truth about how I ended up here and not knowing what I was. I just left out that the Hidden found me first."

"Oh, you simply left it out," he repeats, his eyes now mocking.

Again irritation bubbles up in my chest, and I have to remind myself that he has every right to be mad. The problem is, so do I. I shake that thought away and try to commit to being empathetic and understanding. We're not going to get anywhere by fighting, and judging by the shitty cave we're shacking up in, we need to get *somewhere*.

"I spent a little time with the Hidden, and then I was kicked out. I was trying to get home when you and your soldiers shot me out of the sky. I didn't ask to be taken against my will to Kestrel City. I was forced to try and make the best of a bad situation. Everything else was the truth: I was stuck there and just trying to get back to the gate so I could go home. I found some information about my family in the archives, but I wasn't spying or hiding anything from you for any reason other than I had to protect myself," I explain, my tone pleading for him to see things from my perspective.

"Spent a *little* time with the Hidden?" Treno snarls. "You're mated to their traitorous leader and apparently his Altern. It sounds like you did a lot more than *spend a little time*," he accuses, and all thoughts of being the voice of reason and understanding go flying right out the window.

"I was just as shocked by that as I was to find out I was mated to you," I snap at him, jumping to my feet.

I feel light-headed and weak, but at least I'm up, so I shove that aside and embrace my frustration. I get that he's hurt, but I didn't do any of this out of malice. I deserve to feel bad about how it turned out, but I don't deserve to be beaten over the head with it all. What the fuck else could I have done?

"I was dropped into the middle of a war, through no fault of my own, and forced to figure out how to survive. I didn't know that being physical with anyone would result in a lifelong mating. It wasn't in the *welcome brochure* that no one handed to me when I showed up in this fucking hell hole. In my world, sex doesn't work that way. I had no idea that I could end up in a situation like this."

Treno growls at me and gets to his own feet. He doesn't look as shaky as I do, and that just pisses me off even more. Gone is the sweet and playful male, whose presence felt like cool water on a scorching day. In his place is a cold, hard warlord who apparently isn't going to offer me the empathy I was trying to offer him.

"Well, if you didn't know how things worked here, then you had no business rutting with anyone. Now you've tied me to my enemies, turned my brother against me, and ruined me in ways I don't even know how to come back from!"

"I've ruined you?" I ask, taken aback. Shock and anger swirl in me, and I'm stunned by the selfishness radiating out of him. Does he even care what's been done to me? "Fuck you, Altern of the Avowed," I spit back at him, fed up and stepping into his space like I've forgotten that he's a foot and a half taller than me and probably bench-presses my weight for a warm up. His eyes blaze even brighter with fury, but I continue.

"*I* didn't pursue any of you. Each and every one of you knew I wasn't from here and would have no idea how things worked. I didn't see anyone explaining matings to me *before* they were coming inside of me. You aren't the only injured party in this situation, Treno. I've been fucked literally and figuratively by each of you and what you kept from me."

"You had no right," he yells.

"Neither did *you*!" I snap back, matching his indignation glare for glare. "I'm tired of all you alpha meathead bitches always trying to keep me on my back foot. I'm sorry that I couldn't tell you the truth about who found me first. Trust me, right now no one is sorrier than I am that we're all mated and stuck with each other. But what the hell was I supposed to do? The Avowed would have killed me, just like the Hidden wanted to. I was stuck and just trying to get home. If all you selfish pricks had just let me be, none of us would be here right now. So blame each other, because I'm not here for it anymore."

"My brother—"

"Attacked me, knowing we were bonded. He knew what would happen to you, and if you think otherwise, you're delusional. Loa slit my throat with *his* blessing. So before you go off about him, you should check back into reality, because from where I was bleeding to death on the ground, Lazza seemed perfectly fine with you dying."

I stomp away from him with every intention of storming the fuck out of here—the only problem is, I can't find the fucking exit. I look around completely livid, and it seems the only way in or out of this cave is through the damn hole in the ceiling. Well, shit. I try to call my wings, but nothing happens. Maybe I'm too weak, or maybe something else is wrong with me. I don't get any more time to think through that question though, because Treno closes the distance between us.

I square my shoulders, not even caring if he's going to ring my neck like it looks like he wants to, because I'm going to scratch his eyes out, and then I'm going to wait for Ryn and Zeph to get their aggro asses back here, and I'm going to do the same thing to them. Either that or I'm going to fall over from exhaustion. It's sixes either way at this point.

Like a meteorite, Ryn drops to the ground right in front of me. It's so unexpected that I scream and crouch down, covering my head with my hands like I'm expecting to be pummeled by more asshole gryphons falling from the sky.

"Get away from her," Ryn barks, and I run my eyes over him, checking for injuries.

I stand up and look around, but there's no sign of Zeph.

"Look whose master let him off the leash," Treno mocks, his tone laced with a current of violence.

Ryn smiles, but there's nothing kind or happy about it. "The Hidden don't do that whole master thing. Only you and your brother still think you have the right to own other people."

"The Avowed are not slaves," Treno roars, stepping into Ryn's space. "You've been there from the beginning. You of all people should understand that we protect each other through the Vow, nothing more."

"Right. You only force your mark on people, whether they want it or not, and then control them when they do anything you disagree with. Definitely not slaves, my mistake," Ryn snarks.

"I trusted you. You were my friend my whole life!" Treno growls, and for a fraction of a second, I can see the hurt and betrayal that's surging beneath his anger.

"All of our people trusted you and your family, and look what's become of us," Ryn retorts, and they stand there staring at each other, every muscle tense and ready for action. "Do it," Ryn taunts as retribution lights up in Treno's eyes. "I welcome the challenge of weak males who are ready to die."

My uneasy stare flits back and forth between them. Just when I think they're about to come to blows, Treno steps back, shaking his head, and then moves to a dark corner and sits down. His mismatched eyes are calculating, and his face is furious as he presses back into the shadows and shuts his features off from me.

Ryn stomps over to the fire and rotates the sticks of meat still cooking above the flickering flames. He makes a face as he spins the skewers, and I see that one side of the llama-goat kebabs is pretty charred. My stomach growls, the noise rivaling the most menacing of noises I've ever heard come from any kind of shifter, and it's clear that it doesn't care what state the meat is in.

I feel a little better than I did when I woke up. I'm standing, which is a massive improvement, and I suspect I have grot berries to thank for it. Just the thought of them makes me want to puke though, so I try to focus on something else. Unfortunately, there's not much to focus on other than two very pissed off gryphon shifters. I can feel their fury lapping at me like ocean waves crashing angrily on the shore.

"Where's Zeph?" I ask, because the resentment-tainted silence is starting to drive me a little crazy, and a countdown to the next inevitable blowup might be a good distraction.

"Here," he grumps as he drops to the ground behind me, and I once again scream and grab my chest, hoping it will keep my heart right where it's supposed to be instead of pounding through my sternum as it feels like it's going to do.

"Stop fucking doing that," I snarl-croak as he walks past me and claims his own shadowy corner, which apparently is now going to serve as his sulking throne.

The cave goes silent except for the crackling fire, but there's enough hostile testosterone floating around that I could probably backstroke laps in it if I so desired. My lavender gaze floats to each of my *mates* in their respective corners. And I feel like I'm sitting in the middle of a powder keg.

"So what now?" I ask, the question echoing around the dark stone walls caging all of us in.

This group doesn't exactly feel like they're ready for the *where is this going* chat, but I don't care. I can't stay here and just drown in their bitterness. I'm sure Lazza is up to something that needs to be stopped, and I have some serious revenge to mete out on my apparent sister-in-law.

"Well, isn't that just the question of the hour," Ryn jeers as he angrily pokes at the fire and then adds another log. "I'm sure Lazza is well aware of our plans and hideouts, thanks to my dear ol' sister. Years of planning and putting things into place to help secure our victory are now completely useless. As a rebellion, we just had our wings clipped, and right now we're stuck with Lazza's brother, whose life conveniently now seems to be intertwined with ours, so there's that too."

"You think I did this on purpose?" Treno demands, leaning forward.

Ryn snaps a reply, but I don't pay attention to what it is. I'm too busy staring at the shifter who, up until today, I thought was kind and patient, understanding and support-ive. I didn't know this angry and vicious male was floating around in there too. Given who his brother is, maybe I should have. Treno just always seemed so carefree and jovial, but then again, it's not like I ever saw him in any kind of situation that would have invited this side out of him. He was the Altern. In control. In his element and surrounded by people who wore marks that gave him and his brother power over them.

Guess this further proves that I should be sure exactly who I'm dealing with before I sleep with them. I rub my face with tired hands and ignore my growling stomach as the cave fills with more yelling and accusations. With wobbly steps, I stride over to the fire and steal a meat-filled stick. Ryn doesn't even notice; he's too busy furiously arguing with Zeph and Treno both.

I sit on the warm blanket and ravage the meat. I'm pretty sure I burn off most of my taste buds in the process, but I'm too hungry to have patience. I barely even chew the gamey meat before swallowing it down and ripping off more to fill my mouth. I'm sure I look like some feral animal as I tear into the meal, but I give no fucks. I don't even care that I'm growl-groaning as I clean the stick of meat from one end to the other.

The fact that I can hear the wild noises I'm making should be an indicator that the yelling has suddenly stopped, but I'm too consumed with filling my empty stomach and appreciating the taste to pay much attention.

Damn, this goat-llama meat tastes like popcorn. It has a salty, buttery quality to it, and I find myself wishing I could bathe in this stuff. I lick the stick clean of any remaining juices and then look up to find three pairs of eyes on me. I shrug my shoulders.

"That's some good shit," I declare as I wipe my mouth with my hand and then proceed to lick the juices off of it. Ain't no fucking shame in my starving game.

I look around for a skin of water that I know must be around here somewhere, and Zeph—accurately reading what I'm looking for—picks up one near him and chucks it at me. I pluck it from the air and guzzle almost half of it down before coming back up for oxygen. I sigh contentedly and then turn my attention back to my audience, studying them for a moment. Well, here goes nothing.

"You're not going to like this, but I think I know somewhere we can go," I announce and watch each of them focus even more on me. I swallow down the nerves that crawl up my chest and try to make me rethink what I'm about to say. "I suspect we may find some help there, but at a minimum, I'm pretty sure they could provide some information," I add, already defending the words still sitting on my tongue, as if in some way it will make what I'm about to say less of a bitter pill to swallow. I wait while doubt, questions, and curiosity pool in each of their eyes.

"Where?" Ryn finally demands.

I take a deep breath and slowly let it out.

"To the Ouphe."

4

"What the rut did you just say?" Zeph growls.

"Are you addled?" Ryn counters.

"Why would we do that?" Treno demands.

I sigh.

I point to each of them in turn, answering their questions. "I said the Ouphe. Who knows at this point, and we would go there because I think they may be able to help."

"How do you know?" Ryn asks, getting his question out before the others can voice theirs.

"Because I ran into a little Ouphe spirit or something when I was with you guys, and she told me."

"An Ouphe spirit?" he questions, clearly not buying it.

"Yep."

Treno steps toward me, and my attention goes straight to him. "Where is *there*?"

"I would guess somewhere in the Quietus Mountains. I don't know exactly, but there's a place I was supposed to meet them, somewhere in that area. I had a map before you and your asshole soldiers shot me out of the sky, but I think I remember it well enough to get there."

"You were going to meet with the Ouphe?" Zeph snarls, charging out of the shadows of his sulking corner, and I shoot to my feet to meet his impending rage-filled advance.

"You can shove all that righteous indignation up your tight ass. I get that there's no love in you for the Ouphe, but you don't get to take that shit out on me," I warn. "I wasn't going to meet them. I was *asked* to, but when you threw me out, I was just trying to get home. Regardless of all of that though," I quickly add, cutting off Zeph when he opens his mouth to say something that will no doubt be dickish and rude, "Nadi—the Ouphe ghost chick—thought that they could help me possibly undo the Vow. If we could do that, then there'd be no more issue with Lazza and company, right? No Vow equals no war."

"What do you mean help *you* undo the Vow?" Treno asks warily.

"Turns out my dad was full Ouphe and apparently one of the last Bond Makers left. My mother was half Ouphe, leaving me more Ouphe-tainted than usual. If I can find the language they used to create the Vow, then Nadi thinks I'd be able to break it."

"Falon, you cannot trust the Ouphe. Whatever it is that they've told you, there's a catch or something in it for them," Ryn implores, his features hard and angry and his gray eyes beseeching.

"Maybe," I agree. "But in the grand scheme of things, does that really matter? We can't go to the Hidden. We can't fight Lazza ourselves. This is our best chance at trying to find some secret weapon, some Hail Mary, that could stop all the fighting for good. Isn't that what you were looking for in Kestrel City, some way to end all of this once and for all?"

Ryn shoots a look to Zeph and then locks his eyes back on the fire.

"What's a Hail Mary?" he asks, confused.

"It's a football thing—don't worry about it," I add when I see the *what's football* question form on his lips.

Zeph runs his fingers through his wavy black hair and paces like a caged lion. I can see the fury in every tight coiled muscle in his body. As much as I don't like him most of the time, I have to give him some credit, because I can tell that he's considering what I'm saying. He has as much a right as any to hate the Ouphe, to refuse to ever trust them or go near them again, and yet for the good of his people and everyone else, he's at war inside about what to do.

The fire crackles ominously, hissing like it wants to argue with what I'm about to say, but I ignore it. "I get that this won't be easy. I wouldn't drop it at your feet if there were any other way, but if I'm right, if I can break the Vow, destroy it forever, wouldn't it be worth it?"

"How can we be expected to trust them?" Zeph asks, but his question falls to the dirt of the cave floor unanswered.

I have no idea what to say or if we even can. But we're not defenseless. From what I've heard, the Ouphe have been hunted and run down until they're ragged and desperate. I'm supposedly one of the last with the kind of magic they need to finally dig themselves out of the hole they created, and I figure that will give us the upper hand as long as we're careful.

"We don't have to trust them to use them," Treno states.

"Stay out of this. It has nothing to do with you," Zeph barks, and Treno bristles.

I wonder for a moment how Treno is still on his feet. He had to be as hungry and drained as I was, and yet he's still spewing all the resentment and anger like it's not taking a toll at all. They start arguing again, and I release an exasperated exhale and debate about stealing more food from the fire. These idiots don't seem to be in a hurry to eat. It would serve them right.

They all converge on each other, and I rush to get in the middle of it all. I get that they're mad and hate each other on fundamental levels, but this *bash each other's heads in* mentality isn't going to get us anywhere, especially if I'm going to have to suffer the aftereffects of their fighting too. Right now we really need to put a stop to Lazza and whatever he has planned next.

"Enough!" I scream. My voice cracking like a teenage boy's.

I shove my hands out to keep massive angry shifter bodies from sandwiching me. As soon as my palm touches Treno's chest, he recoils. Hurt sucker punches me right in the stomach. I try to shrug it off so I can get a hold of this messed up situation, but the steady ache in my chest makes it hard.

"She's your mate!" Ryn snaps at Treno, surprisingly not liking what just happened any more than I do.

"Just stop! All of you. Please!" I yell, but my voice is rough and scratchy, and the bite in my tone sounds more like an aggravated nibble. Fuck, I'm tired. "Zeph, where are the Hidden now? Would Loa have told Lazza where to find them?" I ask, trying to get him to focus on something else other than his desire to rip apart Treno or Ryn, depending on who has looked at him wrong in the last five minutes.

"No, Loa was spotted sneaking off, and it alerted us that something wasn't right. We moved everyone soon after. They're safe for now, but it's a large group to keep hidden for long, and I'm sure Lazza will have scouts out looking for them."

I nod and turn to Treno. "Do you know what Lazza will do next?" Treno's clashing eyes move from Zeph to me. I'm not sure if he's going to answer. I can see the battle in his gaze. Maybe he doesn't know where his loyalties lie when it comes to his brother, but I know he's still loyal to his people...to the Avowed.

"He's not going to fight this battle on his own, Treno. Lazza will send people to their deaths to win, and he'll do it whether they want to fight or not. I know you don't want that," Ryn tells him.

I watch the battle in his face, hoping he can see the truth in what's being said. But I'm not sure if he can look past his anger and do what's best for the people he swore to lead.

He shakes his head, and I can't tell if it's an admonishment to me or to himself. "He'll amass an army, and then he'll search every square inch of land until he finds the Vow traitors and destroys them."

He runs his hands through his long white hair, but they get stuck on the tangles and matted pieces strewn throughout his normally smooth locks. I'm tempted to reach up and help him comb out the mess, but that's a stupid thought. He hates me.

"It'll take time for him to organize his army and to find our people," Ryn reassures, and Zeph nods lost in thought.

"I think the Ouphe might be our best bet. I mean, if any of you have a better plan, feel free to voice it..." I look at each of them, giving them time to suggest some alternative option, but no one speaks up. "How far is it from here to the Quietus Mountains?" I ask when it's clear no other ideas are readily available.

Ryn looks at me and then away in thought. "If we could fly, maybe a couple of days, but until we get far enough away from Kestrel City for flying to be safe, we'll have to walk. Maybe a week? Maybe eight days? It's hard to say for sure."

Eight days, can we get there and convince the Ouphe to fight with us before Lazza finds where the Hidden are hiding? I feel like fucking Atlas with the weight of this world on my shoulders. What if I'm wrong? What if Ryn and Zeph are right, and I'm an idiot to trust the Ouphe? What if it bites us in the ass?

I go back and forth in my mind, debating the pros and cons, but the thing I keep coming back to is what else can we do? What other options do we have? We need to try something, because if it comes down to a head-to-head battle, Lazza has the numbers. Even if by some miracle the Hidden can pull off a victory, how much will both sides lose before that happens?

If I can break the Vow though. If I can undo it, then Lazza can't force anyone to do anything, and what reason would the Hidden have to fight their own people anymore? If I can find the language and figure out how to use it, I could help stop this war.

I take a deep breath and accept the responsibility of the task. It settles like a planet on my chest, and I know I'm going to have to get stronger and prepare a hell of a lot harder in order to successfully carry such a heavy burden.

"So that settles it then. When do we leave?"

They're all completely silent as they walk away from me and move back into their respective corners. Zeph disappears back into his shadows, but not before he grabs two sticks of meat from the fire. Ryn returns to his seat by the flames and tears into his own dinner. Treno watches all of it from his corner, I'm sure not failing to notice that there's no more food cooking over the fire for him.

I sigh and shake my head. I stomp over to Zeph and snatch a meat-filled stick from his hand before he can stop me. I jump away as quickly as possible, expecting him to try and take it back, but he just growls and mumbles a bunch of shit I can't hear.

That's probably a good thing.

I grab the blanket that Treno was sleeping on and drag it over to his newly claimed angry corner. I hand him the food and the blanket. He eyes them warily and doesn't move to take them.

"We both know you're weak and that you need this. You can still be pissed at me and at them while you eat. I won't read into your acceptance of food as anything other than you being hungry."

Treno stares at the meat a minute more, and then he concedes. I nod once and drop the blanket at his feet. I move back over to the fire and collect some grot berries and the not-watermelon and set them on Treno's blanket. An irritated grunt sounds off from the shadow shrouded corner, and I look over my shoulder to glare at Zeph. I can't make out exactly where he is in the pitch-black area, but I know his eyes are on mine.

I mouth *grow up* and then turn back to Treno. "The berries taste like ass. You probably already know that, but just in case you don't, those things should come with a warning."

I look over my shoulder and give the dark corner a pointed look.

"You're up and walking, aren't you?" Zeph states evenly, and *touché* sounds off in my mind.

"Please," I scoff. "That's my own stubbornness at play, not your ass berries," I lie.

Ryn snickers, either from the ass berries comment or my bad bullshitting, but either way it's a nice sound to hear instead of all the yelling and accusations. I make my way to my own blanket and try to get comfortable—well, as comfortable as you can get lying on the cold rock-hard ground. I stare off into the dancing flames of the fire and let my mind wander. *How the fuck did my life go so wrong so fast?*

I circle that question over and over again, trying to look at it from every angle in my mind. Where and how did everything go so wrong, and how in rutting Thais Fairies am

I going to get it back on track? I wallow in those thoughts for a very long time, and then everything in and around me starts to blur and I quickly fall asleep.

* * *

A doorbell chimes, waking me up. Groggily I listen to footsteps as they make their way down the stairs. I hear someone flick the light switch on and draw back the curtain to the window next to the door.

I look out my own window to see that the moon is still high in the sky and the stars are out and still up to their mischievous twinkling. It's still night. I hear the door creak open and my gran speak softly to whoever is on the other side of it. I sit up, too curious not to sneak out of my room and have a peek at what's going on, but then I notice my mom standing in the corner, next to my bookshelf.

She smiles at me and I smile back, but something about the exchange feels off. I suddenly feel scared.

"What are you doing, mommy?" I ask softly, my voice heavy with sleep.

"Saying goodbye, My Heart," she tells me, her smile filled with tender affection, but then she wipes a tear from her cheek.

"Why are you sad?" I ask as I feel my own worry and sadness climb to the surface, but my mom walks over and pulls me into her arms, and I suddenly feel better.

"I'm always with you, Falon. Remember that, okay?" she tells me, and I squeeze her tighter and nod my head against her chest.

"We tried hard to hide you from it all, but it found us anyway," she tells me on a sob as she pulls me in even closer. Her hug is bruising and it hurts, but I don't want to say anything. I'm scared. "Just know that you are all you need, okay, My Heart? When the loneliness and sadness feels overwhelming, remember

that you are enough, and you will be okay. I love you, and I'm so sorry."

"I love you too, mommy," I tell her, but all at once, she's gone. I fall to the bed, my mother's bruising hug and words just an echo around me. I can feel her lips against my hair, and yet there's no one here. Confusion fills my mind, and then fear quickly replaces it. I throw back my covers and call out for my mother.

Did I have a bad dream?

Footsteps rush up the stairs and relief filters through me. She's coming. She'll make it all better. My gran's face peeks in through the door, her complexion ruddy and her cheeks wet.

"I had a bad dream," I tell her, and she rushes to the bed and pulls me into her lap.

She doesn't say anything, she just rocks me and cries. This reminds me too much of my dream, and I feel instantly nervous and afraid.

"What's wrong?" I finally ask

"There was an accident, my sweet. Your daddy didn't make it, and your mommy got hurt."

I try to understand what she's talking about, but there's a knock on the door. I look up to find a police officer standing there.

"Ma'am, I'm so sorry to interrupt, but we just received news that Noor Umbra passed before the ambulance could make it to the hospital."

"Oh, no," Gran keens, and she drops her cheek to my head and starts to rock me harder as she cries. I don't know what's going on. I just saw my mommy, and she didn't look hurt. Does she need a Band-Aid? I always feel better after I get a Band-Aid for my owies. I'll wait to ask when Gran doesn't feel so sad. I relax into my gran's hug and think about my dream, my mommy's voice like a whisper in my ear.

"I love you, and I'm so sorry."

5

I wake up with a start and immediately sit up. I press a palm to my chest as if the gesture will help my heart to slow down.

It wasn't a dream.

I don't know why I've never made the connection before, but my mother was there the night she died. She held me and told me she loved me. I hadn't made it up. I try to breathe through the shock of the realization, but I feel like I'm floating haphazardly, and I don't know how to get my feet back on the ground.

The night my parents died feels like it's burned into the fabric of who I am. I've always replayed my gran telling me, the memory changing with time as I grew older and understood more and could look at it through a different lens than the one my five-year-old self saw everything through.

I've always thought of the dream as just that...a dream. I've even wondered if my mind made it up. One last moment with my mother that my psyche so desperately wanted that the want itself morphed into a confusing memory. But looking at it all now, knowing what I am and what they were, it changes everything about that night for me.

If I hadn't left my own body to visit Zeph, if I hadn't experienced it firsthand, I would easily still call it all a dream, but I know better. She was there that night. She could do what I can do. She said goodbye. So many different emotions fight to be let out, but I try to wade through them to make sense of all of this.

I think back through what I thought I knew about my childhood, and try to piece all these surfacing memories into my version of the past. I feel like I'm trying to put a puzzle together with a bunch of pieces I didn't even know I was missing.

My mother and father met and learned that they were mates. It seems like all of that went down at a volatile time. If I had to guess, I would suspect all of this happened at the beginning of a Gryphon uprising, since it was my father who seemed to be unsafe, and my mother's connection to him was what also put her in danger.

Somehow my gran, who wasn't actually my blood relative, but my mother's servant, figured out how to escape, and they all ended up in the world I grew up in. We were hiding. My parents and my gran thought it would be safer, but clearly that couldn't have been the case, because we were still hiding.

I think back to my mother's journal, and something suddenly hits me. The dates I saw in the first book that had my mother's name. She was born in 1619, which is a fact that's hard for me to wrap my mind around, but that's not what's puzzling me. It said to see the archived writings, which I now know was my mother's journal. She writes about being pregnant, but the information in the tome states that the journal was discovered in 1927.

I was born in 1994.

So where is the baby that my mother was pregnant with in her journal? Because there's no way that baby could be

45

me. I assumed it was when I first read her diary, but now I don't think that's possible.

Did they lose the baby? Do I have a sibling out there somewhere? No, that can't be right, why would they raise me and not that child? My parents may have been a lot of things, but they loved me. They wouldn't have abandoned me for anything, and I don't see them doing that to any child they had.

My mother's face from my dream memory of the night she died surfaces in my mind. The way the moon lit up her face, and the shadows tried to hide the sadness in her eyes. I can't even imagine what she went through in life. The running, the possible loss of a child, the struggle to keep me and our family safe, just to lose in the end.

Tears quietly drip down my face. I feel so sad for her. So sad for everything she had to face. She tried to tell me good-bye, to prepare me for her loss and leave me with words she hoped would comfort me in the future. I just didn't realize that until now.

I swipe at my cheeks. I haven't cried over my parents in over a decade at least. It was hard for me at first to under-stand and accept that I wouldn't see them again. That there wouldn't be any more hugs, kisses, and cuddles from my mommy. No more lessons, bear hugs, and wrestling with my dad. It was tough, but eventually life without them was all that I knew. I accepted it and had no choice but to move forward.

So it surprises me that right now, I feel something inside of me splinter, and all kinds of memories and sadness come seeping out of the cracks. I shove the blanket against my face and mourn. I grieve for all the times it would have been nice to have them. The times I needed the kind of affection and softness only a loving mother can give. Or the guidance and strength that my father always had at the ready. I feel the echo of my mother's lips against my head. Hear her soothing voice as she tells me that she loves me and that she's sorry. And that fractures me even more, because I'm old enough to now understand how heart-wrenching that must have been for her.

I sit in my anguish and watch the fire until it's nothing but embers. I watch their red glow as I try to convince myself that maybe I would have ended up here even if they were still alive. It's possible that I could have grown up my whole life knowing what I was and what I could do, and by trickery or choice, I would have found that gate anyway. I tell myself there's no point in blaming or trying to make sense of it all, because in the end, it doesn't matter.

I'm here.

Does understanding the catalysts behind why change anything? No. Regardless of how or why, I'm still sitting in a cave, needing more sleep, while the soft breaths and sounds of deep sleep float all around me.

Treno suddenly snore-snorts and rolls over onto his side. I watch him settle back down in his sleep, and I begin to wonder if he'll ever be able to forgive me. Before I saw his outrage with my own eyes, I would have thought the angry gene skipped him and that his brother got the gryphon's share. He's always seemed so chill before. But now, I don't know what to think. He hasn't left, but maybe having nowhere to go has more to do with that than I do.

A small voice in my head argues that he has to forgive me sometime, we're mates. But the more I examine that thought, the more I doubt it. Mates. What the fuck does that even mean? I know plenty of married people out there who don't like each other. And yeah, yeah, yeah, mates are supposed to be different, some biological and magical thing that sparks up and then fucks with your destiny, but look how well that's going for me so far.

Looks like destiny knows me about as well as I know the gryphons I'm tied to for the rest of my life. I sigh and rub at the ache that's rippling through my chest and throat. My eyes land on the dark corner that soft snores are steadily flowing out of. I don't even know what to make of *him*. I legitimately believed that the next time I saw Zeph, he'd try to kill me. Instead, he crashes through a ceiling and saves my life. Has he forgiven me for what happened in my room? Have I forgiven him?

I run frustrated fingers through my hair. So much damn forgiveness, and lack thereof, just floating around. Everyone in here needs it, no one seems to be in a hurry to give it, and our futures are kind of riding on it. Forgiveness, I dub thee a powerful and elusive little bitch. My thoughts wander to the vault I currently have locked up and chained in my center.

Pigeon.

How long do I plan to stay mad at her? Yeah, she fucked up, but who hasn't at this point? She did sort of try to fill me in...sometimes...when she wanted to, and if I had been really paying attention to what was going on around me, maybe I could have made the connections. That thought sends a new wave of frustration through me. I shouldn't have had to be stumbling around in the dark though; she should have tried harder to explain things to me. She should have had my back.

We've practically been at odds since we first discovered that we had wings. I yelled at Zeph earlier that being his mate should have earned me some benefit of the doubt, but I realize in this moment that I haven't given that to Pigeon at all. One thing after another has caused resentment to build, and it's clearly not one-sided.

We're supposed to be one, but we can't even get on the same page about most anything. There's no trust, no respect, and no understanding. No wonder everything is so fucked up. We've tried. I think back to the training we were doing together when we were in Kestrel City. We were working to physically sort out the differences and transitions between me and Pigeon. But then Treno dropped the mate bomb, and I shut Pigeon out.

I locked her away as though my feelings and needs were more important than hers, and now here we are. Pieces of what we should be. We should have been training our bodies and figuring out how to trust and rely on each other. I thought we were, Pigeon probably did too, but our efforts to rely on one another were tenuous, and the wounds we both had inflicted before by not being there when we needed it were still fresh.

I don't want to hate her anymore. I don't want to be at odds with the other part of my being. I can't do anything that needs to be done without her. I don't want to, and that means that we need to figure some shit out.

I start removing chains from the outside of the vault that I've shut Pigeon in. I think about what I want to say and how I'm going to say it as I work to gain access to the vault door. I need Pigeon to know that we have to be a team. Anything else just isn't going to work. We have to trust each other. Rely on each other. We need to get on the same page about all this mate shit and not hide vital information from each other.

She needs to know that I messed up too. I didn't listen. I didn't try to understand what she needed from me, what drove her instincts. I was so wrapped up in my head and focused on what I wanted that I didn't take the time to really get to know her, to learn about the gryphon that's as much a part of me as...well, I am.

I unlock the vault door and shove it open. I expect Pigeon to be there waiting inside, ready to come out and have the heart-to-heart that we're in such desperate need of, or maybe try to bitch me out, but there's nothing there.

I'm surrounded by black silence.

"Pidge?" I call out hesitantly.

Nothing.

"I was hoping we could talk."

My heart starts to pick up its pace, and I'm suddenly reminded of all the years I thought I was a latent. How horrible it felt to have my animal trapped inside of me with no way to get out. I felt incomplete, like I was defective. I was only a shard of what I could have been, and knowing that was devastating and felt completely wrong.

And now here I've gone and shut her off deliberately. More guilt pools in my gut. I don't want Pigeon, or me, to ever feel that way again. But all I sense right now is the heavy, shame-riddled beat of my heart.

Did I hurt her?

Fuck...could she be lost again, like she was before?

I push into the vault inside of me with a shout. *"Pigeon, I'm sorry. Please come out!"*

Lavender eagle eyes blink to life in the distant darkness, and relief washes through me. Pigeon's features are barely discernible, cloaked in the shadows of the dark place I've exiled her to. She cringes against the light pouring in from the open vault door behind me, and I feel her rage and desolation surge.

"I'm sorry," I offer again in defense of the hurt and rage I suddenly feel rippling off of her, but it's not enough, my words feel inadequate to even me.

The nothingness of where I've banished her to wraps around me like cold chains. Mistrust, dishonor, fury, abandonment, all make up the texture of this place, and I wish all at once that I could yank these things from the fabric of

Pigeon's and my foundation and build on more loving and understanding solid ground.

Tears prick my eyes. *"Pigeon, I—"* My words and heartfelt sentiment are shoved back down my throat when she attacks out of nowhere. Quicker than a striking snake, she slams into me with brutal force. Shocked, I scream and fall back. I land on one hand as I try to catch my fall and throw the other palm out to try and protect myself.

The light in this place dims oddly, and I look up expecting Pigeon to be lording over me, like I did her when I shoved her in here. She's not there. I search for her, ready to fling apologies until one hits its mark, but all I see is the light of the door into this vault growing smaller and smaller. By the time I realize what's happened, it's too late.

"Pigeon!" I scream, panicked, springing to my feet and running for her.

The light is only two feet wide now.

"Pigeon, don't do this! Listen to me, we need each other!" I shout at her as I race to try to escape the brutal trap that I created for her.

"Please, I'm sorry!" I beg as the light reduces to a mere sliver.

"I need you," I plead, but it's too late. My words fall on deaf ears as I slam into the shut vault door where I'm forced to listen to Pigeon locking it from the other side.

"No!" I scream as I bang on the prison walls. *"This isn't going to fix anything!"* I shout at her, but I don't even know if she's there listening anymore.

A cold darkness slithers around me, and I kick at the bleakness, refusing to accept that this is what Pigeon and I have been reduced to. We have to be more than just two warring sides, but how the fuck do we get across the canyon of distrust and pain now sitting between us?

"Pigeon!" I wail as my fists slam against the cool metal of

the vault I'm now trapped in. *"I love you, don't do this!"* I implore, but my cries are only met with deafening silence.

Out of nowhere, I'm hit with a fuck ton of sensations and pain all at the same time. It takes me a minute to collect my thoughts and understand what's happening. I can feel my body ripping apart and reshaping, and yet I have no control over it. I've—*we've* just shifted.

Worry takes over my thoughts. What will she do? Will she freak out and try to escape, getting us all caught? Will the guys stop fighting long enough to calm her down? I can feel her rage pumping through our veins, and the last thing any of us needs to be dealing with right now is a psychotic, volatile gryphon.

I try to believe that seeing her mates all together will be enough to soothe her, but that will only stay that way if they all keep their mouths shut and put her before their issues.

Fuck, that's never going to happen.

I pound on the walls of the vault and scream until my voice is hoarse. She doesn't know what she's walking into with her mates. She tried to rip Ryn apart the last time he pissed her off; will she do the same thing now? *Can she, with our mate connection*, I wonder and then realize she might not care what it does to us.

My voice quits altogether, and I can feel blood dripping off my knuckles from where I'm banging on my cell wall. Defeat filters through me, and I press my forehead to the cool wall and try to breathe through the shame and frustration I'm treading in.

"Fuck," I whisper, lost against the cold barriers caging me in, and the word bounces back against my lips like this place wants me to choke on it.

I close my eyes and shake my head at myself. I should be pissed, but all I can think about is how long did Pigeon scream? How long before her voice gave out? How could *I* have done that to her?

I'm such an asshole.

Pushing away the guilt that's thrashing inside of me, I try to focus on how the fuck I'm going to get myself out of this, because I *have* to get out of this. I have no doubt that, with the way Pigeon is feeling right now, she's going to lock me in here forever.

I can feel my body, so there's that. Right now we're pacing, and Pigeon feels agitated. I can't tap into my other senses, but I'm not completely cut off. So what the fuck can I do with that?

I start feeling around the inside of the dark vault I'm trapped in with my hands, as though my desperation is going to conjure a key. Wait a second! I created this vault. I pictured what I wanted in my head and shoved Pigeon inside. I cringe as the memory of that plays out in my mind —or is this Pigeon's mind right now?

Walk away from the Inception *speak, Falon. That meta shit will get you nowhere.*

Okay, focus. I made the vault. That means I can unmake it, or maybe just change it? I don't want Pigeon to think I'm coming for her, I just need her to hear me. I snort incredulously as an image of a bird cage pops into my mind. The irony isn't lost on me. I focus hard on changing the vault into a bird cage. I make it as much of an eyesore as possible so Pigeon still feels like I'm being adequately punished while I try to fix all that I've fucked up with her.

I recall this creepy old dude who used to walk his parrots around the park. He'd have their dented silver metal cage on a cart, and he'd stroll them around the playground like that. I think he thought he was doing a nice thing. It always bothered me that he never thought to just let them out of the cage to experience the fresh air. He didn't trust them to do what he wanted outside of the cage, so he would never let them out. I hate that I'm doing the same thing.

Anytime Pigeon does something that I don't like, I lock her up. I expect her to be there for me, but if I don't agree with what she wants or says she needs, I shut her out and take back control. I'm no better than the creepy guy walking his caged birds around the park.

I'm not sure how long it takes, but the vault I'm surrounded by slowly but surely morphs into Creepy Park Guy's bird cage. Just as quickly as it does, all my senses slam back into place. Vertigo hits me, and it takes me a minute to figure out what's going on. I'm bigger than normal, which makes sense because I'm definitely not in my human form anymore.

I tower over Ryn and Zeph as they talk to me. The way Ryn's arms are extended, and the rest of his body language, tells me that he's working to calm Pigeon down. But the hurt, confusion, and anger pumping through my gryphon body tell me it's not working. Treno watches from where he's leaning against the cave wall to my right. He looks relaxed, but his eyes intensely track every move Pigeon and I make.

Pigeon opens her beak and screams at Ryn. It breaks my heart to hear the pain in her screech. I hate what our mates have done to cause this, and I hate the part I played in adding to the bleeding hurt in her cry too.

"Pidge," I shout at her from inside my beat-up bird cage, and she reels back as my voice bounces around our mind.

Ryn steps back, apprehension leaking out of his gray eyes. I watch his lips form my name in question, and Pigeon snaps out at him. He dives out of the way, and Treno pushes off the wall like he's upset and ready to step in.

I'm hit with a wave of rage, like a kick to the chest, and I stumble back.

"Pigeon, I'm so sorry!" I yell at her, but she's not having it.

"I know you're mad, you have every right to be, but please hear me out," I beg.

A mental image of a brick wall slamming down between us fills my mind, and I shake my head. I picture myself taking a sledgehammer to it, and it crumbles in front of me like I'm doing exactly that. Pigeon throws obstacle after obstacle at me, and I tear, slice, and smash through them one by one. I'm determined to convince her to hear me out, but that just makes her more determined to throw shit at me.

"I can do this all night, Pigeon," I call out as she slams a steel wall down, and I mentally shove a welder's mask down over my face and spark up a torch ready to cut through it. *"You can do this as long as you want, or we can cut to the chase and figure shit out, like we're going to do in the end anyway. We only have each other, Pigeon."*

She flashes me Zeph's, Ryn's, and Treno's faces.

"Right, and these assholes too...maybe...if they don't kill each other," I agree.

Pigeon pauses her barrage of barriers and studies me for a moment, like she's not buying my capitulation. I stare right back.

"I mean, I'm not happy about it, if that's what you're looking for. They should have told me. You should have told me," I point out. *"I'm not stoked on the situation, and I'm not sure if you've noticed that neither are they,"* I declare, gesturing to our trio of mates, who just so happen to be—surprise, surprise—arguing again.

Pigeon flings frustration at me like bird shit, and flashes me an image of the vault. I instantly feel like crap again.

"I shouldn't have done that, Pidge. I was mad. I had every right to be mad," I quickly add, *"but I shouldn't have shut you out like that. I'm so sorry,"* I tell her, but she flicks the apology away with a wing.

She shows me an image of herself back in the cage and me outside of it laughing, and it feels like a slap.

"This isn't a trick, Pigeon. I will never do that to you again. No matter what. I swear it on everything...like tacos and orgasms and puppies."

Pigeon rolls her eyes, but I feel a trickle of amusement break through the hurt she's feeling.

A roar fills the cave, and Zeph springs for Treno. Pigeon's and my focus immediately goes back to the guys, and I groan and throw my head back in frustration. Pigeon jumps between them and snaps at Zeph and Treno each in turn. They back off immediately, but sorrow washes through Pigeon when Treno and Zeph proceed to yell shit at each other, their insults skimming over our feathers like razor blades. I watch as it dawns on her that this mating situation isn't the happy gathering she hoped it would be.

I gesture internally at our yelling mates and sigh. *"Welcome to the shit show, Pidge."*

6

I can feel when the shock ripples through her. She really thought they would accept each other and everything would work out. To Pigeon, the mate call was instinctual and *had* to be answered. They now belong to her and, in her mind, should happily accept that they now belong to each other too. She doesn't understand all the other complications and nuances that make all of our connections tenuous and strained. She doesn't get the human side of things.

I've been mad at her for not explaining our gryphon side and how it all works, but I've clearly been doing a piss poor job of explaining the human aspects that layer these relationships too. Things like *mortal enemies* and *war* don't seem to trump things like *instincts* and *mate* in Pigeon's eyes. She clearly thinks we should all be shacking up and getting our orgy on.

Elation rushes through me, and I study the misplaced emotion for a moment, trying to figure it out. What the hell is she so excited about?

Before I can so much as question her, we're jumping out

of the cave and out into the night. Panic slams through me as we streak through the air. I don't know how far away we are from Kestrel City exactly, but from what the guys said earlier, it's not far enough, and there are definitely patrols out looking for us.

"Pigeon!" I shriek at her, completely freaked out. We cannot get caught by Lazza. I don't care how excited she is to be doing whatever the fuck she's doing right now. *"Pigeon, go back right now!"* I order, but she completely ignores me.

I don't want to force her or fight for control. I think back to the battle we had for control when Pigeon wanted to take out Ryn. It was brutal and did so much damage to our already troubled and wounded relationship. I don't want to go there again, but I'm not sure what else to do. I want us to figure out how to be together, to listen and trust each other, but we can't get caught, and she's not listening.

My instincts tell me to get rid of this beat up bird cage around me and shove Pigeon out of the way. I can try to help her understand later when we're safe. But that's the kind of shit I've been pulling with Pigeon from the beginning, and I need to show her that I can change.

"Pigeon! You have to listen to me right now, or you could hurt not only us, but your mates too!" I shout at her.

I can feel her focus shift from whatever it is that she's searching for to me.

"You have to land now!" I urge her, panic and worry bleeding out of every word. *"Please just trust me, land and I will explain everything. If you still think it's safe to be flying around, that's fine, I'm not going to fight you. Just give me five minutes now on the ground, preferably somewhere we can't be spotted from the sky."*

I'm not going to lie, I'm a little surprised when Pigeon folds our wings and then drops us toward the ground like a missile. I try to listen and feel the currents around us as we shoot down, checking to see if we've been spotted or if there is danger nearby. It's hard to hear over the wind rushing past our ears, but I don't feel any indication that anything is headed our way.

That does make me wonder where the hell Zeph, Ryn, and Treno are though. I figured they'd be right on our ass, ready to lay into Pigeon about being so reckless.

The ground comes screaming up at us in no time, and about fifteen feet away from crashing like a bug on a windshield, she spreads our wings, catches the air, and lands gracefully on the pine needle covered forest floor. I'm once again completely taken with her agility and grace, and I can sense Pigeon preening and feeling smug as fuck at my appreciation.

I put my knuckles out, expecting a wing five or a talon bump, but Pigeon just eyes the gesture like we're not there yet.

Fair enough.

I quickly explain to her that we can't fly and all the reasons why it's a super bad idea, and once again I'm surprised by her ready acceptance. She flashes me an image of her walking through the forest. I'm nervous about that option and feel like we should just head back for the cave, but there's no mates around us demanding that we need to do that, so I'm torn.

I take a deep breath and say fuck it. *"We can't get caught though, Pidge. So, whatever it is you feel the need to be out here doing, we need to be very careful,"* I warn, and she just flashes the word *obviously* at me.

I snort, and Pigeon starts stalking through the trees.

"What are we looking for?"

Pigeon harrumphs as if she thinks that's a dumb question, but I feel anxiety pool in our stomach. Pigeon flashes me what I'm pretty sure is a bird's nest, and I stare at the image confused and try to sort out what it all means.

Why would a nest make Pigeon feel anxious?

She flashes me images of Zeph and Treno snarling at each other and frames it all with the worry she feels, then flashes me the nest again.

"You think they're fighting because they want a nest?" I ask her, confused. I'm, like, one hundred percent sure I'm not understanding her correctly, but she nods at me excitedly. Guess I speak better Pigeon than I thought I did.

It's cute that she thinks something so simple could help, and I hate to rain on her nest, but this is my chance to help her understand. *"Pidge, they're not fighting because they don't have a nest. They're fighting because they hate each other. They've been on separate sides of a dominance battle for most of their lives. That's where the tension is coming from. Unfortunately, there isn't shit we can do at this point to change that. Maybe if we can end the war, that could pave the way for some common ground, but I don't know."*

I pause, hating to explain this part, but she needs to know.

"Pidge, there's a chance that nothing we can do will ever bring them together."

She seems to consider that for a moment and then flashes me the nest again, like she's certain it will fix everything.

I study her, ready to argue my point and try a different tactic for getting her to see what I'm saying, but I shrug instead. What do I know? It makes no sense to me, but that doesn't mean she's wrong. At this point, what can it hurt?

So I get on board. Let's build a nest.

"What do you need? Like twigs and things?" I ask, liking the contentment that ripples through us when I don't fight her on this.

I look around for some sturdy looking branches, but Pigeon zeroes in on a tree to our left. I gape at it. It's at least twenty feet tall and has a trunk as thick as our gryphon waist. I open my mouth to argue that a whole tree isn't some branches, but Pigeon must speak better Falon than I realize, because she sends me an image of all the branches that are on the tree and her ripping them off with her beak.

I look around us, but there's no sign of the guys or any patrols, so I once again put my *if it makes you happy* hat on. If it gets us on the same page, then what does it hurt? Pretty sure she can't rip a tree from the ground anyway, so it will be a mere gesture of goodwill on my part.

This is exactly how we start repairing things. By trusting each other and supporting decisions that don't make the most sense at the time to one side of us. I can give her this, and maybe in return, she'll do the same when it's something important to me.

"Follow your heart," I concede, and elation floods me.

I can't help but smile as Pigeon circles the tree, assessing the best plan of action to take it down.

"I support that you need to do this, Pidge. I just don't want you to get bummed if this doesn't solve the issues between the guys. There's more to things than just the gryphon side of this," I remind her, and I wonder if Ryn's, Treno's, and Zeph's gryphons are also battling with them like this inside?

Pigeon isn't dumb by any means, but she definitely operates under more instinct-driven guidelines than I do. Are we the only ones? Is this because she was trapped for so long and hasn't experienced life firsthand and hasn't been able to learn the way of it all? Or is this just a gryphon thing?

"Truce?" I ask Pigeon as she traces the height of the tree with her eyes, still sizing it up. *"Can we both try harder to listen and trust each other?"*

Pigeon turns from the tree and studies me for a moment. She flashes me an image of her stomping on a cage.

"I'll never do that again, I really am sorry. Even if I don't understand or agree with something, I promise we'll work it out. No more holding back or shutting each other out. That goes for both of us," I offer, flashing her images of our mates and her with a closed beak. After a moment, she extends her talon-tipped hand for a fist bump, and I brush my small knuckles against hers and feel a massive weight lifted off my chest.

"Alright, Pidge, let's Paul Bunyan the shit out of this tree and get back before we get caught."

I shake my head as she excitedly refocuses on what I think is an impossible task. I'm adding that line to the list of shit I'd never thought I'd have to say to someone. These days that list is getting seriously long.

Pigeon flashes me an image of her handing me a beer can, and I crack up. Well, she'll probably get me killed, but at least I'll go down laughing. I guess I should find some comfort in that.

* * *

"What the hell?" Zeph shouts as Pigeon hands over the reins of our body so I can explain why she just shoved a massive tree through the roof hole of our cave.

Thanks, Pidge.

I climb down the branches, which is no small feat since I have no fucking clothes on. Again, *thank you, Pidge.* My feet hit the floor of the cave, and Ryn pulls off his shirt and hands it to me. I don't have time to thank him or try not to drool over his muscles before Zeph is in my face. I ignore the feel of his body against mine as he invades my personal space with his anger issues.

Shit, we need to stop surprise shifting, because we are

running out of clothes. I get now why all of their clothes have ties holding them together on the sides. It's so the ties break and not the clothes themselves from a shift, but I'm not seeing any more ties around here. The clothes we have now are thanks to a raid on someone's laundry line, but surprise shifts have resulted in two pairs of pants and a shirt having been ripped apart, and that leaves us with only three pairs of pants and two shirts.

"Why is there a tree sticking out of our roof?" Zeph asks, shoving a branch away from his face as he does and pulling my thoughts away from our clothes issues.

I sigh and pull Ryn's shirt over my head. "Because Pigeon decided she needed to build a nest."

"And you're just letting her?" Zeph demands, his words oozing all kinds of judgement.

"Yes, I am. And guess what? So are you, because your snapping at each other is the reason she decided it needed to happen in the first place. Apparently, she thinks a nest will solve all of your issues."

He gives an incredulous snort.

I glare at him.

"Don't worry, I tried to explain to her that there is no cure for your dickish personality, but it seems she takes this whole mate thing a hell of a lot more seriously than any of us do."

"What is that supposed to mean?" he challenges.

"It means exactly what I just said." We stare each other down, and I pour ice water all over the heat that tries to crawl up my thighs and settle low in my belly.

Yep, Pigeon is back, and she's returned with a healthy dose of annoying ass hormones. I was really hoping now that we're all officially mated—ugh—she'd cut that shit out. It seems I've seriously underestimated her nympho ways.

"Where the hell were you guys anyway? What kind of mates let their other half just take off when it's dangerous?"

Ryn scoffs. "Oh, we didn't, we all tried to go after you, which means we all crashed into each other as we tried to fly out at the same time. By the time we stopped fighting long enough to decide who goes first, you were nowhere to be found."

I can just picture the *Three Stooges* scene in my head, but instead of finding amusement in it, I just feel tired. How the hell are we going to win a war when they can't even work together long enough to fly out of a fucking hole?

I look around. Well, technically none of us can fly out of the hole now because of the whole tree thing, but hopefully Pigeon can make short work of her nest, and the tree stopper in the roof will be gone in no time.

I press in closer to Zeph and drop my voice. "Can you rein in your hate long enough for us to do what we need to do, or should I rethink who goes on this trip and who doesn't?"

Zeph's honey eyes flash with rage, but I don't let it sting me. I'm not trying to embarrass him by calling him out in front of the others, but his attitude needs to be addressed before we start our search for the Ouphe. If it's not dealt with, we could have serious problems because of it.

Zeph, Ryn, and Treno can't spend the whole time bickering. Aside from it grating on my fucking nerves, it makes Pigeon do dumb shit like rip trees from the ground. We can't afford for them to be too busy arguing to spot a scout or something else dangerous and deadly. I get the impression this place has no shortage of shit we don't want to run into, and unfortunately, they're the only ones who know what we are up against. We can't afford for any of us to be distracted by petty hate.

The fact that I'm the only one who seems to realize that,

speaks volumes. These guys aren't dumb, they're the leaders of their people. But right now, they can't seem to shove the hurt and history away long enough to tap into who they need to be so all of us can get shit done.

"Are you questioning *me*?" Zeph growls low and menacingly.

His tone sends all kinds of pleasurable flashes to my clit, and I roll my eyes. *"Pidge, cut that shit out!"* She snickers, and I groan internally.

"You bet your asshole-ish ways, I am. I don't want to die because you can't behave," I snap back.

Treno makes a noise that's somewhere between a snort and grunt of agreement. I turn to him.

"You're not much better," I accuse. "You both have issues you need to sit on until we've figured out a way to win. Don't forget you're in this with us. We don't have to like each other, but we need to figure out a way to work together, because more lives than just ours are counting on us figuring out a way to end this war. There's no time for petty bullshit and hurt feelings."

Treno stares at me like he's not sure if he's impressed or offended by what I'm saying.

"What about you?" Zeph challenges. "Can we trust that you won't betray us or use your abilities against us? Will you run the first chance you get or accept your place in this fight and see it through?"

Anger boils up inside of me, and I can feel my face go red with fury. If he wants to talk about betrayal, we can go there. I've got plenty more to say about what he and Ryn did and what they kept from me. Even Pigeon is flashing me images of when he saved Loa and kicked us out of the Eyrie. We got our throats slit because of that, and she's just as pissed about his tone and the insinuations in it as I am.

I work to calm myself down. I want to punch the giant

fucker in his smug face, but I mean what I say about squashing our issues so we can get to the Ouphe and hopefully get help. Decking Zeph right now, however good it may feel, is not the example that needs to be set in this moment. So I swallow my offence and vitriol down.

Tastes worse than those damn grot berries, but I do it.

"Yeah, Zeph. You can count on me to see the freedom of the Gryphons through."

He studies my face for a beat and then surprisingly backs off.

"We should go," he orders, walking over to his dark corner and picking up a pack. Light is starting to filter in through the branches of the tree Pigeon and I shoved into the roof of the cave, and I realize that it must be dawn already. Well, there goes my plans to go back to sleep.

Outrage hammers in my chest, and at first I think Pigeon is also pissed that we're not going to go back to bed, but she flashes me images of her nest and all the work she put into getting that damn tree here.

Shit.

"Pidge, you promised you wouldn't get mad if they didn't appreciate your nest gesture," I argue, but she huffs, clearly not sticking to that agreement. Crap, how the hell can I smooth this over, we just got back on good terms. *"We can build a nest when we get to the Ouphe. I'll help you rip out as many trees as you want."*

"What's wrong?" Ryn asks me.

I look from his concerned face to the tree sticking down into the cave and back. "Um...Pigeon's not ready to leave; she's super into wanting to make a nest or something."

"Pigeon?" he asks, puzzled.

"Yeah, that's what my gryphon likes to be called."

Zeph and Treno both grunt in irritation at the same time. For two people that hate each other, they sure do think alike. I'm about to defend Pigeon's choice in names when Treno speaks up.

"This isn't the time for useless female urges. Like you said, lives are counting on us. Save the preening and roosting. This is war, not a mating."

Zeph grunts again, his back to us, but it's clear he's agreeing in his own fucked up way. I personally don't care, but Pigeon reacts like what they are saying is a direct attack against her. Hurt and anger clash inside of me, and she stomps off to the dark recesses of my consciousness and lies down, burying her face underneath her onyx wing. I study her reaction and the feelings she sends whirling around inside of us. She feels rejected and hurt, and I hate it.

My eyes and face harden as I look at Treno. "I get what you're saying, but we both know there are ways to get your point across without being a piece of shit about it. You want to be mad at me, have at it, but if you think I'm going to stand by and let you hurt *her*," I seethe, pressing my palm to my chest, "...then you're in for a rude awakening. Stay the fuck away from me until you can figure out how to be fucking respectful...both of you," I growl, catching Zeph's eyes as well. "She deserves better than that."

I call on my wings, ready to fly the fuck out of here and find the Ouphe myself. But my feathers brush against bark and pine needles, and I'm reminded that there's not enough room to fly off thanks to the fucking tree. These dicks don't appreciate shit.

"It was a good tree, Pidge; they weren't worthy of it," I try to reassure her, but she stays quiet.

I turn instead and start climbing the tree to get out. At least the wings will cover my ass as I do.

I high five myself for owning this whole *find the bright side* attitude. Fuck knows I'm going to need it traveling with this group of uncouth numpties. I make my way out of the cave more winded and sweatier than I probably should be from climbing that damn tree. Good thing we'll be walking for a good portion of this craptastic adventure we're about to embark on, because I clearly can use the cardio—and a shower. I smell a level of ripe that no one should have to endure for too long.

This should be fun.

7

"I hate this place," I mutter as I stare at the pile of grot fruit in front of me. "Why can't we hunt?" I ask again for the sixth time since Ryn dumped *dinner* in front of me on my blanket.

"We can't build a fire out here. It's too dangerous," Ryn answers.

"We haven't been making good time, and we're still too close to possible patrols to risk it," Zeph adds, giving me a look that says my slowness is to blame.

I stare at the pile of vile fruit and try not to groan. "And why can't Pigeon hunt? She likes raw meat," I ask again.

Zeph huffs, and Treno pulls his blanket tighter around him, which has been his tell of annoyance the past three days.

"Pidge—your gryphon—needs a lot more food to sustain her in her form. She'd have to find a whole herd of something to hunt, and that would also possibly draw attention. We can't risk it. Just eat the berries. They're the best option we have, and they're not that bad," Ryn reassures me, popping a berry into his mouth and chewing it, like that proves it's edible.

All it proves is that he possesses fucked up taste buds. These berries are the worst. We've been eating them for days, because—lucky us—they grow all over the place in the forest. They are some kind of superfood apparently, as it doesn't take many of them to fill you up, they're packed with a bunch of nutrients, and they help with healing, but they taste like vomit, and I just can't put myself through eating them again.

Pigeon won't even touch them, and that's saying a lot, because she makes questionable choices and clearly has messed up taste. Which is only further proven by the collection of grumpy jerks currently sitting around us that she likes to call mates.

I thought I had figured out a way to solve the grot fruit problem last night. I figured I could simply swallow them whole and avoid the nasty innards that taste like putrid betrayal. But just when I thought I had outsmarted the evil little berries, I started to digest them.

I then spent the night burping up the rancid taste of their juice. It was a lose-lose situation for all, especially when the gas kicked in. I was banished to walk downwind all morning, and let's just say I no longer judge animals who fear their own farts.

So lesson learned: apparently, chewing the nasty little fuckers makes them a hell of a lot easier to digest, but then you have to suffer with actually tasting them. Either way, I'm fucked, and I hate this place. Maybe some granola, vagina-steaming, health nut might be able to choke them down for the benefits alone, but Gwyneth Paltrow I am not.

I can't do it. I lie back on my blanket and try to ignore my empty stomach. Maybe tomorrow night when I'm really starving, I can force myself, but tonight it just doesn't feel worth it. I stare up at the stunning starlit night and once again search for any constellations that exist in the sky I know back home, but I can't make familiar shapes out of any of these stars. Guess I'll just have to create my own.

"You should eat, Falon, tomorrow will be another long day," Ryn tells me, like it's breaking news.

Every day will be a long day until we find the Ouphe, and that's *if* we can find them. I outlined what I could remember of the map the other day for them, and they all kind of looked at me like there was no way I had that right. Something about uninhabitable badlands or whatever, but it's definitely where I was told to go. Zeph's now convinced that we're being led to our deaths for sure, but he was outvoted, and alas here we are, still slowly making our way closer to who the hell knows what.

Either way, Pigeon and I already decided that she is going to walk tomorrow so I can have a break. I'm pretty sure that makes the grot berries officially her problem now.

Treno stands up and gives us his back while he arranges his blanket. He's off to the side like he's trying to pretend that he's not with us. It gets cold at night, but it seems everyone is too pissed and stubborn to huddle together like good sense would encourage.

I watch his back as he flings the blanket out and lays it gently on some bracken. I study the matching black symbols marked high on each of his shoulder blades. I trace the skinny rhombus and the small pearl-like circles that surround the thin diamond. Each mark is identical, and I can feel my shoulder blades itching from where I know the same marks now reside on me.

I want to ask what they are, but now is not the time. Not when he's still set on hating me.

I think back to the marks I know I used to have on my own body. If I still had them, would Treno have gotten them too after our mating, like I did his?

A rumble of irritation bubbles up in my chest. It seems

Pigeon isn't a huge fan of my line of thought right now. She hasn't been too keen on thinking about her mates at all lately. I try not to feel boastful about the fact that things aren't turning out the way Pigeon wanted. I did try to warn her about crushing on assholes.

Pigeon flashes me the memories of me screaming Zeph's, Ryn's, and Treno's names, lost in the ecstasy of incredible orgasms, while they pumped away between my thighs. I roll my eyes and try to dismiss the heat I feel in my stomach at the images.

"That's just sex," I tell her dismissively. *"Any asshole can give you an orgasm if they're skilled enough, it doesn't mean anything."*

To back up what I'm saying, I flash her images of all the other times I hooked up with people, but that just seems to irritate her more. She's like an ex who wants to get all bent out of shape over who you were with before them.

"You were there for every single one," I point out to her.

Yeah, I thought I was a latent and she was a wolf back then, but we still had somewhat of a connection. I could feel her when she was very agitated or wanted to exude some good ol' fashioned dominance. She liked pushing to run the show when it came to my hookups in the past. Aggressive was our middle name.

She flashes me images of Ryn, Treno, and Zeph again, clearly trying to communicate that things are different with them. It seems she doesn't want to recognize that I was no more attached to them when we fucked than I ever have been to any other guy. The only real difference is that *she* was attached.

Several images blink through my mind. Pigeon is trying to figure out how to solve the *asshole* problem occurring in our three mates. I snort in amusement. *"Many a woman has tried and failed to suss out the solution to that one, Pidge. I wish you luck, but I'm not holding my breath that there's a way to fix that. Especially not with these guys,"* I tell her, amused.

"What's so funny?" Ryn asks me. I look over my shoulder to see him settling in next to my blanket.

"Pigeon's deciding between ripping everyone's heads off and trying to figure out how we can all be one big happy family," I tell him, the snark thick enough to cut with a knife.

"Well, that should keep her occupied for the rest of our natural born life," he replies, and I try not to release an amused snort.

I know Ryn is feeling bad and wants to get on my good side, but it's going to take a hell of a lot more than apologies and some attempts at comradery for me to trust him.

"Yeah, I had similar advice to dole out," I admit, focusing back on the twinkling sky.

I can feel Ryn's eyes boring into the top of my head.

"I was thinking"—he clears his throat nervously—"that maybe we should work on some of your training while we're making our way to the Quietus Mountains."

"She doesn't need to know how to fight. She needs to figure out how to break the Vow. That's all she should be focusing on," Zeph cuts in.

"Excuse you." I glare at him. "I will do everything I can to figure that out, but I can't do much until I talk to the Ouphe. What does it hurt to get better at swords and shit?"

I think back to the young gryphon Sarai and how badly she kicked my ass with a sword. I could definitely use some work.

"You remembered enough of the language to try to use it on me. Maybe you just need to eliminate all other distractions," Zeph commands, shooting a pointed look at Treno.

I sit up and spin to give Zeph my best *get the fuck over it* look, but I kick a rock as I try to swivel, and fuck it hurts. My feet are already beat to shit from not having shoes this whole time, so I pull my poor little pained foot in my lap and fold myself over it as I wait for the pain to recede.

"What kind of soft world do you come from if the small amount of walking we've done leaves you so hobbled?" Zeph observes, clearly not caring about my soft feet and their issues.

He's in a shit mood today, which really isn't different from the shit mood he's been in the entire time I've known him, but for whatever reason, I get the impression he's looking for a fight this evening.

Now, if I could only get my foot to stop hurting long enough to give him one. "A better fucking world than this one, I'll tell you that much," I snarl at him, flinging a look of disgust at him and the pile of berries still tainting my blanket. "I'd kill for a fucking taco right now. And judge all you want, but a car sure would shorten this little adventure by a shit ton. You can stomp around this forest like you're a big tough guy, but you can't drive a manual, and in my world, that separates the men from the boys. So may the rocks bless *your* barefooted path," I snap, suddenly homesick and dying for a massive bowl of chips and salsa.

Oooh or some mashed potatoes. I'd happily cut a man for a piece of chocolate cake, no questions asked. But no, I get grot fruit and popcorn meat. Okay, maybe the popcorn meat isn't so bad, but I miss peanut butter and Oreos.

"I don't know what any of that means," Zeph snaps back over his shoulder.

"Exactly. You want to judge me for how I'm surviving in your world? Well, buddy, you wouldn't last a day in mine."

"Please. From the looks of things, your people can't even walk!"

I yank a witty retort from my mind and load my tongue with it, ready to aim and fire, but a whimper-snarl from

Treno has me unloading my mouth and looking over to him. Treno has his fingers buried in his hair, and he's partially bent over like he's about to pray or something. It seems I'm not the only one hitting my limit with all the bullshit.

Every muscle in his body looks tense, and I wait for him to explode, like I'm watching the wick of a firework burn down. When he doesn't immediately turn to us and tell us all to *shut the rut up*, I'm surprised. Another pained noise comes from what sounds like gritted teeth, and his hands fist even tighter in his hair. My irritation is immediately replaced by concern, and I abandon my blanket and move to check on him.

"Treno?" I ask hesitantly.

I wish his name didn't sound so small coming out of my mouth, but he's definitely still pissed at me, and I worry if Treno tries to rip my head off for getting near him, then Zeph will get the fight he's looking for. He seems to have a *I can be a dick to her, but you can't* code of conduct when it comes to Treno and how he interacts with me.

"Are you okay?" I ask moving toward him, and Ryn and Zeph both stop bickering and turn to take in what's going on.

Treno releases a choked gasp, and then his hands move from his hair to his throat.

"Fuck, I think he's choking!" I scream, running to close the distance between us. Ryn and Zeph shoot to their feet as I scramble to Treno, grabbing his shoulder and wrenching him around.

Zeph and Ryn are shouting something behind me, but I can't hear it over the terror I see in Treno's mismatched eyes as they connect with mine. His mouth is open in what looks like a silent plea, and fear hammers through me as I take in his fingers clawing at his throat.

"He needs the Heimlich!" I yell over my shoulder, but

when I try to pull Treno up so I can move behind him, a wall of pain unexpectedly slams into me, and I find I can't move.

I'm so stunned by the rippling agony, and my senses are so completely overwhelmed by the flood, that I sort of just fold in on myself. My legs go weak beneath me as I instantly start suffocating. I grab for my throat and try to gasp for air, just like Treno is doing, but it's like something is trying to pull the oxygen out of every cell in my body. I'm suffocating, but I also feel like I just might implode at the same time.

Treno rolls to his side, his face starting to go purple and his lips slowly tinting blue. My eyes fill with the same terror I saw in Treno's gaze, and I look over to see Ryn and Zeph drop to the ground, pain instantaneously etched in both of their faces.

What the hell is going on? I look around to see if I can find the source of what's happening, but I don't see anything.

"The bond," Zeph chokes out, pointing to Treno before whatever is happening to us steals the last of his ability to speak, or move, or do anything other than start to die slowly.

The bond is doing this to us? I ask myself as I try to make sense of it all. I feel my brain starting to grow more sluggish, and it gets harder to grasp the threads I'm trying to hang onto. Is someone doing this to us through the bond? I blink slowly and start to feel my body relax in a way that makes me even more terror-stricken. My body is giving in, when I want it to battle. *But battle against what*, I scream at myself as I fight futilely against the black specks now dotting my vision.

8

A flash of light explodes to my right, blinding me, and by the time I blink my eyes back into focus, I spot a man standing over Treno like he's looking for something on his body. Alarm joins my panic, but it's getting hard to keep my thoughts focused. Everything is starting to feel fuzzy and muted, and my body just lets go, all fight officially sapped from every cell in my body.

"Fuck!" the man growls. "How is your brother getting to you again?" he demands, frustration bleeding out of his tone.

Lazza? Lazza is doing this?

"Where is it?" The man with the cropped white hair and Cristal-colored eyes grumbles. "I took care of the Vow. Lazza shouldn't be able to get to all of you still," he defends.

He took care of the Vow. Who is this guy? When did he take care of the Vow?

"Where is the rune Lazza is using right now?" the tall beautiful man demands of Treno, but Treno can't answer as his arms fall limp and his head starts to loll back.

"By the stars, of course your bloodline has been sneakier than they should have been. Why didn't I see that though?"

he asks himself, oddly. "Where's your other mark, Altern?" he frustratedly snarls again before he flips Treno onto his other side and searches his body.

"If I have to touch your cock to look for this thing, I'm not going to be pleased," the unfamiliar man grumps. "Where are you hiding your sneaky little rune?" he sing-songs, and then his eyebrows shoot up with knowing.

He abandons his efforts to untie Treno's pants and brushes the white strands of Treno's hair back from the side of his head. He looks behind his ear and then shouts. "Got ya!"

The man presses his hand over Treno's left ear, and a glow comes to life under his palm.

All at once, the crushing feeling in my lungs, throat, and limbs abates, and I gasp to pull oxygen into my body. I hear the others doing the same, coughing and heaving as we all try to recover from whatever the hell Lazza just tried to do to us.

I keep my eyes trained on the stranger as he pushes away from Treno and looks around at the rest of us while shaking his head. His champagne-colored eyes seem to be debating something as he takes us in, and then his gaze lands on mine. His concerned eyes soften, and he comes nearer.

I wheeze and stiffen.

"Pidge, I may need you," I tell her, checking in quickly to make sure she's okay. I feel her observing everything intently, guarding and assessing the situation, but she doesn't seem to feel threatened by whoever this is, so I take that into consideration as I refocus on him.

"Don't be afraid, Falon. I'm not here to hurt you. I've been watching your threads closely and saw you were in need of me again. That's the only reason I'm here," he explains, but I have no fucking clue what he's talking about.

Watching my threads?

"I hoped, when I took care of the Altern's Vow, that you would be able to make it to me on your own—and that maybe all of you would be in a better place when you did—but I think given what just happened *again*, it might be best to let go of those hopes and just get the group of you to safety."

"Who are you?" I croak, rubbing my neck as if that will make it all better. Damn, between my throat being slit and whatever Lazza just did to phantom strangle us, I'm worried my vocal cords may never fully recover.

Zeph would be so pleased.

"I'm sorry. I've been watching you for so long it makes me feel like we're old friends," he tells me on a laugh. "I'm Wekun," the strange champagne-eyed man declares, offering his hand.

I give it the side-eye. There he goes with that whole watching thing again. I scan his chiseled frame and take a moment to study his handsome face and stunning eyes. Nope. Still not okay with the whole watching me thing.

Before I can say anything about how *not cool* stalking is, Wekun looks to the side. "Now, now, Syta, is that any way to thank the person who just saved your life?" Wekun asks, and I follow his stare to find Zeph crawling to his feet with murder in his golden gaze.

"For all I know, you're the one who tried to kill us in the first place, Ouphe scum, and you're just blaming Lazza so we fall into your trap. You seem to have a habit of showing up when tainted magic is in the air and claiming that you're there to help," Zeph growls and then spits on the ground, punctuating exactly how he feels about our visitor. Surprisingly though, Zeph doesn't make another move against Wekun, even though I can see in his eyes that he wants to.

"Habit of showing up?" I ask, confused, my eyes bouncing from Zeph's indignant glare back to Wekun.

"Zeph," Wekun chides like he's scolding a naughty toddler. For some reason, it makes me like him already.

"You know each other?" I ask, trying and failing at figuring out what the hell is going on.

"I don't know about *know each other*, but we've met him before," Ryn explains, getting to his feet. He looks just as pissed as Zeph, and I'm trying to understand why.

Maybe the lack of oxygen fried the last of my working brain cells. "Can someone just fucking tell me what the hell is going on?" I croak, reaching my limit for near-death experiences and cryptic half-stories.

"He showed up back at the cave. Lazza tried to go after Treno and us through his Vow mark. This Ouphe walked in out of nowhere and stopped it," Ryn explains.

Me, standing outside of my body as pain washed through me, surfaces in my mind. I remember Ryn and Zeph scrambling, and then I saw a flare of light—not unlike the one that occurred right before Wekun showed up just now. I recall the faint image of a figure appearing in the cave, awash in that bright light, and I make the connection to what Ryn is talking about.

"You helped us before? Why?" I ask, turning back to Wekun.

His eyes light up with affection, making the pale gold color sparkle in an incredibly enticing way. "Like I said, I'm here to help. I should have seen that, at some point, their family would have put another connecting rune somewhere, although I'm sure they never thought one brother would use it to try and kill the other," he tells me, like that should make complete sense to me.

I stare at him for a moment. "Am I supposed to know what any of that means?" I finally ask when my brain doesn't catch what he's throwing at all. Nope, I fumble that shit like my name is butterfingers, because I am not receiving anything he's sending my way.

"We told you last time that we didn't need your help. We also told you what would happen if you ever showed up again," Zeph growls and takes a threatening step toward Wekun.

He just chuckles like he's not about to face down the big scary asshole Syta of the Hidden and then tsks when Ryn also moves to join Zeph against him.

"No appreciation ever from the mates," Wekun sighs, exasperated.

I scramble to my feet and intercept the ungrateful mates Pigeon has stuck me with. "Are you guys kidding? This guy shows up and saves our asses not once, but twice, and your response isn't to thank him, but to threaten him?" I demand.

"You can't trust anything the Ouphe say; they always have ulterior motives and schemes going on," Zeph defends.

I dismiss the sting I feel from that comment. I don't know why I'm shocked to hear it. I'm part Ouphe, and Zeph has always been clear in how he feels about me because of it. I know his and Ryn's prejudices run deep. Being irritated with their current reaction of judging Wekun based off of what he is instead of the fact that he's helped us is probably a waste of my time, but I can't help it.

"Are you both forgetting that we're trying to get to the Ouphe so that we can ask them for help?" I remind them, as though somehow the predicament that we're all in just slipped their minds.

"No, *you* are going to the Ouphe to ask for help. *We* are just making sure you aren't used against us," Zeph clips.

I stare at him blankly for a moment. Did he really just say that to me? I know I heard the words, but my heart and mind don't seem to want to let them take root. During my time in Kestrel City, I saw peeks of Zeph that showed me parts of him that were so much more than the angry, vicious, knife-tongued male who's staring down at me right now. I've tried to understand where his vitriol comes from. Empathized with him and hated the awful things he'd experienced that shaped him into who he is today.

But right now as he stares down at me with taunting, hate-filled, honey eyes, I can't for the life of me remember why I've ever bothered to give him the benefit of the doubt. Hurt and anger unfurl in my chest and slowly claim everything that I am.

I look at Ryn as I try to breathe through the swell of emotion, but he says nothing to counter the words that just slipped out of Zeph's mouth. I shake my head; of course he'd stand up for his Syta over me. He always just goes along with what he's told, such a good little puppy.

I'm an idiot wasting my time with these fools.

"Falon," Wekun speaks up, his face filled with pity and concern.

"Don't you speak to her. You're not going to taint her mind, we won't allow it," Zeph snaps at Wekun, and Ryn puts a hand up to keep Zeph from moving any closer, nodding silently at me and where I'm standing in proximity to Wekun.

I look over at Treno, too disgusted by Zeph and Ryn to stare at them for a second longer. He's quiet and still, lying on the ground, but the color is back in his face, and I can see that he's alive and breathing. His eyes are far away and filled with pain, and my throat grows tight as I take him in.

"Treno, are you okay?" I ask, moving closer to him, the drive to comfort him overtaking the logic that he probably doesn't want me near.

My voice seems to snap him out of whatever he's thinking about, and his eyes fill with anger and fix on me. "Lazza just tried to kill me," he snaps out, and even though he doesn't say *because of you* with his words, his eyes flash exactly that for the briefest of moments.

I stop my advance and realize that Wekun is still by my side. More hurt pings through my battered body like I'm a pinball machine. He wants to blame me instead of blaming his brother for being a prick?

I study him on the ground and feel myself hardening inside. It's as though their hate and mistrust were the water my insides needed to start churning everything I am into concrete. And now, with each glare and nasty word, the cement in my soul is slowly hardening until there's nothing left but stone.

I can take responsibility for connecting Treno to Zeph and Ryn without their knowledge. I didn't know either; however, that little fact doesn't seem to matter to anyone. I'm just some Ouphe-tainted who clearly can't be trusted. But I'm not going to just sit here and get blamed for the actions of a psycho, because it's convenient to aim all the anger at me. I'm not going to let their hate infect me, or stand for the unspoken accusation that somehow I would do something to hurt the Gryphons instead of try to protect them.

I've hit my limit. I'm over these fuckers.

I check in with Pigeon, and she's just as disgusted with their behavior. She wraps a warm wing around me and flips them a taloned bird.

"I've tried to take the high road," I start, looking at Zeph, Ryn and Treno in turn. "I've tapped into my empathy. I've done my best to put myself in your shoes, to understand how hard this situation is for all of you. But have you assholes even tried to do that for me? Nope. Not for one fucking second.

"You all think it's okay to just dump your anger and pain all over me. You think that for whatever reason, I have to just take the bullshit. That I'm stuck with you and that's all there

83

is to it. You want to think the worst of me, have fun. You want to blame me for your problems and pretend like your dicks didn't help to put you in this situation, go for it. Rewrite history all you want. Do what you need to do to cradle your fragile egos and stroke your weak manhoods. But you can do it without me."

I look over at Wekun, rage simmering in my gut. "You want to help me?" I ask, revisiting what he said earlier.

"I do."

"Then get me as far away from these pricks as you can, please," I tell him, hating the crack of emotion that ripples through my words. I blink back the tears I feel in my eyes and rip the cracks inside of me open so that all my fury can flood out and staunch the wounds these three have gouged into my soul.

Wekun gives me a sad smile.

"Gladly," he agrees, and then he reaches for my palm.

In the time it takes to flap a wing, I'm no longer in the cold dark forest, surrounded by gryphons with anger issues. Now I find myself standing inside a massive tent, the kind I've seen in period movies or at Renaissance festivals.

"Holy shit. You actually did it," I exclaim, looking over at Wekun, completely shocked.

Awed, I look around at the sparse dark wood furniture that's been placed on top of overlapping, beautiful, jewel-toned carpets. The large rugs are laid out on the ground so the floor is completely covered and cushy. Inside the canvas walls, the tent is spacious. There's a large bed and side table, a seating area that has massive cushions that look very inviting and relaxing, and on the opposite side from where I'm standing is a small washroom with a copper bathtub, a sink-like basin for washing hands, and...a large bucket.

It says a lot about how fed up I am with Pigeon's mates, because I don't even question how smart it was to just up and pop away to who knows where, with a person I don't know, until right...now.

Like he can sense my instantaneous concern and discomfort, Wekun squeezes my hand. "Don't worry, Falon, I portalled your mates to the Gryphon camp that's just next to ours. They don't know where they are, and they think I took you, but I feel like that might be just the reality check they need at the moment, don't you?"

I pause, not sure what to say. There's a part of me that feels bad. They were just magicked somewhere unknown and might be going through some issues with that. Then another part of me screams that I need to get over it. I can't keep operating like Zeph, Ryn, and Treno have common courtesy, decency, or genuine concern when it comes to me. If not for the fact that their lives are tied to mine, they probably would have killed me or left me behind a long time ago. I promised I would help end this war, but I didn't promise to let them shit on me and emotionally beat me down while I do.

"Where are we?" I finally manage as I drop-kick my empathy and try to adopt a more hardened mien. Zeph is right, this world isn't easy on soft feet or soft hearts.

"Oh...right, sorry!" Wekun offers sheepishly, his smile apologetic and kind. "Falon, welcome to the Ouphe stronghold," he announces, pulling back the front drape of the canvas walled structure we're standing in and revealing a tent city as far as the eye can see.

Well, fuck me, we're exactly where I was trying to get.

I step under Wekun's arm, and thick cool air greets me. It's quieter than I would have expected from a place that clearly houses so many people. Something about this place reminds me of images that I've seen of refugee camps in my old world. The tents are various sizes, but all made from an animal hide that's the color of light sand and has a suede look to it—only way thicker than any material I've seen back home.

People move around the camp, going about their business, and they don't even bother to look over at Wekun and me as we stand and stare and I take it all in. The ground is covered in a soft, rich looking soil the color of espresso. It looks wet, but although the sky is overcast and gloomy, nothing else around me gives the impression that it's rained in a while. The air is dry and brittle, and I get the distinct impression that the spirit of the people who live here just might be too.

There's a palpable sadness in the air, a tension reverberating all around me, that I feel. Nadi said that the Ouphe have been waiting for a Bond Breaker to come and help them, and right now I can sense how true that is. I know that in the eyes of the Gryphons, the Ouphe are to blame for all of the wrongs done to them. I don't know if that's completely true or not, but I can see that the people who live in this tent-dotted stronghold are suffering.

This place feels broken.

9

I look to Wekun, concern bubbling up in my chest, but I'm not sure what to say. Questions alight in my eyes, and he just nods his head solemnly like he can read my mind, or maybe it's my face that's communicating *what the fuck* loud and clear. Either way, he obviously understands what I'm saying without speaking a word. Maybe I'm wrong, maybe I need to see more of this place than one minute of observation, but if the people here are as downtrodden as it feels like they are, how the hell are they going to help us?

I've been picturing a place like Vedan in my mind. The way the Gryphons talk about the Ouphe like they're still this hated ruling class, and the cliff castle they built that hid a city in its bosom, they've completely fucked with my expectations of what we would be walking into. This doesn't feel like a proud, strong race of beings, they feel...terrified.

I look over and catch eyes peeking through a crack in the doorway fabric of a tent across from me. As soon as my eyes land on theirs, the fabric closes all the way and they scurry off, like they're petrified that they were caught.

"Come, we have about five minutes, but we can talk as

we go," Wekun explains, walking out on the well-traveled pathway that winds between tents.

"Five minutes until what?" I ask as I fall into step next to this incredibly attractive stranger who—for some reason—I feel like I can trust implicitly.

He smiles, and I try not to drool or read into it. I crack a whip at my libido. It's gotten me into enough trouble already. I'm not fucking anyone else, maybe ever again. Man, that's going to suck.

"Five minutes until your mates start tearing this camp to the ground in search of you."

I snort. "Blame the horny half bird inside of me for those three. They're her mates, not my mates. I wouldn't have picked that assortment of assholes if my life depended on it."

Wekun gives me another hump-inducing smile. "It may very well depend on it. You need to lead them home," he tells me cryptically. I push the automatic trust I feel for this guy aside and study him. He's very tan, and I can't tell if it's from a lot of time out in the sun or if it's genetics. His white hair is buzzed, which isn't a hair style I've seen in this world, and his champagne-colored eyes look like they swirl with a whole fuck ton of secrets.

"Who are you again?" I ask, needing to know more and questioning why I haven't asked before now.

Has this world fucked me up? I've been forced to go with the flow so much that it's some kind of fucked up habit for me now. If this dude was driving a creepy white van and pulled up in front of me, smiling and telling me to hop in, would I do it now without question? I shake my head at my behavior and tell myself to get it together and trust no one.

I take a step to my right, creating more distance between myself and the mysterious Wekun. He smiles, like he thinks I'm adorable. Shit. Can this dude read my mind?

"I'm like you, Falon, a Bond magic user."

I stop in my tracks and narrow my eyes at him. "Wait. I thought Nadi said there were no more Bond magic users left. That's why it was so important for me to come here," I ask, confused and immediately more suspicious.

Fuck. If Zeph was right about this being a trap, I'm never going to hear the end of it. That is, if we don't die.

"There are other Bond possessors, you'll be meeting your Sept not far down the road, but Nadi didn't lie when she said you were the only one who could fix the Vow."

"But if you're a Bond user too, then why can't you do it?"

"Because I'm not the right kind of Bond user for the job," Wekun tells me. He waves me forward, and I start to walk again.

"I'm confused, there are right and wrong kinds of magic users?"

"Not wrong users, per se, but Bond possessors can specialize in different aspects of the magic. We all have our strengths, so to speak. Take me for example, I'm a Bond Weaver, or at least that's what the Ouphe—or Sentinels, as we call ourselves in the new world—like to call me. I can see connections that affect our race for good and bad. I have developed abilities that allow me to influence things for the good of our people. I can portal between our worlds, connect those who should be tied together with magic-laced runes, awaken dormant magic, and also block active magic in runes. That's what I did for you and your mates, I shut down the two runes that Lazza was trying to use against you," he explains.

"So I won't be able to do any of that?" I ask, perplexed.

"Oh, no, I wouldn't presume to tell you what you can and can't do once you wake up entirely," he tells me, his eyes very serious. "All I can really say is that you alone are uniquely capable of breaking the Vow."

"And why is that?" I ask as we turn left and continue to wind through more tents. Some people are watching us now, and I can see the exchange of curious and cautious whispers as we make our way through camp.

"Because your father was Awlon the Dark, and your maternal grandfather was Verse Solei, the last Bond Forger. They were two of the five Ouphe who created the Vow. The three other Vow Founder's bloodlines have been destroyed. You're all that's left of the magic that created that Bond, which is why you're the only one who can break it."

A snarl fills my ears at the same time panicked cries register. I pull my thoughts from the bomb of information Wekun just lobbed at me, and focus on the three pissed off gryphon shifters who are standing in a circular clearing, surrounded by people who are scrambling to get away from them and a handful of beings who look like they're in charge of this place.

"I won't ask again, where is my mate?" an enraged voice demands, and as the frantic crowd starts to thin, I see that it's Ryn who's squaring off with a female who's taller than him and all lean muscle.

"And I'll tell you again, I don't know. You three popped up here alone. How are we to know what happened to her?" the female argues, frustrated.

She's almost as tall as Zeph, but her muscles are lean and feminine. The sides of her head are shaved, leaving a strip of white wavy hair to flow back from her face and down her back. She has scars all over her arms and what looks like a set of three claw marks that slash through the middle of her face. The raised scars give the effect of war paint across her cheeks and the bridge of her nose, and she's all the more fiercely beautiful for the imperfections. This is definitely not a female I'd want to fuck with.

I observe the way the other gryphons with her defer to

her lead, and I deduce that this tough-as-nails-looking gryphon runs shit in this camp. She's wearing a similar Narwagh armored clothing that many of the Hidden used to wear, and my heart leaps with excitement when I take in the pants her legs are clad in.

I look to Wekun. "Well, she looks like she's got things well in hand," I tell him, turning to leave.

I don't want to talk to Ryn, Treno, or Zeph, and honestly I don't care if they're upset that they don't know where I am. They can find someone else to shit on all the time. They're surrounded by Ouphe-tainted gryphons as big and as menacing looking as the three douchebags are. It's a sea of white tones of hair or ghostly streaks as far as the eye can see.

I realize that many of the Ouphe I saw in the other camp didn't have that same white hair, purple eyes thing going, and I make a note to ask Wekun about why that is. He turns to follow me away from the gryphon showdown.

"Falon!" Ryn calls my name, and I groan.

Fuck. I wasn't fast enough in sneaking away.

I don't bother to turn around, I just keep walking.

"Falon, you will come here right now!" Zeph orders, like I'm a misbehaving dog.

Savage rage slams through me so hard that I can barely breathe through it. My wings shove out of my back, as though my body is arming itself, as I whirl around and fix a scathing glare on my three mates.

"I am not yours to command!" I bellow at them, my voice louder and filled with potent power.

Everyone around me—including Zeph, Ryn, and Treno —goes still, their eyes filled with shock and unease. Purple streaks of something crawl up my limbs and disappear into my skin, like I'm some kind of electromagnetic force and this purple energy is drawn to me. I'm reminded of the plum-colored pulse I sent out when shit was going down in Kestrel City with Lazza.

My breaths are heavy, weighed down by wrath and indignation. My pure black wings give a little snap, and I can feel Pigeon's *take that* in it. I turn and continue to leave, not a sound of protest lobbed at my back.

Wekun is quiet at my side, but I can feel excitement wafting off him in steady waves. Another flicker of purple climbs up my torso, and I point at it.

"What the fuck is up with this?" I ask, "...and where can *I* get some pants?"

Wekun cracks up and wraps an arm around my shoulders, pulling me into a side hug that squishes one of my wings. "That, Falon, is how you're going to help save everyone, but first let's get you cleaned up, and then I'll explain everything."

Steam rises up all around me from the warm pond I'm standing shoulder deep in. It feels so good I could probably orgasm right now if I just think about it long enough. I don't because that's weird, and Wekun is lying on the shore, facing away from me, explaining what the fuck is going on. I figure a bunch of random moans and sex gasps is not the impression I should leave on this helpful stranger, so I rein my shit in.

"Wait," I tell Wekun, pausing the comb I'm running through my hair to get all the snarls out, and turn toward him. "So the Ouphe, or Sentinels—or whatever—fucked things up for themselves so badly in this world that they created the gates so they could escape? *Then* in the new world—my world—they tried to rule over everyone again, wash-rinse-repeat, and now they're once more in hiding?" I ask, half in shock and half to clarify that I'm understanding what he's telling me correctly.

"Pretty much," Wekun concedes.

"Talk about not learning from your mistakes," I mumble, shaking my head. "I mean, how can you convince yourself that you're a superior species and then get hunted to almost extinction in not one...but two worlds?"

Wekun shrugs and picks another leaf off the weird looking tree he's lying under and sucks on the stem. The trunk looks petrified, like it's more crystal than bark, and the leaves remind me of green flowers; they're like roses made out of leaves. Wekun keeps sucking on their stems, so I'm guessing they're sweet, but grot berries have traumatized me, and I don't trust anyone's taste buds in this world.

Although maybe Wekun could be an exception, because it turns out he's not exactly from this world. He's not solely from the world I grew up in either, but travels back and forth as needed, doing what he can to protect what's left of his people.

"The Sovereign of the Sentinels just changed, and I have a lot of hope that things will finally move in the right direction. She's surrounded by good minds and hearts, and I have faith that she'll do right by our people...or Vinna will kick her ass."

"Vinna? Is that like the Ouphe version of karma or something?"

Wekun laughs. "You know, she just might be," he tells me with a chuckle and amused smile on his face.

"So I'm a Sentinel?" I question as I put everything he's told me together and continue to brush my hair.

"Part of one; the blood's running through your veins, but so is that of the Gryphon's. In my opinion, it makes you stronger. All the strongest Bond wielders and magic users I've seen are always a mix of Sentinel and something else.

All of your Sept bring new things to the table, it's quite exciting," he tells me, his head resting on the crook of his arm as he stares thoughtfully up at the overcast sky above us.

"My Sept?" I question as a particularly gnarly tangle meets the teeth of my comb, forcing me to get all aggressive and show it who's boss. The water of the hot springs agitates against me as I get all confrontational with my hair. At least it's white again, but I can't get it as clean as I'd like it until I deal with the uninvited dreads I started to form thanks to my recent adventures.

Pigeon impatiently taps her talons inside of me as she waits for her turn to play in the water. I ignore her, no intention of rushing the first bath I've had since the night Loa slit my throat.

"Yes, all Bond possessors have a Sept. It's like your family, or casters in our world call it a coven. With Bond users, you can call on each other's abilities and magic when a Sept is complete. It makes you stronger and more protected."

I raise my hands in victory when the nest of hair finally submits. *One down, who the fuck knows how many left to go.* I'm in a hot spring, learning all about magic and the worlds and how I fit into all of it, and yet the thing I seem to be most excited about is getting clean.

Maybe it's the fact that I've been *oh shit* deep in this world and all of its crazy for so long that some hot guy— who can pop in and out of existence—telling me I'm some magical being from a dying race just isn't the surprising revelation it would have been months ago.

Technically, Zeph's been hating on me for being exactly that from the get-go. It's not like I didn't know about casters and shifters and other things that go bump in the night before. Granted, I haven't heard of the Ouphe or Sentinels, but given that they're in hiding, that makes sense.

"So where's your Sept? Do they pop in and out, fixing things like you do?"

Wekun stills for just a fraction of a second before continuing to casually suck on the stem of his leaf flower, but I catch the reaction.

"They're dead. I'm the last of my Sept," he tells me evenly, like it's a simple fact, but I catch the hint of sorrow in the word *last.*

"I'm sorry," I offer.

He smiles sadly but doesn't offer any more information. I don't feel right about prying, and I turn away to give him the moment I sense he's in need of.

"So my Sept will be other Bond magic holders like me, right? Am I supposed to go looking for them? Are they in this world? How will I know who they are?" I start again after a minute.

"When your Sept is complete, the Sept rune you all have will activate and pull you together."

Concern and sadness crawls through me, and I sink down into the water a little more. "But I don't have runes anymore, Wekun, so how is that going to work?" My voice sounds small, and I try to shove away the memories that flood me of my dad taking the marks on my skin and the pain.

In truth, I have Treno's runes, but I don't get the impression his marks are the Sept rune that Wekun is talking about. Unless Treno has Bond magic. He's never told what he can do and how, so I have no idea.

"I'm hoping I can fix that," he tells me, and I pause and turn back to him. He takes in the shocked look on my face and offers me a warm smile. "Awlon occluded your core somehow, but the purple magic that was crawling all over your skin? That was your Sentinel magic, and it showing up like that proves that it's not dead, just hindered. I'm hoping I can undo what he did to hide your abilities and what you are."

I take a deep breath and tamp down the flash of excitement that flickers through me. There's a part of me that's begging to be made whole and a part of me that's nervous about what that means for me. I shake that thought away. I said I'd do everything to help the Gryphons, and that means being as powerful as I can be, regardless of how much that scares me or whether it makes me more of a target than I already am.

"Even if I can't restore your marks and abilities, your Sept rune isn't something you're born with. It shows up when it wants to, when magic has compatible Bond wielders for you. I've seen Sept runes that are triggered by loss or trauma, or one day they just show up out of the blue for no obvious reason whatsoever." He rubs a hand over his buzzed white hair and half shrugs. "There's really no rhyme or reason when it comes to magic. We've been gifted with the ability to use it, but no one knows how or why it works the way that it does."

I run the comb through my hair and do a little underwater dance when it finally glides smoothly through all my locks. I open my mouth to ask Wekun how he knows I will have a Sept or pack of Bond homies, but a group of male gryphons tromping my way makes me pause. Sinking down until water edges my chin, I back up in the warm pool of water that's being fed by a quiet, misty fall. The pool I'm in trickles down into several other pools below me, like a stairway of natural jacuzzis that ultimately lead to a calm river that steals the water away to who knows where.

The group of male gryphons part, and I see Treno, Zeph, and Ryn. I realize that the gryphons surrounding them are serving as guards, and I find myself wondering what went down after I left them to deal with things on their own. As though the three of them can suddenly feel my eyes scanning over them, their heads snap to where I'm currently bathing.

I freeze, not sure how I feel about seeing them again. A handful of hours apart isn't nearly enough to begin to recover from all the bullshit. I feel Pigeon fluff up all her feathers, equally agitated by their presence. Wekun must sense the change in atmosphere, because he suddenly sits up and looks over in the direction of the guards.

Zeph's eyes flick over to Wekun and then back to me, and fury ripples through him. He takes a step in our direction, but two of the guards around him move to get in his way. His nostrils flare, and the tic in his jaw starts up. He's clearly pissed that I'm bathing in front of Wekun, but he's once again letting his temper get the best of him. Wekun couldn't care less about my naked ass.

Zeph mumbles something, and I look to find both Treno and Ryn shooting daggers our way too. I turn, no longer willing to absorb any more of their anger, and the guards guide them to a lower pool that's thankfully far away.

I'm silent for a moment as I try to wash the rage that was just aimed at us from my skin.

"Wekun, can mate bonds be severed?" I ask as I rinse my hair and body one last time, ready to get out and get on with things.

It's quiet for several beats.

I look over at him so I can gauge his response. He's looking down at the group of gryphons, his eyes fathomless and far away. I watch him for a moment, and just when I accept he's not going to answer, he does.

"Yes, they can be severed. It's brutal, and I don't recommend it, but it has been done."

I turn away from his sympathy-filled, champagne gaze and stare down at Treno's runes on my chest. Thoughts swirl in my mind, and I wade through them as I trace the black marks with my eyes.

"When you try to bring my runes back, I'd like you to sever my mate bonds too."

I look up at him, so he can see the determination in my face and in my eyes. I want him to see that my request isn't a rash decision, and that spite isn't the catalyst for my appeal.

I let the pain I feel bleed into my gaze, and I open myself up so that he can witness the emotional wounds I've been collecting from being attached to these males. I'm slowly dying inside, and not just me, but I need him to witness how wrong and awful the mate bonds are for them too. I know we'll all be better without each other.

He studies me for a moment and releases a resigned exhale.

"If that's what you want," he starts, pausing like he's waiting to see if I'll take the words back.

"It is," I answer instead, relief swirling in my chest, as the rest of me hardens with resolve.

I take one last look at the lower pools and the three gryphons currently cleaning off in them. Ryn looks up at me. I know he's too far away to have heard anything, but his eyes are conflicted all the same. We stare at each other, and his gray and white wings spring from his back. He doesn't take his eyes off of mine, and they flicker between frustration and sorrow. I turn away and climb out of the hot spring. Wekun turns away, but I can feel my mates' eyes on me, and goose bumps crawl up my arms.

"Let's do it then," I tell Wekun as I reach for the makeshift towel that's been laid next to the pile of clothes he acquired for me.

Pigeon sends me a flash of desolation and then a steady stream of resolve. I withdraw inside myself and give her a hug.

"I'm sorry, Pidge. If you don't want this, I won't do it, but I think it's for the best," I tell her, and she butts her feathered head against my chest. I run my fingers over her soft angled ears and give her time to show me what she wants. The elation she felt when the call went out to each of her mates flashes in my mind. She shows me the rightness she felt when the call was answered, and I can feel her contentment radiating through me.

But then image after image of Zeph's, Ryn's, and Treno's angry faces, their mouths warped as they spit hateful words that hurt not just her, but me as well, flow in my head like a river of pain. Their secrets and rejections wrap around our heart until we don't feel like us anymore. Pigeon tears at the hurtful bindings with her razor sharp beak and shows me pictures of the two of us flying and talking and laughing.

I smile and feel a tear slip down my cheek. *"I want that too,"* I tell her, burying my face in the soft feathers of her neck. *"I'm sorry I couldn't make them love you the way you deserve, Pidge,"* I tell her quietly.

She drops her head on top of mine, and we just sit like that for a while. Both of us mourning the loss of what will never be with our mates and accepting our future without them.

10

I step out of my newly acquired pants and set them aside gently. I just got them, and I hate that I'm being asked to abandon them so quickly. They're a little big, but it's better than traipsing around in an oversized shirt, free-lipping it, and trying to pretend like the crotch rot from not bathing in weeks is no biggie. Now at least the chafing rash caused by my thighs rubbing together from too much evil walking can finally start to recover.

I pull the weird tank top dress down from the top of the screen I'm changing behind and slip it on.

"Why haven't you explained how underwear works to the Ouphe-Sentinels of this world?" I ask Wekun as I pull the maroon fabric down over my ass until it falls to my knees.

I step out from behind the screen and motion to my weird outfit. "Why do I have to wear this, again?"

Wekun doesn't look over, as he's too busy positioning the big fluffy cushions on the floor of the corner of his tent. I take it that's where this whole rune restoration thing is going to go down, and move toward him.

"If this works, it's not going to feel good. Your body is

going to behave like it's going through an awakening. You'll thank me for the lack of restrictive clothing," he tells me over his shoulder.

"I won't thank you if my vagina's business is being flashed to the whole camp," I retort as I sit on a cushion and yank the hem of my tunic tank top down.

"I'll be the only one in here; your vagina and its business are safe with me," Wekun declares on an amused snort.

I watch him as he continues to make a pillow nest. In my past life, I would have taken his words as a challenge. He's good-looking, nice, probably knows what he's doing between a girl's thighs. I would have relished the opportunity to make him see me as desirable and then happily walked away when I had gotten what I wanted from him.

But now, I must have turned over a new leaf, because I find myself not caring whether Wekun sees me as anything. It's almost a relief in a weird way that he doesn't care, that he's not flirty or subtly pushing boundaries.

I sigh and wonder if I'll ever be the same after all of this is over. Once these mate bonds are broken and this war is over, what am I going to do? I guess I could live in the Eyrie, give all the houses there running hot water, or maybe I find a little patch of land and build a cottage and collect...fuck, they don't have cats. I try to think of the alternative to a cat lady spinster, but I don't know if there is one here.

I pause, contemplating if fairies like to be kept as pets, and then internally facepalm because I'm an idiot. Wekun can travel between worlds, so he can take me home when all is said and done. If I break the Vow, then I'll have done what I promised to do and there would be no point in staying in this world anymore.

I could leave.

The thought sends me reeling. I don't have to be stuck here. I've been searching for a way to get back and here it is, standing in a pile of pillows. Astonishment rocks me, and I suddenly find the words to beg Wekun to take me home sitting on the tip of my tongue. I stop them from spilling out. The realization that I can leave all at once feels a little too *counting your chickens before they hatch*. First the mate bonds need to be severed, and then I need to actually figure out how to break the Vow. Once all of that is done, I can bring up my plan to Wekun. I'm sure he'd be happy to help, it's what he seems to be all about.

"Okay, how does this work and what should I do?" I ask, ignoring the nervous wobble I hear in my voice.

"Lie down here," Wekun instructs, patting the pillows in the center of his nest. "I'm going to put my hands on you in search of a thread of your magic. If I can find one, then I more or less tug on it and see what I can unravel—"

"And if you don't find a thread?" I interrupt to ask.

"Then I may not be able to do anything. I won't give up, but it would make everything harder," he tells me solemnly.

I nod and take a deep breath. Well, here's hoping he can find something, because I have the sinking suspicion I'm going to need it if I want to help the Gryphons.

"Wakanda Forever," I exclaim quietly to myself, like I'm hoping somehow the words will pump me up and prepare me for what may or may not happen.

Both options suck dirty dick, because if he finds a thread, I know this is going to hurt. I can recall the memories of when I first got the markings when I was little and what my dad did to take them away. I've never felt anything like that kind of pain. Well, not until Zeph knocked me out of the sky and smashed me into the ground.

If Wekun doesn't find hints of my magic, then everything I've been planning and striving for is about to get a little more impossible. I hope for the sake of the Gryphons who are about to destroy one another that I can find a way to put a stop to it.

I scoot over and lie down in front of Wekun. His Narwagh-pant-clad knees rest against my side, and he bends over me with his hands outstretched. He closes his eyes as though he's centering himself or perhaps praying. Maybe he's whispering his own *Wakanda Forever*.

My eyes trace the lines of the cream-colored tunic he's wearing and watch as he takes a deep breath, releasing it slowly. I try to relax and stare up at the ceiling of the tent as his warm palms move up to rest on my chest. He pauses for a minute and then moves down my sternum, like his hands are a metal detector and he's trying to listen for the right cadence of beeps to tell him he's hit the jackpot.

I become all too aware of my breathing as he skims slowly over my body. I'm nervous. Worried about what happens if he finds something, worried if he doesn't. Pigeon sends me a wave of reassurance, and I give her a grateful smile. We've been doing so much better together; checking in, taking the other's feelings into account. I haven't been able to let her out to stretch too much, but as soon as Wekun gets us sorted—one way or the other—we'll start training again.

I try to go through the list of things we need to do in my head as Wekun's hands roam over my arms and then move back to my stomach. Pigeon and I need to find the words to break the Vow. We need to convince the Ouphe and the Gryphons here to help us. And then we just need to win the war.

No pressure.

My heart picks up a little as Wekun's searching palms dip lower down my abdomen. His skin skims the fabric of the thin tank top dress I'm wearing, and my body wakes up and heats, regardless of the platonic way my brain is saying it should react. He stops suddenly just above the apex of my thighs, and I try not to snort.

Who doesn't want a magical vagina?

The rapacious little shit has gotten me in enough trouble though, and I don't know if I'd trust whatever Wekun is obviously feeling to be the guiding light for Gryphon salvation.

"Got it," Wekun announces calmly.

Fucking hell. Well, this just got infinitely more awkward.

Pigeon makes that chuffing sound that she does when she's amused, and I roll my eyes at her. I swallow down the wisecrack I have for Wekun, because he's clearly concentrating so hard.

A jerking sensation hooks through me. Thankfully, it doesn't come from my crotch, but rather my chest, but I'm all at once overwhelmed by the feeling that something is being threaded through me. It's as though each cell that I possess is the eye of a needle and Wekun is carefully fitting a warm, stinging string of magic through each opening simultaneously.

I gasp as the slight burning sensation goes from uncomfortable to agonizing in less than a blink. My back bows off the large pillows I'm lying on, and just as I feel the bloodcurdling scream claw its way out of my throat, I'm ripped away from my body.

I scramble to try and hold on to myself. I feel Pigeon's talons scrape down my arm as she tries to reach for me, but I'm suddenly hurtling back through the star-filled sky as though I've been lassoed and I'm being dragged to fuck knows where.

My body crashes against stone, but surprisingly it doesn't hurt. I work to pull oxygen into what I'm pretty sure is my incorporeal body and look around. Shock slithers through me when I immediately recognize where I am. I'm sitting inside the gazebo that Nadi brought me to, surrounded by the overgrown and long abandoned Ouphe city of Vedan. I'm back in the heart of where the Hidden used to live.

Only it's not Nadi glowing green and sitting next to me.

I stare at the man for a moment and try to make sense of what I'm seeing. It's impossible, and yet there he is. Black hair and lime green eyes take me in, patiently allowing me time to recover from the bewilderment he must know I'm experiencing.

"Dad?" I whisper, still not trusting my eyes or the words spilling out of my mouth. "Am I dreaming?" I ask as his eyes light up with a familiar light and his lips spread into a joyous smile.

I look around again, wondering if this is just another memory my conscious has become aware of, but that can't be it, I've never been here with him before.

"How?" I breathe out, barely audible, my heart hammering in my chest, and tears prickling my disbelieving eyes.

He opens his arms and leans in to give me a hug. My first reaction is to flinch back away from him. I hate that my body immediately reaches for protection away from him instead of toward him, but I've seen too much to fully trust him anymore. I don't know who he is. I've realized that I never did. Not him, not my mother, not my gran. I was left in the dark, thrown to the gryphons, my body and soul abandoned to mop up the mess that was left in my parents' wake.

My dad is shocked by my reaction, and he pauses, studying me for a millisecond before dropping his arms. I don't miss the sadness that bleeds into his lime green eyes, but what does he expect? He's supposed to be dead.

"Falon," he finally speaks, my name like a worship-filled prayer floating on the air between us.

The sound of it breaks me in ways I didn't know possible. I clutch my chest as a sob bubbles up out of it. Flashes of my memories, new and old, move through my mind, and I have to fight not to see him through the five-year-old lens that I used to know him through.

"How are you here?" I demand, my tone laced with bone crushing sadness.

"I am, and I'm not," he tells me cryptically.

My brow folds with confusion.

"Your magic called to me when it tried to awaken. I bound a piece of my magic to yours so if this ever happened, I could explain, make sure you were okay," he tells me, and I'm surprised by the explanation.

"Make sure I was okay, or try to stop it?" I ask, wishing accusation wasn't dripping off of my every word.

"Falon," he chides quietly, and his eyes drop from mine and look down at his hands. "I can imagine what you must think of me, but I swear to you, I was just trying to keep you safe, keep you alive."

"But what you did to Gran...to me," I counter.

"I know it may look brutal, but she was too trusting, she thought her people would keep you safe, but I knew that wouldn't be the case. If she had told anyone, they would have hunted you down and slaughtered you, like they did..." He pauses, pain taking over his sadness, and I try to read his features to understand what's causing it.

Agony and guilt pour out of him, and I watch as my dad, my hero, wipes tears from his cheeks and breathes deeply as though he's trying to piece himself back together one inhale and exhale at a time. His hurt calls to my own, and sorrow leaks down my face as I reach out and thread my fingers with his.

"Your mother and I had a little girl before you," he confesses on a tormented sob. "She didn't...they didn't allow

106

her to...to live. We barely made it through alive, the damage they did to your mother, we didn't think we could have more, and then you."

My dad partially folds in on himself as his words rip open wounds inside of him that are incapable of healing. I wrap my arms around him, instantly feeling guilt and sorrow and shock at what he's saying. I suspected a miscarriage or something, but this...

"If Sedora had told anyone, if somehow the Sentinels and Gryphons found out that you existed, they wouldn't have stopped until they ended you. I couldn't let that happen, Falon. I know what we did was wrong, that if our line ended, it would shatter all the wrong that we had enacted, but you were too precious. I was too selfish. I loved you too much. I'm sorry," he tells me brokenly, his tone pleading.

"It's okay, dad. I'm so sorry," I offer, my attempts to comfort him feeling flat.

There are no words that could ever make what happened okay. There's no saying or anecdote that will soothe the continuous ache and loss that I can see rippling through him right now. I instantly feel horrible for how angry I've felt at him, and my mom, and gran. They were all just trying to do the best that they could.

"I'm sorry, dad," I tell him over and over again, until he wraps his arms around me and we trade places in our efforts to try and console each other.

And then it dawns on me what he said.

If our line ended, it would shatter all the wrong that we had enacted.

My heart hammers painfully hard in my chest, and I pull back so I can look my dad in the eye and see the truth.

"Dad, are you saying if I die, then the Vow will break automatically?"

His lime green eyes answer before his mouth does when they fill with shame and resignation. I watch as tears spill out of his black lashes, and they feel oddly like a death sentence. I pull in a shuddering breath and reel at the truth of that. My hands come up and cover my mouth, like that will hold in any selfish objection.

I don't want to die.

My dad takes in the horror pouring out of my watery gaze, and he quickly starts to shake his head. "It's not the only way, Falon," he tells me in a rush. "You have the ability to break the magic."

"No, I don't," I argue, pulling back even more. "I didn't even know what I was. I fell into this world blindly, and I've been fucking up ever since. How do I have the ability? Wekun doesn't even know if he can reverse what *you* did to me," I tell him, feeling bad for pouring more anger and hurt onto his already bleeding and open wounds. But how could he think I could still do this when I've been blocked and impeded at every possible turn since before I even knew this world, and the Vow, existed?

I've been set up to fail from birth, good intentions or not.

I shake my head and stare at the dead city around me. Will this world claim my body like it has this place? Cover it in moss when my soul is gone and pepper flowers across my hollow shell? Will it honor the sacrifice being asked of me? Mourn my loss and grieve for the impossible legacy being laid at my feet?

"Falon, you know the words. They're ingrained in who you are, in the magic both your mother and I passed down to you. I know you can do this, I know you can remember our lessons and find exactly what you need to make it right," my dad tells me, cupping my cheeks as his fervent eyes hold mine. "You're stronger and better than the Sept whose magic flows in your veins. I know it's not fair to put so much on you, but My Heart, if anyone could do this, it's you."

The strange pulling sensation that brought me here starts again in my chest. Panic flares inside of me.

"Dad!" I cry out, suddenly scared and not ready to be stolen away.

"I love you, Falon. I believe in you. You've been pure light and love even before your first breath."

He wraps his arms around me, and I hold tightly to him as though somehow it will anchor me and I won't be pulled away.

"I don't want to go," I plead with him, and I feel him kiss my tear-stained cheeks.

"I don't want you to go either, My Heart, but we're always with you. You're never alone."

I'm yanked from his strong hold, and I cry out and thrash against the force that's tearing me away.

"I love you, dad, I'm sorry," I scream at him, sobs ripping out of my chest as though I'm watching him die all over again.

"No, I'm sorry, Falon. All you have to do is remember, My Heart! Just remember!" he calls after me, and then just like that, I'm pulled out of Vedan and staring down at the cliff castle that served as my first home in this world.

I'm once again surrounded by the night and its teasing, unfamiliar stars. I race backward, but in the distance, I see looming purple mountains and a bright light that almost looks like a spotlight shooting up into the sky. It's radiating out of the base of a mountain that almost resembles a fist. It's surrounded by two, taller, triangle tipped peaks, and I don't know what it means, only that the strange manifestation of light is burned into my mind as I'm flung back and slammed into a body that's drowning in pain.

I'm so overwhelmed by the agony that I can't even speak.

I open my mouth to scream, but only a hoarse crackle exits my throat, and I realize I've already screamed my voice away. My skin burns like someone doused me in gasoline and took a match to my sodden existence.

"Falon, your magic's awakening. It will be over soon. Are you sure you want me to break your mate bonds? I'm worried you can't survive it," Wekun tells me through the smoke of my melting soul.

My jaw is clenched so tightly that I feel like the bones are going to shatter any moment, but I manage to unhinge them somehow and grit out, "Do it."

Wekun places his hands on my chest, and the searing sensation blazing through me morphs into something trying to cut out my soul and shred it into a million pieces. I feel Zeph, Ryn, and Treno, writhing in their own pain, clutching their chests, and gasping against the cutting of the threads that hold us together.

My awareness of Treno goes first. He just blinks out of existence for me as though he no longer walks this world. Panic slams through me, and I can't help but feel terrified that in doing this, I might have killed him.

I claw at my chest as I feel Ryn's threads start to shred. He screams as they do, and I can feel him reaching out to capture them, holding the threads to his chest like that will be enough to reattach them. In one torturous breath he's there, and in the next, Ryn is gone.

I scream at the loss of him, my voice gravelly and filled with pain. I can taste the blood in my throat and the damage my cries are further doing to it. The absence of Ryn and Treno almost hurts worse than severing them did. I don't understand the why of it, only that I know in this moment that I will never recover. I will never be the same after this loss.

Pigeon wraps my consciousness up with her warm feathered and furred body, and I can feel her suffering alongside me as, one thread at a time, we ruin and reject what fate's decreed for us.

Zeph's essence threads itself through my mind, and he takes a hold of me. I'm surprised by the strength I feel, and the questioning touch that caresses the threads between us.

"Don't, Falon," I hear him plead quietly in my mind before the pain and trauma of what's happening takes over everything, and I feel myself start to shut down in defense against it.

I cling to consciousness, like I'm hanging off a cliff and I know if I let go, I'll plunge to my death. The black abyss below me promises nothing but more loss and pain, and I know I can't let myself fall. I call on every ounce of strength I have, and despite the disconnecting of threads that I felt before, power shoots through me and bleeds out, wrapping around Zeph, Ryn, and Treno and stamping ownership all over everything they are.

I feel their gryphons, their fear, their hurt, their anger...their claim. Treno's connection to his other half feels like mine to Pigeon. Ryn feels more braided and interwoven with his beast, and Zeph's lines are so blurred I can barely see where he and his other half end and begin. His gryphon is so tightly wrapped around him it's as though without it, Zeph could no longer be anchored to the world.

Pigeon rears up inside of me, like she can't help but peek at the pieces of them they would never show us. I feel her sadness and hurt, her desire for more, and then all at once it's gone. I feel nothing but cold hard emptiness as the blackness I'm fighting works harder to claim me for its own.

11

_____

"What have you done?" Treno demands, his voice pulling me from the in-between I'm floating in as my body adjusts to everything that just happened to it.

I didn't pass out, which I'm pretty fucking proud of. I'd wing five Pigeon if, you know, I could move.

"Only what she asked me to do," Wekun defends evenly.

"You have no right to try and take her from us!" Ryn bellows. "It's not just her decision to make!"

I can't open my eyes, but I can just picture him, stepping threateningly into Wekun's personal space. Oddly, I become aware of purple threads inside of me that seem to lead from me to Ryn. I look over in my chest to see another set that connects Treno and me. I would groan at their unwelcome anchor in my soul, but I don't think I'm completely awake.

"It is Falon's decision whether or not she wants to be with you three. She's the only one who can make that choice," Wekun lobs back. "Don't come snarling in here at me. If you had been more careful with her and who she is from the beginning, she wouldn't have tried to cut your bonds."

His words make my chest ache.

Tried? Does that mean it didn't work?

I swim through the distress that fills me at that thought and try to surface from the numbness I'm treading in. The purple threads feel heavy inside of me, and I need to know what that means. Am I free, or did I somehow strengthen what I was hoping to break?

"Where's the Syta?" Wekun asks. "He's usually the more volatile of the group, why is he not here lumbering around and being all threatening?"

I would snort if I could. It's almost as though Wekun likes pissing Zeph off, but his question makes me pause, because it is weird that he's not here blanketing everything in his outrage.

The room goes quiet.

"He's not dealing so well with these," Ryn states, and confusion stabs at my numbness. "He told us to make sure that Falon was okay, but he's in a bad place right now..."

Something in Ryn's tone calls to me, and I force my battered consciousness to look down at the threads I know lead to Zeph. I reach out to the purple tether that's not supposed to be there anymore, and in a breath, I'm pulled from where I am with Wekun, Ryn, and Treno, and yanked toward Zeph.

A roar slams against me, shocking me as my feet touch soil. I blink the darkness all around me into focus and find myself at the bathing pools. Another cry fills the night around me, and I can hear the panic and terror in it. I try to shake the disorientation I feel from my senses.

What did I just do?

Am I doing that dream thing again? I've never been able to control it or make it happen at will. I look down at myself and scrunch my toes in the damp soil surrounding the bathing pool. I don't feel like I'm dreaming. This lacks the somewhat fuzzy quality I always felt when it happened before. I feel like I'm actually here, but I have no idea how.

I'm pulled away from my confounding thoughts with a jump, as Zeph crashes into the water in front of me with a horrified bellow. The warm water of the hot spring sprays up all around him as he runs deeper into the pool and falls to his knees.

My first reaction is that he's under attack somehow, because he looks like he's running for his life, but as I look around, there's no one but us here. He starts to scrub furiously at his skin, and the torment laced in his every movement has me running into the water to help him with whatever is hurting him.

A whimper escapes him as I close the distance, but Zeph doesn't even look over as I make my presence known. I round on him and see he's scrubbing at rings of black marks that now wrap around his arms. His eyes are far away and lost looking, and his movements are frenzied. I'm taken aback and confused for a moment.

Where did these marks come from?

It's as though he doesn't even know I'm standing right in front of him, and I reach out for him, not able to stop the drive slamming through me to help him in some way. I'm not sure what's going on or why he's so spooked and terrified.

I freeze as my arm comes out in front of me and I see the same rings of marks on my body. Understanding sucker punches me in the mouth, and I immediately know what's setting Zeph off.

He's wearing my runes.

He's covered in marks that represent the people who destroyed his entire life, raped his mother, killed her and then his father. People who swore by these marks, brandished them like weapons, betrayed his family, slaughtered his brother before his eyes, started the war he's currently fighting. Zeph has worked his entire life not to ever bear a rune that could ever enslave him and bring him to his knees against his will. And now, he is covered in them, on his knees, trying to wash them all from his skin.

My heart breaks.

I may not like him or appreciate what's gone down between us, but I wouldn't wish the panic and pain I can see in his golden gaze—and feel in my soul—on my worst enemy.

I'm not sure what to do. How to help Zeph navigate this. He seems out of it at the moment. He's manically scrubbing and clawing at himself, but his eyes look as though they're reliving all kinds of horrors.

Fuck!

I thought Wekun was going to break the bond, that even if my marks came back, it wouldn't affect anyone but me. I didn't think something like this was a possibility.

Water laps at my waist, and I frantically search through my guilt for a solution. *Okay, Falon, think.* I need to snap him out of this in a way that doesn't make him want to snap my neck. I reach for him again, my hands now shaky and unsure. I hesitate just before I connect with his hands. I don't want to set him off even more by touching him in a way that could be more triggering. I think through the horrible things I know he's been through and try to suss out a way I can touch him that isn't going to make what he's experiencing so much worse.

He's been held down, held back, forced to watch and endure.

I decide not to try and touch his arms or shoulders. I don't want him to think I'm just another soldier here to make him hurt.

Another pained whimper comes out of the massive male

in front of me, and I fucking loathe that I have no idea what to do.

I bring my hands up, and before I can really think it through, I cup Zeph's cheeks with my palms. He doesn't react in any way that makes me think he can feel me, but his gryphon doesn't appear and literally bite my head off either, so I go with it. I crawl over his frantic hands as they continue to scrub at his now bleeding skin until I'm settled firmly in his lap.

His eyes are still somewhere else, and I press my forehead and nose against his as I cradle his head and start to hum, my mouth centimeters away from his. He's panting through whatever flashback he's currently being forced to endure, but he breathes in my song each time he fills his lungs, and I decide to give whatever the fuck I'm doing time to hopefully draw him out a little.

I press my head against his firmly so he can feel me, but my touch isn't demanding or cruel. The tips of my fingers edge his wet black hair, and the scruff of his new beard feels prickly against my palms. I stare at his haunted, scrunched eyes and just hum.

I have no idea what I'm even singing. The damage I've been doing to my throat over and over again doesn't help to make the tune any more identifiable. I sound like Scuttle and a toad's tone-deaf baby.

Gradually I fix my cracked and battered voice onto Radiohead's "Creep." I mellow it out, humming the Daniela Andrade cover of the song that I like to play on repeat when I'm feeling moody. I sing it on a loop against Zeph's frenetic breaths, my face touching his and my hands holding him.

I feel his tense muscles slowly relax, but I don't let myself celebrate. Nothing about this situation is worthy of any level of elation. He pulls in a deeper breath than the others that came before, and I go from humming to softly singing the words to my moody song choice. I try to picture the tune and lyrics seeping into him and helping to invite him out of the dread that's consuming him.

Zeph's hands stop moving behind me, the scrubbing coming to a stop as I tell him the musical tale of how I'm a weirdo. Surprise ricochets through me when I feel his large hands wrap around my waist and pull me tighter into him. I don't miss a gravelly note as he inhales me and his clenched eyelids begin to smooth out.

My thumbs trace his cheek bones as I sing about wanting a perfect soul. His chest starts to move in time with mine, and then all at once, honey-kissed eyes are staring directly into mine. Pain bleeds out of his stare, so I just keep whisper-singing to him, my own eyes telling him that I'm here. That he's safe and not back anywhere that could be causing the haunted look in his eyes.

We stay like this for a long time, me singing the same song over and over again as I sit in his lap and do my best to hold his fragile pieces together. I'm not sure how many hours separate when I first got here until now, but the water is warm and pressing lazily against us as his thumbs start to brush against my ribs in time with the languid beat of my borrowed tune.

I don't ask him what happened or if he's okay. They're stupid questions I refuse to lend my splintered voice to. I can see it in his eyes and feel it in his body that he's not ready to leave this moment yet. I'm in no rush; this is the least I can do. They're my marks that are etched into his skin and terrorizing him, this trauma is on me.

I think that Wekun can probably do whatever my dad did to me and make them go away, but Zeph isn't ready to hear any of that yet. So I wait patiently and start the song over for the hundredth time.

"You tried to break the mating?" Zeph suddenly asks me, his voice quiet and even.

I stop my song and immediately feel the peace it brought slip through my fingers.

"I did," I admit, my thumbs going still on his cheeks.

He doesn't say anything, and my confession floats around us, slinking in and out of the silence that settles between us.

"The Ouphe enslaved my people," he tells me, his face hard, but his eyes beseeching like what he's saying isn't easy for him.

"I know."

"I'm covered in their magic."

"Yes, you are."

He pauses for a minute, and I see unmasked vulnerability flicker in his eyes. "I don't know how to live with that."

His confession soaks into me, and I nod my head in understanding. "You have two choices then," I start, my eyes flitting back and forth between his, our faces still pressed together like we're telling secrets. "We either figure out how to get rid of them..." I pause for a minute to let that option resonate and land where it needs to inside of him.

"Or?" he presses when he's ready.

"We learn how to use them so *they* can never be used against you or your people again."

A spark of uncertainty alights in his gaze.

"I'm going to break the Vow, Zeph," I tell him, the words a promise. "Once that's done, the magic that bound the Gryphons to the Ouphe is dead. I'm not sure what each mark on our bodies can do, but if any one of them can help us bring down Lazza and what he represents, then maybe it could be worth it to wear them for a while."

"For a while?" he questions.

"Speak to Wekun, find out what all of this means, and

then decide what's best for you," I encourage him, trying to help him see that he can take back control over these runes on his body. He can decide if they're allowed to mark his skin or if he wants them removed.

After a minute, he nods. His hands tighten slightly around me, and I'm abruptly aware that my thighs are wrapped around his torso, my lips a feather's width away from his, and my maroon tank dress is floating up around my waist, meaning there's only his pants separating his bits from mine.

We're tangled in a very intimate position, but our connection to each other couldn't be any further from intimate if someone strapped it to a rocket and sent it hurling off in the direction of the moon.

I'm pressed tightly against him, and oddly, it didn't feel weird until just now. My body responds to him despite my head saying *oh come the fuck on.* Unfortunately, in moments like this when Zeph peels back the layers and shows that there's more to him than anger and brutality, it's hard not to get reeled in by the other facets of him.

But my reality is that the tenuous connection that existed between us has been beaten to a pulp. As much as part of me wants to close the miniscule distance between our lips and slide his hands over to cup my breasts, I've played with his fire already—and been burnt to cinders. I won't risk it again.

Zeph's eyes stay fixed on mine as I shutter myself against him. His honeyed gaze flashes with penitence before resolve takes over. His large hands skim down the sides of my ribs, testing my will power.

I wish I didn't know what he felt like pressing himself inside of me or what it was like to kiss him. It would be nice to no longer remember the feel of his chest beneath my palms as I ride him or what his weight is like on top of me as I orgasm.

It makes all of this so fucking complicated, because my body feels right against his. I just wish my soul did.

I climb out of his lap and ignore the way his fingertips skim down the side of my bare hips and thighs as I do. I can see that he wants to press for something physical between us right now. Like he wants to fuck the vulnerability he just experienced away, replace the trauma he just suffered through with connection and orgasms.

I can't lie, there's a part of me that still wants that too, but I refuse to be used and trampled again. I need to talk to Wekun and find out what went wrong, see if there's a way to fix it. I want more than hate fucks and *help me forget* intimacy. I want the way Moro looks at Tysa after they kiss, like she's oxygen to him, like his world couldn't possibly exist without her. I'm not stupid enough to think I'll ever find that here.

12

Z eph lets me go as I step back and put distance between us. Cold air saps the warmth of the water from my body immediately as I step out of it, and I start to shiver. I think of the bed in Wekun's tent for some reason, piled high with furs. In a flash, I'm no longer standing ankle deep in the bathing pools, but dripping water on Wekun's fur covered bed.

What the fuck?

"Oh good, you're back," Wekun exclaims from the pile of pillows he set up for my magic retrieval. He looks exhausted, practically dead on his feet as he gets up and gestures toward the front of his tent. "The other two left not too long ago in search of you," he informs me, pulling a dry shirt from a trunk and chucking it at me.

So it wasn't just that dream thing I can do, I realize as I look down at my dripping body.

"What the fuck was that?" I demand, completely unnerved.

"You're a slipper," he tells me as he falls back onto the bed I'm now climbing out of.

"Say what?" I ask, heading to the screen I changed behind earlier.

"There's a mirror in the corner behind you. It's not the best, but it's all I could find out here."

I look behind me at his instruction and find what looks to be a slightly tarnished piece of reflective metal. I pull off my sopping top and stare at the distorted reflection I create in the makeshift mirror. I have runes everywhere. My arms have the same three bands of markings, spaced out on my forearm, that Zeph—and I suspect Treno and Ryn—now has. Above my elbow are four more spaced out bands, but these are much thicker and prominent.

I have a little flower-like symbol with four petals just under the nail of my ring finger, and three other runes that run down the digit. A thick black band, which looks to be a garter belt of runes, encircles each of my thighs. The markings sit high up on my thighs, and I turn to see they wrap all the way around.

Treno's marks run vertically down my calves, and I spot the same skinny diamonds surrounded by dots on both of my shoulder blades. What's new though, is line after line of even markings that run down the right side of my back. The structure of the runes looks like writing of some sort, and I immediately wonder what it says. I face forward once again and see more of Treno's marks in a line above my left breast, and on the right side, in the same formation, are matching runes to the ones on my ring fingers.

I lean closer to the mirror and scan my body for any other marks. I catch a hint of black under my chin and tilt my head back to see what it is. On the underside of my chin, there's a circle made of a thick black line. I drop my head down and step out from behind the screen.

"What do all of these mean?" I ask, gesturing to the new marks on my naked body.

Wekun looks over to me at my question and then slams his eyes shut. "Whoa, Falon. What the hell, are you trying to get me murdered?" he asks, covering his already closed eyes with his hands as though that will keep my nakedness from seeping in.

"Murdered?" I question.

"Yes, you know, from your warm and fluffy mates, who already look at me like I have ulterior motives when it comes to you."

"What happened? I thought you were breaking the mate bond. I felt it snap with Treno and Ryn, and then all of a sudden..."

"Are you still naked?" Wekun asks me, irritated.

"Yes, because if I get dressed, then you can't see all my runes, and I want to know what they are. We both know there's no attraction between us, so stop acting like a baby and just tell me what's all over my body so I *can* get dressed."

"Fuck my life," he growls.

I stand there, refusing to make this a big deal. Shifters get naked around each other all the time. Plus, I've seen—and worn—the barely there dresses that make up Gryphon and Ouphe fashion; there's no way he can pretend to be overly shy when chicks here practically flash vagina lips on the daily.

He must sense my stubbornness, and with an exasperated sigh, he drops his hands from his face. I cover my breasts as much as possible with a hand and forearm, and drop my other palm to cover my vagina in an effort to save his virtue. Wekun looks over at me warily and quickly scans my body. He twirls his fingers, indicating that he wants me to turn. I do, moving my hand from my crotch to cover my ass crack as I go.

I stand with my back to him for a beat and look over my shoulder when I hear fabric rustling behind me, as though he's climbing off the bed. Wekun comes closer, his eyes fixed on the lines of runes that run from under my shoulder blade to the top of my ass cheek on the right side of my back. He reads the symbols left to right like you would a book, and it confirms my suspicion that it's some kind of written message.

"You can cloak," he tells me, his tone shocked, and he runs a fingertip over a handful of lines on my back. "I've never seen anyone with these marks, but that's definitely what they're saying. Vinna has new ones too; the mixing must be creating new abilities," he states contemplatively, still studying the lines like he's triple-checking that he's right.

"What does that mean?"

"That when you activate this sequence, you can blend into your surroundings to the point that no one can see you. I don't know if that means invisibility all together or more of a chameleon effect?"

My eyes go wide, and I try to look down at the marks on my back, in shock. He touches my shoulder blades. "These are spears of some kind," he tells me. "And these four bands are how you can slip through space."

"Slip through space?" I question.

"Teleport...like you just did earlier when you disappeared for five hours. It looks like you can physically move from one place to another, like I can, but you're also able to separate from your body and move around that way too. Sentinels call it projecting, and it's very rare, although at this point with *your* Sept, that shouldn't surprise me."

He runs a finger down the thin bands of symbols on my forearm, and I turn to face him.

"These are shields. But interestingly, they shield you from outside attacks and also from yourself, you must have a weapon that takes a lot of skill to wield. Your runes will protect you from it." His eyes drop to the rune garters high up on my thighs. "I'd guess it's these. They look like symbols for long swords but different." He shrugs as he crouches down so he can study them closer.

I'm feeling a little lab rat-y, with the way he's looking at my runes. He vacillates between intrigued scientist and reverent worshipper, and I can sense he's cataloging things while also wading through awe. I'm surprised by his astonished reaction altogether though. The guy can portal between worlds at will, but he thinks *my* runes are cool?

"These are your mate runes," he identifies, pointing to my ring finger and the line of marks above my breast on the right side. "Treno has runes that allow him to control water. That's what this line on your left side is. It's not a natural elemental affinity, because it's just for the one element, but it's a strong mark."

Wekun stands up and lifts my arm: between two of the thick bands of runes on my upper arm is another of Treno's marks. It looks like something a kid's Spirograph toy would make. I had one when I was little; I used to love putting my pen in the different pattern wheels and circling it around, making endless amounts of perfect spirals and intersecting shape patterns on paper. I could sit and do it for hours, and this mark is ovals and triangles that all cut through each other to make a cool symmetrical pattern.

"These are blades too, not swords though...something smaller."

"And this?" I ask, tilting my head back and pointing at the circle under my chin.

Wekun smiles, satisfaction lighting his features. "That, Falon, is your Sept rune."

"We can't find her anywhere, are you sure that—" Treno's question chokes off as he storms inside the tent and quickly takes me in. His eyes jump to Wekun's close proximity to my very naked body, and his purple and blue gaze flashes with fury. "What in the rut do you think you're doing?" he bellows, stomping over to place himself in front of me.

Wekun wisely slips himself to the opposite corner of the tent, his hands up and his face and body radiating innocence.

"I'll rip your eyes from your head for looking at her and then choke you with your own severed hands," Treno threatens.

I wince at the visual.

He takes a step in Wekun's direction and then stops himself. Treno seems momentarily torn between wanting to rip him apart with his bare hands and protecting my naked body from Wekun's unwelcome gaze. Treno has the same marks on him that Zeph does, that I do, and I realize that Wekun never answered my question about what went wrong when trying to sever the mate bonds.

"He wasn't doing anything, Treno. He was just telling me what my runes mean. I asked him to," I defend, reaching up to his massive shoulder and trying to pull him back.

He doesn't budge.

"That's not his place, not like that, and not with a mated female," Treno argues, fury and self-righteousness wafting off him in waves.

I snort. "Then whose place is it? And we're not mated. This is none of your business," I counter.

He rounds on me, stepping forward until his tunic-covered chest is pressed against my naked one. "I could have told you what my marks mean, and the fact that you're still wearing my runes, and I'm now adorned in yours, proves that we're as mated as we ever were."

I narrow my eyes and shake my head at him. "You had plenty of time to fill me in, Treno. You were too busy blaming me for your problems and your brother's attempts to kill you."

"Falon," he implores, cutting me off and lifting his hands to gently cup my shoulders.

I shrug him off. "No. You have no right to come barging in here and accusing anyone of anything. Wekun is trying to help me, which is more than I can say of anyone else."

"We're mates, Falon, this will take time for all of us to adjust to, but you need to hear me on this," he orders.

"I don't *need* to do anything," I snap, stepping back from him. "What we are is temporary, because I'm going to fix it. It will be better for all of us in the long run, you'll see."

"*We* are not temporary. It doesn't work that way. You may not want to listen right now, and I'll respect that, but you can't shut me out forever."

"Watch me," I growl and reach for the dry shirt I hung on top of the screen. I pull it on over my head, needing the buffer between me and Treno to help fortify my indignation and my choices.

"You can leave now," I tell him, giving him my back as I pick up a comb from the side table next to the bed.

I brush through my frizzed locks, the ends of my hair still wet from sitting in the bathing pool with Zeph. Concern and curiosity over where he is and if he's okay trickles through me, but I turn the worry tap off and tell myself he's not my problem. Well, hopefully not for much longer anyway.

Treno is still behind me, radiating irritation. I can sense that he wants to say something, but he holds back. Good. Because I don't want to hear shit he has to say.

"This isn't over," he finally grumbles, and then he spins on his heel and storms out.

"Yeah...fuck you," I mumble under my breath as I comb through more snarls.

I miss conditioner.

"Sorry about that," I offer Wekun on a tired sigh.

I pull several furs off the bed and drag them over to the pillow nest that's calling my name.

"You look shot as fuck right now, so I won't push you tonight, but when you feel up to it, can we try to break the mate bonds for good?" I ask, my voice breaking slightly and forcing my vulnerability to leak out against my will.

"Falon..."

I stop what I'm doing and turn to Wekun. The way he just said my name is screaming that there's going to be a bunch of words that pour out after it, and I'm not going to want to hear any of them.

"I tried," he tells me somberly. "It appeared to work for two of your connections. I felt them break, just like I was expecting. But then with the third... When it came to Zeph...maybe it was your awakening that messed with the strength of the connection. Or in your case, it might be that severing things just isn't possible. I couldn't cut the cords between you, and not only that, when I tried, it almost drained me completely, and the next thing I knew, the two connections I had already severed were back and fortified as fuck. I've never seen anything like it. I understand why you're making the choice that you are, but there's nothing more that *I* can do at this point to help you break away from them."

His words burrow into me, cutting me deeply as they go. Desolation pours into the wounds, and I collapse onto the cushions and stare at nothing as I try to think through a future where I'm stuck with mates like these. Choosing to sever our ties hurt, but I knew it was the right thing to do. Pigeon even knew it was what was best for us. And now, to know that I'm stuck? I look up at Wekun, devastated.

Sympathy fills his features, and he runs a hand over his

shorn white hair like he's trying to think of a way to make all of this better.

"There's another Bond Weaver in Tierit— that's where the Sentinels live in the other world. She's ancient, so if anyone would know of any other ways, it would be her. I can check with her. Well, if her watchdog, Issak, will let me get near her that is. He doesn't like me, which is an effect I can have on mates. He's not mated to Getta, just indebted to her, I think, but still." He shrugs his shoulders. "I honestly have no clue what his story is. He came over with her when she crossed...it's an odd friendship."

My mind prickles with recognition for some reason, and I examine his words, looking for the trigger.

"Anyway, let's get you set up here and start working with your runes and what they can do. I'll sneak off the first chance I get and see if I can get in to speak with her, find out if she knows any other ways."

I nod in agreement at his plan, and exhaustion washes over me. I quickly get myself comfortable and pull the furs up around me. Wekun stumbles toward the bed and falls face first against the lumpy mattress. I swear he's out before his body is done bouncing from the impact.

I release a weary breath and study the runes on my finger.

"What the fuck are we going to do, Pigeon?"

She pulls her head out from under her wing, swaying like she's too tired to balance properly. She flashes me an image of scissors cutting string, an *X*, and me fucking each of our mates in turn.

I scoff. *"Did you really just tell me, 'If you can't sever 'em, fuck 'em'?"* I ask incredulously. *"That is not the same thing as if you can't beat 'em, join 'em,"* I scold.

She just makes that chuffing noise she does when she's amused, and her face disappears back under her wing.

I watch her for a moment as her breaths grow heavy and steady with sleep. One minute she hates them, the next she's ready to forgive and move on. I can't even keep track anymore of what she wants or doesn't want.

They say women are hard to figure out, well, they sure as fuck never met a female gryphon. Talk about taking confusing to a whole other level.

I try to list what still needs to be done, while my body winds down and prepares for rest. I realize that, as difficult as everything has been already, I'm pretty sure that the hard part of all of this has just begun.

I sigh and drift off to Pigeon's gryphon-porn-filled dreams flooding my mind.

Fickle fucking buffalo wing.

13

"The last thing any of us should be doing is sticking our noses into Gryphon business. Yes, we are obligated to help fix what our people did to them, but even if we have the best of intentions, they're not going to see it that way," a female Ouphe from the crowd comments, and everyone gathered in the center of the camp starts talking all at once again.

Several of them raise their hands to be called on so they too can voice their opinions. The middle-aged salt-and-pepper-haired lady who seems to be running the show here calls on a man.

"Even if we wanted to help, how are we supposed to identify which gryphons are good and which are bad?" he asks, and sounds of agreement from people around him rise up into the air.

I open my mouth to say that Lazza really is the only threat that needs to be dealt with, but if I can't figure out how to break the Vow, one side will be fighting the other side, and this guy has a point.

"We could provide aid and healing to those who are willing to take it from us, but we can't forget that many of the gryphons on both sides of this fight will happily kill us on sight. I don't know whether we'd be of much help or more of a distraction," a younger, pretty female calls out.

I release a deep sigh. I was hoping the Ouphe would be willing to help us, fight with the gryphons, and shore up the numbers against Lazza's army, but I'm realizing that my hope was really fucking short-sighted I can see the willingness in many of the Ouphe's faces, to help in what ways they can, but they make really good points about the fact that many of the gryphons who will be there won't take kindly to their presence. There's still a lot of work to be done on the front of Ouphe and Gryphon relations and peace treaties.

Wekun and I are leaning off to the side against a cart and watching the Ouphe have their say about what's going on in the world between the Avowed and the Hidden. There are some gryphons spotted around the perimeter, including Ryn, Zeph, and Treno, but they're keeping to the outskirts and staying quiet.

"They've hunted us to the brink of extinction; they can't come to us for help now," a man growls, and low murmurs of assent surround him. "No one came to our aid when we were forced to escape to this putrid wasteland and eke out our survival. Where was Awlon the Dark and his progeny then?"

The man spits on the ground, and I feel far too many eyes turn to me. Hostility ripples out toward where I'm perched, and it crawls up my skin in warning.

"No one person or bloodline was to blame for what happened," Wekun interjects. "The Ouphe as a collective voted on the Vow and the Accords, and they passed with favor. We are all accountable for what our ancestors did," he volleys into the crowd. "We must all work to do better and be better for our future generations."

"*Our* future generations?" the man argues, fixing his

angry gaze on Wekun. "You only pop in when you're here to pluck strings in a favor of a future only your kind can see. You ran for the gates and a new world, abandoning the rest of us to suffer and get picked off. Don't talk as though we're one people when you know that's not true."

Wekun shakes his head, like he's disappointed. "Are we back to that again?" he asks, scanning the crowd like his question is for all of them. "Some Sentinels chose to leave, others chose to remain, what happened after was the consequence of that choice, on both sides. How is one side held accountable for the tragedies the other suffered? Tierit and its people have also known hardship and struggle; we're hidden from the world there, just as you are here. Blaming others for our problems serves no purpose," he points out, and the gathered crowd grows quiet.

"I think we've had our say," the leader of the camp announces, her eyes fixed on me and Wekun. "I don't think we are in the position to truly help. You should speak to Cree and the Gryphons, they would be in a better position to help," she tells me, and I nod.

"Thank you for trying at least," I offer, but she just looks at me weird. I remember that the Ouphe and Gryphons aren't big on manners and just smile at her and wait for the crowd to disperse enough for Wekun and me to take off so we can go speak to the gryphons.

"Is Cree the female with the cool mohawk and scars?" I ask Wekun as we're waiting.

"The very one, although you might not want to bring up the scars."

"Oh, is she sensitive?"

"No, but it will start her down battle memory lane, and we could be there for weeks as she tells stories and forces us to drink."

I chuckle and shake my head. "Yeah, I'm not going to lie, I could be down for that."

"You're just trying to get out of training," Wekun accuses, and I shrug, not even trying to deny it.

"I still don't understand why I can't just work on things on my own," I grumble. "I'm not saying that they can't get rune lessons too, but it doesn't *have* to be together," I point out.

Wekun went and organized a little group training with me and the mates I apparently can't escape. I was glad to hear that Zeph was doing better and working to embrace what happened and find a way to make it work for him, but I'd prefer they did it far away from me.

"Get over it, Falon, it's time to Sentinel up and do what needs to be done," he announces, slapping me on the ass like I'm some obstinate horse that needs to get a move on. Three growls simultaneously fill the air around us, and I roll my eyes and rub my ass cheek.

"I should let them take you out," I threaten Wekun, who simply glares at me, unamused by the joke.

"Then you'd really be stuck with them," he points out as he takes the lead through the remaining crowd in the direction of the gryphon camp.

"When are you going to go have your little chat with the other Bond Weaver in Tierit anyway?"

"When you are good enough with your runes that I can leave for a couple days," he calls back over his shoulder.

Well, crap then. Guess it's time to Sentinel up...whatever that means.

We make our way to the gryphon camp quietly. I'm not going to admit this to Wekun, but I'm actually excited to start working with my runes. I'm just not overeager to be working on them with an audience of inconsiderate mates, who all just so happen to know that I tried to undo our bonds. So far, I'm not sure what to make of how they feel about that. Treno seemed annoyed, Zeph seemed surprised, and I don't know what Ryn's feelings are on the matter, I haven't seen him yet.

I sort of feel like I've been caught doing something I'm not supposed to, but that doesn't quite capture the awkwardness I feel today facing them. If it had worked, it would be a different story. I could just keep it moving and ignore them. But it backfired and somehow connected us even more, and that's just plain fucking awkward for me. I feel like fate is laughing its ass off right now, and I'm just supposed to go about my day like I can't hear it cackling and calling me out.

On the plus side of things, I woke up this morning feeling more alive and invigorated than I have ever felt before. I can sense something different, and very powerful, flowing through my veins, and I'm eager to tap into it and see just what I was always meant to be able to do. When Pigeon was freed, I felt more complete than I ever have before, but now that everything inside of us is unlocked, we're both flying in and around cloud nine.

We wind through tents, and I can feel the guys some-where behind me, tracking our every move, but I don't look for them. I'm not sure why they're so interested in keeping an eye on me, but I suspect it has to do with what Zeph said in the forest the night he brought all of us here: they're there to make sure I don't betray them in some way.

Two large male gryphons with staffs step in front of Wekun, and we stop. "What business do you have here, String Puller?" one of the beefy males asks.

As much as Wekun has helped me navigate everything going on around me, I'm starting to get the impression that he's not the most popular guy around the camps. I don't know if it's simple hate for Bond magic, what it can do, and over all mistrust directed at those who possess it? Or if it's something about Wekun in general that rubs people the wrong way, but he doesn't have the fan club around here I would have guessed he'd have based solely on his looks.

"We're here to see Cree," he answers simply, not at all perturbed by the way they're speaking to him.

"She only wants to see the female," the other massive male grunts out, and Wekun nods once and steps aside.

He gives me a thumbs up, which does nothing to calm my sudden nerves at all. I have no idea who this gryphon is other than she's the boss around here. I feel like Zeph or the other two would be better choices to ask her to join us in our fight to defeat Lazza and the Vow, but for some reason, it seems this task has now officially fallen to me.

Yay.

I shrug and give myself the old pep talk standby of *what the hell, here goes nothing* as I pass Wekun and follow the two ripped gryphon guards past several tents before they open the flap to an especially large one and gesture for me to go in. I walk in confidently, and Pigeon gives me an approving nod. I figure it's best to come off like a badass bitch when meeting other badass bitches, so I hold my head high and take in the space.

It's immediately clear that this is not the leader's quarters, but more of a meeting room. There's a large table that currently has a map spread on it, and Cree and several others are standing around the table, pouring over the details on the rolled out parchment. There are braziers with small fires set in each corner of the room, but the flames that flicker inside of them are green. I suspect they've been magicked in some way to provide heat without burning down the fabric of the tent they're positioned next to, but what do I know, maybe fire in this place is always green.

Cree looks up, and her aubergine-colored eyes land on

me. "Ah, I was wondering when I'd get to meet the infamous Bond Breaker," she comments, running her eyes over me.

Clearly, gossip travels fast in this camp too. I've not formally introduced who I am or where I come from to anyone in either place, and yet it seems to be common knowledge nonetheless. I'm not sure if I have Nadi to thank for announcing my existence or Wekun, but it's obvious I'm being discussed in many circles, and judging by some of the looks I've gotten while moseying around camp, not all of it's good.

"We'll discuss this later," she dictates to the others gathered around the table, and they all nod and immediately leave.

She's not terse, simply commanding, in every sense of the word. She has that same air about her from when I saw her in action with Zeph, Ryn, and Treno the first night we arrived. She is not to be fucked with, and I find myself wondering how I can develop a similar countenance.

I imagine her mates wouldn't question her worth or loyalty. They're probably crawling all over themselves to keep such a powerful female happy.

"It's nice to meet you. I'm Falon," I offer.

I have to consciously remind myself that handshaking isn't a thing here, so instead of offering my palm to her in greeting, I lace my fingers together behind my back and wait.

"Falon...interesting, and what brings you to me on this piss soaked morning?" she asks, a hint of amusement in her tone.

I have no idea if it's my name or my presence that's entertaining her, so I just keep it moving. "I'm sure you're already aware of why I've arrived in the camp, and that I'm hoping to find help to fight Lazza and break the Vow once and for all."

"I am aware that you spoke with the Ouphe before you came here, and that they denied your request for help."

I study Cree for a moment. Her words imply some level of insult in my not coming to her first, but her tone is even and very matter-of-fact. I'm not sure if I should be reading between the lines or taking her at face value. Pigeon sits up and studies her too. I decide I can't be bothered with games or trying to figure out if one's being played right now.

"The Ouphe were worried about how any help they offered could be perceived by the Gryphons," I explain. "I hadn't thought about that before speaking with them, but after listening to the discussion this morning, I agree that there's too much negative history between the Ouphe and the Gryphons for them to really be of any help. The leader is going to work on finding out if they have any materials that might point me in the right direction as far as figuring out how to break the Vow, but that will be the gist of their contribution to our efforts."

"*Our* efforts?" Cree asks, and it reminds me of the Ouphe that questioned Wekun in a similar way.

"My efforts, alongside Zeph, Ryn, and Treno's," I correct.

"Yes, that's right, you did come with quite the collection of powerful males. Many a female have been preening."

I try not to roll my eyes and grunt out a *tell them good luck with that*. Cree watches me like a hawk, studying me and my reactions, but I have no idea to what end.

"Would that bother you, if the Syta and two Alterns entertained the females of this camp?" she asks smoothly, and I once again have no idea what the game is here.

I look to Pigeon, but she seems just as intrigued and confused.

"I don't own them; it's up to them how they choose to spend their time here. I won't speak on their behalf one way or the other."

Cree nods and then waves at the guards standing just inside the front flap of the tent. One of them slips out immediately. Uneasiness washes through me.

"And how about you, Falon, are you looking to tie yourself to our people?"

Cree poses the question as innocently as she has the others, but I sense the trap in it immediately. She doesn't trust me, and I get the distinct impression she's looking for leverage. She wants collateral, something she can lord over me. Maybe she needs something that helps her feel confident that the lives of her people will be safeguarded if they fight, or maybe she just likes pulling strings like Wekun. Either way, I instantaneously feel like I'm in some fucked up chess match, which sucks because I'm a checkers kind of girl.

"No," I admit, in answer to her question. "I'm not interested in tying myself to anyone from any side," I add.

"Hmmm," she hums, her tone tinged with a hint of judgement. "I've heard as much."

The flap of the tent opens, and in walks Treno, Zeph and Ryn. Their faces are stony, their movements stiff, and I swear I can hear the wheels spinning in Cree's head as they're lined up in front of her. She pushes away from the table and circles them, her purple gaze raking over their figures carefully, as though she's committing every curve and dip to memory. But I get the distinct impression that she's watching me more than them.

Does she want a reaction?

"Falon and I were just discussing your potential interest in females in this camp. She stated she didn't want to speak on your behalf, so I thought it best to go right to the source. You three know how this is done. Our ways haven't changed in how alliances are formed during times of war. If you want us to fight, then you give us something to fight for," Cree states, stopping her circling and settling behind Ryn.

Four pairs of eyes land on me, and the sets belonging to Ryn, Zeph, and Treno do *not* look happy. If they're trying to send me some kind of subliminal message though, it's lost on me because these fuckers always look pissed off these days.

"We are all aware of how things are done," Ryn starts, his tone irritated. "However, we're all mated and not in a position to make alliances in that way."

As though Ryn's words went in one ear and right out the other, Cree steps up behind Ryn and presses into him. Her palms skate across his chest as she wraps her arms around him from behind. Ryn stiffens, and every inch of him radiates how uncomfortable he is, but it seems Cree doesn't give a shit. I wait for Ryn to grab her hands and shove them away, but he doesn't. He also doesn't look over at me as she nuzzles her cheek against his neck.

I look to Zeph and Treno, trying to understand what the fuck this chick's deal is. Treno just looks blankly at the ground, and Zeph looks conflicted but doesn't move either.

"What the fuck are we missing here, Pidge?" I ask.

Cree nips at Ryn's neck, and he flinches but still doesn't stop her. Anger at not understanding the nuance of what's happening surges inside of me. Cree is tough as fuck, that's clear, and she has hair I'm massively jealous of, but the fucked up vibe coming off her right now is not sitting right with me.

"Cree, maybe you can clarify something for me," I tell her, and her face lifts until she's no longer looking at Ryn like she's going to devour him, but her gaze is once again fixed on me. "Where I come from, we do things a bit differently, so you'll have to forgive my ignorance, but when you talk about how things are done around here, is consent not a factor? I mean, clearly *you* don't care about how pathetic or desperate you look pushing up on someone who's clearly not interested, but is that just you, or is it a Gryphon thing altogether?"

"What did you just say to me?" she asks, evenly pulling her hands from around Ryn and now moving in my direction.

"I asked if you have any shame?" I tell her. "I used more words than that, but I'm happy to dumb it down if you need me to."

"So you do speak for them then?" she presses.

"I'll speak on behalf of anyone being pushed into something they clearly aren't interested in," I correct her.

"Good," she responds simply, and then she gestures to the guards in the room who all converge on us.

"Take them to the pit please; I'll be right behind you," Cree instructs, and with that I'm suddenly being herded out of the tent and away from the Psycho Syta of this Gryphon camp.

The guys don't say anything, but they look tense as fuck. I know I'm missing so much right now, but they have looks on their faces that tell me I'm going to get ripped apart if I even ask for them to fill me in on what the fuck is happening, so I just keep it quiet.

Pigeon feels agitated inside of me, so I focus on calming her down as we're ushered through the camp to a large sunken rink of packed dirt. The word *pit* is accurate at least.

This should be fun.

14

I look behind me to see Cree steadily trudging our way. And goody, she has what looks to be the entire camp on her heels. She passes me like a force to be reckoned with and hops down into the pit. She starts to untie the armor encasing her body, and I look around a little more cautiously.

If she tries to force herself on anyone, I'll fucking rip her to shreds. I don't give a fuck what happens to me in my efforts to do so. It dawns on me that I'm massively outnumbered and, as indignant as I am, I may not be able to stop it, but I shove that away. I'm not the same person I was when I first landed in this world. I'm not powerless.

"My Pride," Cree calls out. "I humble myself before you today to answer a challenge that's been laid at my feet."

My brow crinkles in confusion as gryphons all around me hiss in anger at her words.

Did I challenge her?

"We've been asked to join the fight against Lazza and the Vow, but the petitioner is untested and therefore unworthy. How can we follow *that* into battle? Sacrifice our lives and our futures for someone who won't even claim her mates!"

The crowd boos and shouts out their anger, and my mouth drops open. "You don't know what the fuck you're talking about, lady," I snap at Cree.

Apparently, my mouth gives no fucks, because I just pop off. And what's weirder is as soon as I open my mouth, the crowd quiets, which means every word that slips off my tongue is heard loud and clear.

"Do I not?" Cree counters. "Your scent isn't on them, you don't sleep in the same place, you left them in a dangerous situation with not a care in the world about what we might do to them, you offer them to other females. Why would we fight for someone who looks at us and our ways so heartlessly?" she demands.

I see red at her words, and the next thing I know I'm jumping down into the ring too. I hear the guys shouting my name, but I ignore it. There is no fucking way I'm going to get painted as the bad guy here. Fuck this bitch.

"I did not offer them to other females, I said I don't own them or their decisions," I shout out as I close the distance between me and Cree. "You don't know shit about me. Those fuckers have walked all over me, lied, withheld information, blamed me for shit I have no control over, and destroyed any kind of connection we could have ever had together. If that's the kind of shit you and your people value, then fuck you," I snarl at her and then turn to our audience. "But you know what, I'm still going to break the Vow and do what I promised to do, regardless of the fucked up ways any of you see the world."

I turn back to Cree and continue my rant. "You want a fight, you got one, but let's keep it real, it's not because you're standing up for some kind of code. You're a bitch with a chip on your shoulder and nothing more."

Pigeon wing fives me, proud of my little speech. Excitement flashes through her as I start to untie my pants and strip down like Cree is. She's probably going to kill me, but I don't even care anymore. I'm tired of being pushed around. If I die, I'll still fulfill my promise. All I know is, there better be a massive burger waiting for me in heaven...with bacon on it and a pool full of fries.

"Maybe we have a worthy opponent on our hands after all," Cree declares, and then in a blink, she explodes into a massive fog gray gryphon with bright purple eyes.

"Alright, Pidge, this is all you?"

Pigeon rips out of my chest like a freight train, and we're attacking before the change from me to her is fully complete. I forgot how utterly fearless she is when she fights, and I clap and cheer her on when Cree rears back in surprise.

She promptly gryphon slaps us into next week, but the element of surprise was good while it lasted. Pigeon shakes it off and flips back at her again, like some bouncy ball of feathers and promised pain, ricocheting around the pit, taking hits, but doling them out too.

We're fast, and Cree doesn't quite know what to do with our manic advances. It seems *balls to the wall* is not the fight setting she's used to facing. I can feel her studying Pigeon. Like a cat watching a fly, just biding their time before they...pounce.

All at once, Pigeon and I are flying sideways through the air until we slam into the edge of the pit. Cree just swatted us like we were nothing more than an annoying mosquito. The crowd around us roars their approval, and Pigeon and I scramble to our feet just in time to take the full weight of Cree pouncing on us.

She shoves us to the ground, and Pigeon roars out in pain and frustration as claws rake down our back. She's toying with us. Pigeon and I are in no position to overtake her, but she's not done having her fun. Cree digs her talons under one of our wings and wrenches it back hard. We scream at the same time she trumpets glee.

Rage builds inside of me as Cree starts to pick at us with her beak, her other talon-tipped hand working to get under our other wing. She wants to break us as badly as she can before ending this. I can feel the lesson she wants to stamp all over this pit with our blood, and defiance surges through me. Pigeon is lost to the pain, and it takes her a long time to register the words I'm screaming at her.

"Shift, Pidge! Let me out!" I demand, ignoring the confusion and concern that flickers through her before Cree's back paws dig into our flank. It feels like she's trying to rip us in half.

"Pidge, shift!" I bellow at her again, and this time she chucks the reins at me, and I pull her back inside of me.

Cree is a million times heavier when I'm me than what she felt like on top of Pigeon, but I don't waste any time before I unleash the power that is damming up inside of me. I scream as it pulses out of my body in purple waves, the blast shoving Cree off my back and across the pit.

I let go of control of our body and shove Pigeon back out, and in a stride, we explode into our gryphon form and leap for Cree. She's quick and rolls to the right, kicking out at us as she does. But we get our claws in her chest and tear at her as we're shoved away. We scramble back and both get to our feet, cautiously assessing for a minute before charging toward each other again.

"Shift, Pidge!" I scream out, and she does without question, just as Cree rears up ready to do everything she can to knock our head off our shoulders.

Just like we used to practice back in the fields around Kestrel City, Pigeon gets sucked back into our core, leaving me to run right at a fucking monster. I skid like I'm stealing home base and punch out with my fists like I'm hoping my power will right hook her into oblivion. Panic rips through me though when no purple power of doom shoots out of my hands, and instead I find myself gripping some kind of weapon in both my palms.

Time slows as I skid closer to Cree, the hilt of two swords in my hands. Only they're not swords exactly, because the blades look broken.

Fuck.

Where the gleaming metal of a sword blade should exist, it looks more like interconnecting vertebrae. Only instead of bones making up the unusual spine-like appearance, sharp pieces of metal interlock with each other. I flick my wrist, testing out the weird weapon, and the metal pieces suddenly move like a whip. Shock punches through me when my innocuous wrist flick sends the blade pieces snapping out and burying themselves in Cree's descending arm.

She screams and instantaneously yanks her hand back, and the weird whip-sword blades dig into her flesh even deeper. Astonished, I'm still holding on to the handles as the blades of the whip grow taut from her reeling back, and I'm suddenly flung to the side and then up into the air. The handles of the weapons are wrenched from my grip, and I immediately release my hold on our body so that Pigeon can once again come surging forward.

She bends us and flips us midair, using our aching wings to right our trajectory so we're no longer flying away but barreling right for Cree again. Her arm is mangled and bleeding, and she clutches it closely to her chest as we charge into her with all our might.

A large *crack* bounces off the walls of the pit as our massive feather and fur-covered bodies collide, and Pigeon snaps out and digs her sharp beak into Cree's shoulder.

Momentum has us both ping-ponging off the pit wall, and we're all claws, snarls, and hooked beaks as we tear at each other.

Somehow Cree gets us on our back, and as she snaps for our face, I feel Pigeon recede again.

"Fuck!" I scream, not ready for her to hand me back the reins, so I try to make the whip swords appear in my hand again. They don't. Instead, I get some *Chronicles of Riddick* shit that pops up in my hands, and I find myself squeezing two black grips with blades that curve around my knuckles like back-to-back *J*s.

Cree's beak snaps out at my face, and on pure instinct, I shove my blade-covered fists out, the sharp black blades instantly connecting with her neck. Cree freezes, her gryphon face less than six inches from mine. My blades are buried in the feathers of her neck, warm blood now dripping down my fists.

We're both panting and unmoving, as though someone hit pause on the battle and we're waiting for them to hit play again. I'm completely surprised that Cree doesn't just close the distance and rip my face off. I'm pretty sure she'd kill me before my blades could slice her head off, but maybe they're sharper than I realized.

A familiar chuffing noise creeps out of Cree's maw, and I realize that everyone around us is completely silent. No one is cheering or jeering. It's as though they're just as shocked by what's happening as Cree and I are.

Cree steps back, and Pigeon and I tense, ready for her next attack. It doesn't come. Only more of that gryphon giggle fills the pit as Cree distances herself from us, slowly loping toward her scattered pile of clothing and armor. I scamper as far away from the foggy-colored gryphon as I can. I move away until the side of the pit caresses the naked skin of my back. My Nike Swoosh shaped blades are still clutched in my hands, mostly because I have no idea how to get rid of them or really why I even have them in the first place. I watch Cree through suspicion-laced blinks and heavy breaths, feeling like this is somehow just another one of her tricks.

Her gryphon folds in on itself until Cree is all that remains, as naked as I am and surprisingly battered. Blood trickles down her throat, her shoulder, her back, her thigh. Her arm is fucked up, and I'm stunned to see the wounds of her gryphon have manifested on her body too. Pigeon's pain and injuries always feel separate from mine, with the exception of our wings. Not taking my eyes off of Cree for a second, I run my fingers over my shoulder where I know she did her best to rip it apart, but there's just smooth skin.

I can feel Pigeon hurting inside of me, and yet I bear no marks of what we just endured. I need to ask Wekun if that's normal. I tense as two burly guard-looking guys jump into the pit and saunter over to Cree. She chuckles and bats at their hands as they wipe blood from her body and press their hands against her wounds. *Not guards*, I tell myself as I watch the exchange, *healers*. I'm reminded of the healer that Treno brought to me in Kestrel, and I find myself completely fascinated as I watch her injuries knit back together simply from the touch of these two males.

I flinch, and my attention is yanked away as a gargantuan body slams down to the earth next to me, and I look over to find an enraged Zeph ripping his shirt off and stepping in front of me. Ryn lands on my other side, and I feel Treno pound to the ground behind me.

Zeph fits the neck of his tunic over my head and threads my hands through the too long sleeves like I'm some inept toddler incapable of dressing myself. His touch is surprisingly gentle, but he doesn't say anything as he works to cover me up. He doesn't have to; the rage coating his counte-nance says quite enough. He's fucking pissed.

The two healers finish up with a smiling Cree and turn in my direction. Zeph, Ryn, and Treno all tense, but shock-ingly they stay quiet. A large muscled arm snakes around my shoulders and chest, and I'm carefully pulled back against Treno. I'm so shocked by the possessive display, but there's no time to really say anything before the two healers are standing in front of me.

Their eyes scan my body, and I see a flicker of surprise in both of their gazes when they don't find me in a worse off state than Cree. "You're not hurt?" one of them asks, lifting the hem of the tunic like he expects to find it hiding copious amounts of blood and gore. Ryn's hand shoots out and clutches the male by the wrist, a low warning growl rever-berating out of his throat.

"My gryphon is hurting more than I am," I interject as the healer's eyes narrow on Ryn. "I'm not sure if you can do anything about that."

He refocuses his attention back on me and nods. "Where?" he asks, his periwinkle gaze roaming over my face.

"Do you need her to come out so you can see?" I ask, unsure how this works exactly. I sort of passed out the first and only time I came in contact with a healer in Kestrel City.

"No, we can reach her through you, but if you tell us where she's suffering the most, that's where we'll concen-trate our ability," he explains.

I look back and forth between the two and realize they must be related. They have different shades of golden blond hair, one slightly darker than the other, but they have the same nose and the same blue-purple toned eyes.

"Our wings, her back, her hips, and her neck. I think she

got whiplash from a couple of those swipes to the head," I confess.

Treno's arm tightens slightly around me, and the healing brothers both nod and step closer to me. One of them presses his palms to the sides of my neck while the other lifts Zeph's shirt and snakes his hand up my back from the bottom. Treno doesn't move away from me, and the healer has to wedge his hand between my back and Treno's front.

It's awkward as hell, but I keep my mouth shut, as everyone around me is feeling entirely too volatile, and I am not going to be in the middle of this shit show if it blows up. Out of nowhere, heat from the healers' touch slowly builds and then gently pushes into me. I gasp at the sensation of their magic stretching out inside of me, and Pigeon unfurls as the warm tendrils reach her and start to do their thing.

Smoky billows of healing magic move through my chest, and I almost feel high from the sensation of all my minor aches and pains being wiped away alongside Pigeon's wounds. My head lolls back against Treno's chest, and every muscle in my body relaxes. It's like this shit takes care of emotional wounds in addition to the physical ones.

"Damn, that's some good shit," I mumble, and one of the healing brothers chuckles.

Pigeon and I both feel all floaty and warm as a thumb grazes my jaw. I focus on the touch and stare right into a pair of periwinkle-colored eyes. The brother with the lighter golden blond hair gives me an inviting smile, and I return it without any thought as to what I'm doing.

Pigeon perks up in that way that I've learned to be very wary of, and it snaps me out of my floaty haze. I immediately sober and shoot her a glare.

"Don't even think about it," I snap at her.

She flashes me an image of the brothers and how she feels high as fuck, but I shake my head at her. *"We've collected enough fucking trouble as it is,"* I remind her, and she gets all pouty but thankfully doesn't argue.

A large hand trails down my spine, and fingertips skim the side of my ass cheek, as the other healing brother pulls his arm out of my shirt. Another warning growl sounds off from behind me, and both Zeph and Ryn quickly join in. If I weren't so shocked by the show of solidarity between the three of them, I'd tell them to cut it out.

The healing brothers step away, and one of them shoots me a wink that earns him a snarl in triplicate. He doesn't seem bothered by the reaction of the big scary males surrounding me, which makes me question his sanity, because Ryn, Zeph, and Treno really aren't the kind of males anyone should want to fuck with.

Zeph and Ryn both step in front of me, not blocking my view, but more taking up a protective stance. The level of menace seeping off of them makes the hair on my arms stand on end, and I'm grateful not to have that shit aimed at me for once.

Cree is completely dressed again, and she walks to the middle of the pit and raises her arms as though to silence the watching crowd. The only thing is, they're all already quiet. You could hear a feather fall in this place.

She smiles, and the appearance of it makes her whole face light up in this genuine and beautiful way. "She's worthy," she announces quietly, and the emotion that pours into those words takes my breath away. Cree pauses like she needs a moment to gain control of the flood of feelings flowing through her. "We have waited for so long…" she starts again, her eyes shimmering with unshed hope, "and now it's time."

The roar of approval that bellows out of all the gryphons surrounding us shocks me. Wekun explained that the gryphons here were exiled for one reason or another, and

I'm completely taken aback by the longing and determination I feel all around me, to take back what was taken from them. I look around, and for the first time, I don't see a fragile and wilted people, I see belief and fortitude.

It fills me to the brim with conviction and hope. Now all I need to do is find the words to break the Vow.

15

"So I said to him, I wish you could use the sword between your thighs as well as the one in your hand."

Raucous laughter shoots up all around me, and Cree downs her drink and wipes her mouth as her tankard plops back down to the table.

"And that's how I got this scar," she states, pointing to the nick in her ear.

I give a small chuckle and take a tentative sip of my own drink. It's mead, which should make me happy, but I find myself drifting off to thoughts that just don't support frivolous joy at the moment. Maybe I've reached the sad-drunk portion of the night, or maybe there's just too much going on for me to really let go. Plus, Wekun was right, Cree can talk about her scars like Bubba Gump talks about shrimp.

They're all entertaining stories, and it seems everyone around us has their favorite they like her to tell, but my heart isn't into the carefree night it seems Cree and her people are up for. I'm happy to say that after the fight, Cree seems more normal and less "covetous bitch."

I must have passed all her tests, because she's been

nothing but welcoming and kind since we all traipsed in here to indulge in some day drinking. The sun has long since tucked itself into bed though, and I keep thinking about my dad and everything he told me the other night when my marks returned. His sad eyes and strong hug haunt me tonight. I can't help feeling like time is running out and I'm still trying to put everything together.

I take another sip of my drink and force a smile as more laughter titters around me. I pretend like I'm participating in the girl chat, but I'm far away in Vedan, and in Colorado, trying to remember the things my dad taught me. I keep expecting the words to tumble out of my mind like a long-lost key clanging to the ground and making its presence known, but nothing happens. He said I already knew; the problem is I can't remember.

Maybe when I'm done here, Wekun can try to hypnotize me or something, because the answers are in my head, I just need to shake them out somehow. I look up, feeling bad that he wasn't allowed to join in on the fun. I tried to vouch for him, but it's clear the gryphons aren't a fan. I thought that maybe they take issue with the kind of magic he has, but Bond magic is laced in my blood too, and here I am. Guess it still is a Gryphon versus the Ouphe thing, even if the camps here are reliant on each other. That appears to be a begrudging thing they all try to ignore.

Someone else is telling a story now, but I can't focus on it. I can feel Zeph's, Treno's, and Ryn's eyes weighing me down, and their presence makes everything feel even more complicated. I've been ignoring them all night. Wisely, they haven't approached me, but the stage five clinger alert is fucking strong.

I try to push thoughts of them out of my mind for the thousandth time tonight. There's no amount of alcohol that will help me untangle the mess between us; I just wish my body and mind could come to some sort of agreement on that. It also doesn't help that Pigeon is once again in a forgiving mood. Shit is so much easier for me when she hates them too.

The intense need to pee suddenly takes over my senses. I quickly chug down the rest of my drink so my relieving my bladder doesn't completely fuck with my buzz, and focus on trying to get my fizzy body to whatever bucket around here has been designated as a bathroom.

I push away from the table, and Cree looks over at me expectantly.

"I need to piss like a racehorse," I announce, and she smiles, confusion sparkling in her glassy gaze.

Shit, they don't know what horses are, I realize.

"It's an animal we have where I'm from. They have four legs, long noses and they run really fast," I quickly explain. I take my index and middle finger and crisscross them quickly as I try to explain that they run. I then make my hand rear up and release a *neigh*, which for some reason, makes all the females sitting at the table with me crack up, like I just told the best joke.

I shrug and chuckle, their mirth a little contagious, and then my bladder gets all threatening, and I quickly make my way out of the tent that serves as this place's bar, in search of a tent or bush I can piss in.

Bush it is, I decide as I stumble behind the bar tent into the night in search of a good place to do my thing. I spot one of those weird looking crystal trees and stomp over to it, unlacing my pants and crouching down, the trunk hiding me from view. My mind wanders as I water the vegetation, listening to the sounds of the night all around me as my head swims.

I give myself time to drip dry and tilt my head back to the sky. "That group of stars kind of looks like a broken wing," I point out to Pigeon, but she's three sheets to the wind and is currently trying—and failing—to pin down her own tail.

"I always thought it looked more like a Thais Fairy," Ryn announces from somewhere behind me, and I jump at the sound of his voice and almost land my ass in my own puddle. I manage to grab onto the tree trunk and save myself, but it was a close fucking call.

"You need a bell," I grumble as I pull up my pants, glaring at him over my shoulder as I move to the other side of the tree.

"You need to be more careful, two other males followed you out here," he tells me.

I gasp dramatically. "Oh no, not two males." Rolling my eyes, I huff out a breath. "Maybe they had to pee too, Ryn," I defend, leaning back against the crystal trunk of the tree so my swaying body can settle before I try to make my way back to my tent.

Ryn moves closer. "Or maybe they wanted to mess with things that don't belong to them," he counters quietly, reaching out to capture a lock of my white hair between his fingers.

"Oh, so I'm a *thing* now?" I snark, batting his hand away from me. I push away from the tree trunk, shaking my head. "Doesn't matter, call me whatever you want. I don't belong to you," I tell him, ducking between him and the tree.

He puts an arm out and stops my escape.

"We belong to each other, Falon," he declares, stepping even closer to me. "That's what happens when you're mated."

He brushes hair off my shoulder, and I have to stop myself from leaning into him.

I snort. "Mated?" I question. "We fucked and somehow we're tied together, but we're not mates, Ryn. Not in the way that word is supposed to define a relationship. There's nothing sacred or special between us. We're strangers, ones that don't even like each other."

The crystalized bark of the tree digs into my back as Ryn flattens his body against mine. My breasts are pressed tightly against his muscular chest, and his leg settles between mine. He runs his fingers down my hair, and I despise that I don't want him to stop. I should push him away, crush his effort the same way he's pulverized my trust. I should leave him hurt and wanting, the way he and the others have left me too many times. The only problem is...I don't want him to leave. I want him to show me why fate has kept us locked together. I want him to prove why I shouldn't break the bond.

My mind and body war with what I want versus what I deserve, and I'm lost to the confusion of the battle. He feels good against me. He feels right. And in a world and time where everything is so wrong and uncertain, I need this.

"We started off badly, there's no denying that, but it doesn't change what you are to me, Falon. I know I hurt you, but if you'll stop running from me, I can show you how I can make it better. I can do things the way I should have done them from the beginning. I can show you why we're right for each other. Don't you want that?" he asks me, his lips so close that I can taste his desire. "We don't have to be strangers if you'll just accept me."

Ryn's tone is molten and pleading, and I hear a hint of sorrow laced with the heat and the hunger.

"Ryn..." I breathe out heavily, and I can't tell if his name on my lips is an invitation or a chastisement.

I can't get the image of him holding our severed bonds to his chest and desperately trying to reattach them. The pain in his face haunts me, but so does everything that's happened between us. The mistrust and accusations, the fighting and betrayal.

I don't know if it's possible to come back from that.

His lips are on mine, and I'm opening to him before I can question what I'm doing. He kisses me and throws me off my axis, just like he has from the first moment I saw him on the balcony in the Eyrie. He cups my face and devours me, mind, body, and soul, and as much as I question coming back from all the awful things that have happened between us, I know in this moment, that there's no coming back from this either.

As hurt as I've been. As lost and as broken as he's made me feel, you can't kiss someone with this much passion if you have no hope for more.

He can't sear his lips and soul to mine, pour his sacred promises into my mouth, caress his passion against my own, if I don't feel all of those things too.

I pull away from Ryn's lips, panting and confused. His thigh rubs against my sex, and I'm practically grinding against it as the rest of me tangles around him. I don't drop my hands from around his neck or open my eyes, because I'm not ready for this moment to be over...and it has to be over.

I can feel Ryn's unspoken apology in his kiss, his words, and in the way that he's holding me right now. I'm woman enough to admit that as much as I don't want there to be anything between us, there is. But if I accept him, then I know Zeph and Treno will come too, and I'm not there.

"Ryn...I can't..." I start, but his lips steal my words.

"You can. You just choose me like I'm choosing you, and we fight for that," he tells me, as though it's all that simple.

"If it were just you, Ryn, then that argument might work, but it's not."

"I need you. *We* need you, and you know you need us," he argues.

I sigh and try to pull away from him. "What *do* you need, Ryn? Because I need trust, respect, and validation. I need to feel important and cared for, and I need to be understood. All I get from the three of you is venom, blame, and resigned affection. Suspicion laces your every word to me, and your loyalties are divided, Ryn. You can't decide if you're Zeph's Altern or my mate, and I deserve more than the scraps you three throw my way to keep me compliant and pliable."

"We know that, but you won't even look at us," he tells me, ducking down so that his eyes are at the same level as mine. "We're trying, Falon, but you don't see any value in it. You want to cut us out of your essence instead of letting our tenuous connections grow into more."

He huffs out an exasperated breath.

"We didn't do things right, but they're done. No Ouphe magic in the world will allow us to erase it, but why are we irredeemable to you?" he asks quietly, and the sorrow in it hurts more than I thought it could.

"I don't know, Ryn, why was I never worthy of any of you in the first place?" I ask as I fervently try to blink back the emotion welling in my eyes. "You refused to see me from the beginning, to trust me, to acknowledge our connection and what it meant. You three all taught me very important lessons about what the term *mate* meant to you," I lament. "You can't get mad at me now for simply taking your lead and learning to see things the same way."

"Falon, you're not seeing, you're hiding. Zeph is wearing your runes even though they haunt him. He's trying...for you. Treno says you need time and space, that we owe you that much, but I think you need to wake up. Navigating the current between us is never going to be easy, but you wouldn't want it if it was. We made mistakes, but we called to you for a reason, and you called to us right back. We fit. It may not be pretty or look the way you thought it would, but we fit all the same. You need to admit that to yourself and accept it so we can move forward."

"I need to go," I tell him, wedging myself out between his warm body and the tree behind me.

"Don't run, Falon."

"I'm not, I just need to think...and to sleep, and to not be drunk when I'm trying to figure shit out."

The image of Wekun's tent and my bed of pillows pops up in my mind, and the next thing I know, I'm not standing with Ryn in the brush bordering the Gryphon camp, but I'm once again in Wekun's tent.

"Fuck," I snarl and run my fingers through my hair.

I pull at my roots, as though that will activate an instruction manual for these fucking runes and what they can do.

It doesn't.

First thing tomorrow, I'm training with Wekun, I tell myself. *No more whining and putting shit off.* Clearly, I have no control over my abilities, and that is not a good thing when we'll be heading into war any day now.

The Bond Weaver is nowhere in sight as I fling the entrance to his tent to the side. I stomp out and make my way back toward the Gryphon camp. Ryn is going to think I pulled a bitch move and ran away like a coward. Even though I am done with the discussion we were having for tonight, I don't want him to think that I didn't hear him and that I'm not going to give what he's saying thought.

He did give me a lot to consider. I just need to do that when I'm completely sober—and he's not pressed up against me, clouding my good sense.

It takes me several minutes, but I cross the line between the Ouphe side of tents and the Gryphons'. Winding my way through the camp, I move in the direction of where I know the bar tent is located. I figure Ryn will have gone back there as soon as I disappeared.

"She's being harder than a rock troll's prick," a voice declares to my right, and I pause mid-step when I recognize that voice as Ryn's.

"We've been hard on her, so are you really surprised?" another deep voice replies, and I'm surprised to hear that it's Zeph's.

They're inside the tent I'm currently standing next to, and I pause for a moment, not sure what to do.

"I thought she would understand. I knew it wouldn't be easy, but I thought she would see what we have been up against our whole lives and that we *had* to be careful. Loa is just more proof of why we couldn't simply rely on our instincts: they've been used against us for so long," Ryn confesses, and I bristle at the sound of Loa's name.

I want to destroy her. I've never wanted to hurt someone as badly as I want to hurt her. I take a deep breath and file my vengeance-filled thoughts away. I'll think more on that later when I don't need to focus on spying on the guys.

"She doesn't see things as one-sided the way we have though," Treno offers. I stare at the side of the tent in shock. Are Zeph and Ryn really having a heart-to-heart with their mortal enemy? Is Treno seriously talking to them like equals? "We all keep forgetting that this isn't her world; she doesn't have the same prejudices as we do. She takes everything and everyone at face value, and truly we can't expect any different. None of us gave her time to make up her own mind before we pushed our will and the way that we see things onto her."

"But what choice did we have?" Ryn asks him.

"Maybe none, given what we're up against, but what choice did she really have either?" Treno volleys back.

"She was shoved into this world, and we all demanded that she make a choice before her wings ever caught the current. We did the best that we could, but so did she," Zeph states, and the tent goes quiet.

"So what now?" Treno asks.

"We do better," Ryn answers simply. "She doesn't want to listen, but the bond works in our favor: she physically responds when we're close. It's natural for mates to crave one another, and she gives into it instinctively when she forgets to fight it."

I shoot an incredulous look at the tent. I'm going to punch Ryn in the dick the next time I see him, giving my weaknesses away like that to the others.

"She still wants to sever the bonds," Treno informs them, and deep growls bleed out through the tent.

"That tree rutting Ouphe told her he couldn't do it," Ryn supplies.

Well, well, well. I suddenly don't feel so bad about eavesdropping, when they've obviously been doing the same thing.

"He's going to ask someone else about other ways to do it, but some female Ouphe threatened to hit me with a pot if I didn't get out of their camp, so I didn't catch who. We need to keep an eye on him," Ryn adds. "I told her we were all going to fight for her, that we were all working to show her that the mating matters to us."

"And what was her response?" Treno presses, like he's a kid at a sleepover hanging on every word his friend is delivering about his crush. It would be kind of cute if the foundation between us wasn't layered in *fucked up*.

"I think, despite everything that's happened, she wants to believe it, but she's going to think that all we are is what she's seen so far."

"We'll just have to show her more then," Treno declares, and Ryn grunts in agreement.

I'm so floored by what they're saying, and the fact that the Altern of the Avowed and the Altern of the Hidden are the ones saying it, that I don't even feel the person behind me until their huge hand is covering my mouth, and their other arm is holding me tightly against them. My feet lift off the ground, and I try to kick out as I'm pulled away from the tent and whatever the guys are saying now.

"It's not nice to listen to conversations that you weren't invited to be a part of, little sparrow," Zeph whispers in my ear. He nips at my lobe as he holds me even tighter against him, and my fear is quickly replaced by irritation.

I try to bite the hand that's pressed over my mouth and squirm out of his hold, but all of a sudden, my stomach drops and we're no longer standing in front of a tent, but inside a cool dust-covered room.

We both tense, Zeph still holding on to me tightly, and I mumble *fuck* against his palm. I think I slipped us somewhere, only this place doesn't look familiar at all.

"Cum on a tree sprite," Zeph whispers quietly, his hold on my mouth and waist weakening slightly. I look behind me and see recognition in his eyes, and I immediately realize that I didn't slip us anywhere...he did.

16

I swear, as soon as I figure out how to slip from one place to another on purpose, I'm never going to walk again, but until that happens, this shit is annoying. I look around the unfamiliar room, taking in the lumpy mattress and the handmade wooden frame. There's an armoire in the corner, and the walls and floor are made of old wooden planks.

The place has a distinct cabin vibe, but more rustic and handmade than anything I've seen before. There's a large window to my left that's letting moonlight trickle in to kiss the dusty surfaces, but when I look out, all I see are...tree branches.

"Where are we?" I ask, pushing out of Zeph's hold.

He lets me go, but when the floor creaks ominously underneath me, I instantly wish he hadn't.

"It's safe," Zeph reassures me. "My father laid the floor himself; it will hold us."

"Your father?" I question, turning from the branch-hindered view back to Zeph.

"I lived here until..." he trails off, but I can fill in the blanks on my own. He lived here until they were murdered.

I look around the room and wonder if this was Zeph's or if it was his parents'. When Dri told me about what happened to Zeph and his brother, I assumed it happened in Kestrel City, but I'm starting to grasp that might not be the case.

"Are we in a tree?" I ask, as the branches on the other side of the window catch my attention again.

"We are."

Zeph's voice crackles with emotion as he walks to the bed and runs his hand over the comforter that's covering it. The air in here is stale, and everything looks like it has surrendered to disuse and age. Leaves are prying their way into the room at one corner, like the tree this place is nestled in decided to start to reclaim it.

I suspect there's more house on the other side of the closed door, but I suspect cracking it open to see would force Zeph to deal with more than just stagnant air and dust bunnies. His whole world started to crumble inside of these walls.

Dri said that after Zeph's parents were killed, he and his brother were forced to go live with Lazza and Treno's family. I look out through the window and spot other houses in the branches of colossal trees, and wonder which house belonged to his betrayers.

"My brother and I used to sleep in this room," Zeph tells me as he sits on the bed, a plume of dust rising up to greet him.

"He was older, right?" I question gently, my tone telling him he's not obligated to answer if it's too much.

"By a year. Issak was a good big brother," he tells me softly, and I ache for his loss.

The name sparks something in me, and my brow folds in question. "Was Issak a common name?" I ask curiously, I've heard it twice now, which suddenly seems odd to me.

Zeph shrugs like he's never really thought about it. I make a note to ask Wekun when I get back. I lean a shoulder against the wall and quietly try to give Zeph as much time in this place as he needs. I'm curious as to why he brought us here, but I realize that it may not have been a conscious decision, but more of a fleeting thought our new ability grasped onto somehow.

"Lazza had a tainted mind even when we were young. People don't like to admit that about eyas, but sometimes you can see the rot early."

I drop my head and nod in understanding. I had limited contact with Lazza, but I could definitely see that. I didn't sense an ounce of compassion in him either of the two times I was in his presence.

"Issak found a nest of sparrow hatchlings in the training yard one day. He didn't say much after we were taken away, but when he found the little creatures, and it was clear the parents weren't coming back, he became single-minded in caring for them. I can see now that he was working through what had been done to us, maybe shifting his loss and hurt onto the tiny birds, but every day I saw more and more of my brother come back."

Anguish throbs through me, because I can see where this story is going. I shove away from the wall and move toward Zeph as he stares at his hands blankly and continues.

"Lazza didn't just kill them, he tortured them. Unlike his parents, however, he didn't have the power to force Issak to just sit and watch like he had to with our mother and father. When Lazza broke that last little hatchling's wings and then started in on its feet, Issak snapped. It all happened so fast; I should have helped him, but I was just so stunned. I didn't move, not to help the little sparrows or my brother, and then..."

"They killed him," I finish, and Zeph nods.

"I thought he'd be scared, and that *was* in his eyes when I pulled him into my lap and tried to stop the bleeding while also trying to get us away from the riots. But there was so much anger in his eyes too, anger and...relief. I've never stopped fighting since. Not against the Avowed, my past, the Ouphe...you."

Zeph looks up, his golden, honey-colored gaze fixing on mine, and I'm taken aback by the regret I find in it. "I don't know if I'm capable of putting aside the fight. It's what's kept me going for most of my life, but I don't want to fight against you, little sparrow. I don't want to destroy what we should have as mates."

I stare into Zeph's eyes as his confession sinks into me. His stare is filled with conviction, but I can see that he's adrift too. That he's just as lost as I am when it comes to figuring out how we all fit together. I question if what he's saying is enough, enough to build on, to try to start fresh, but I need more than words. I need the kind of proof that only comes with time. I need to see the day-in-day-out kind of effort his conviction is promising me.

"Okay," I concede after a while of us studying each other and trying to read into the other's gaze.

"Okay," he repeats, a questioning lilt in his tone.

"Okay," I confirm, my eyes and resolve sure. I exhale, and the concern and anxiety that felt like it had settled in my marrow abates. I look over and trace the lines of the window. An idea occurs to me, but I need to figure out how to get out of this room. "Come with me," I tell Zeph as I move closer to the window.

Crap. It isn't the slide open kind.

I reach for a lone chair that's been propped in the corner and grip it by the back. I bring it up like I'm ready to hit a home run.

"What are you doing?" Zeph shouts out, grabbing for the chair and pulling it out of my hands.

"We have to get out of here somehow, and I don't know how to use the slipping thing properly yet," I defend.

Zeph reaches over me to a handle on the right-hand side of the window. He gives it one good twist, and what do you know, the whole frame opens out into the night, like a door.

"Oh," I chirp in surprise, "...that's a cool trick."

Zeph shakes his head and snorts, and I just shrug as I call on my wings. The black as coal appendages shove out of my shoulder blades, and I bite back the smile that wants to take over my face when Zeph's wings immediately pop out too.

"Show me Lazza's house," I ask as I climb out of the window onto a branch that's as thick as a car.

Zeph doesn't say anything as he follows me out, but he does step around me to take the lead. I expect him to question why I want to see it, or to maybe shut down at the thought of having to go back there, but he just walks out on the limb until the air is clear of branches below him, and then jumps off.

It's like watching a graceful diver leap out into the air, ready to twist and flip his way into a perfect score. He spreads his arms like he was made to do nothing more than ride the wind, and his ebony-dipped wings flare out powerfully to catch a current that forces him to arc up into the air.

I smile as I watch him own the air, and Pigeon sits up excitedly inside of me at the prospect of flying. I chuckle at her.

"Let me do something first, and then it's all you, Pidge," I promise her, and she gives a satisfied nod and sits back, ready to enjoy the show.

I leap off the branch, not nearly as gracefully as Zeph did. I'm more cannonball to his swan dive, but who cares?

When the wind is rushing past you, and gravity is threatening to bring you to heel, all that matters is your wings on the wind and the way it makes your soul soar like nothing else will.

Zeph zips past me, and I giggle as I redirect and follow him like a bullet that's hot on his trail. The *faster* that I'm ready to lob at him dies in my throat as he pulls his wings in tighter and shoots through the sky like a comet. I give chase, and I'm just about to catch him when he flares his wings out and drifts slowly onto a branch. I follow suit, stopping in front of a massive house that's been built into the trees.

I try to picture what life had been like for the gryphons and their tree houses. I can practically hear the giggles of kids swooping around as they played tag or whatever it is gryphon kids love to play. I can see mothers and fathers watching their children from the branches of their home, calling loved ones home for dinner, or getting ready to celebrate one of this world's many festivals.

It makes me sad that gryphons were forced to abandon this way of life. Now they reside in Ouphe abandoned castles and cities, and even though I know nothing about tree houses and what it was like to grow up in a community like this, I hope the gryphons can find their way back to all of this once the fighting is over.

I watch Zeph for a moment as he takes this place in. I'm not sure what's running through his head, but it's really none of my business. This is where his fight started, and this is where I hope he can find a way to make that drive work for him instead of against him. I don't want Zeph to lose the fire that's guided him for so long, but when this war is over and there's no Vow anymore to fight against, what will be left for him? He needs to find more in his life that makes it worth living than hate and the need for retribution.

I nod once and then rip off a branch the size of my arm,

stomp toward the house of horrors, and swing hard at the window. I let the branch fly from my hands, and the sound of shattering glass fills the air all around me. I don't look over at Zeph to see what he thinks of my sudden tantrum—what he wants to do with his time is his business—but me...I want to tear this shit to the ground with my bare fucking hands.

I want to erase the legacy of pain and hate, destroy the home that fostered such torment. If I could light this bitch up with fire, I would, but since that's not a power I have, my anger will have to do. I kick at the front door until it's half hanging off the hinges and break off another branch to throw through another window. I go to work, grunting and screaming when it helps me, but otherwise I'm quiet and focused solely on destruction.

Something crashes to the ground on my left, and I look over to see Zeph pulling boards down and chucking them as far as he can throw. His face is fixed in fury and determination, and we both work alongside each other, doing what we can to rid the world of this shit hole, one piece at a time.

I'm panting and sweating in no time, but there's not enough damage for me to stop. *Damn, where's a bulldozer when you need one?* Pigeon perks up, as though Bulldozer is her middle name, and flashes me images of her ripping a fucking tree from the ground, roots and all. I chuckle and gesture for her to have at it. She cracks her neck from side to side, rolls her shoulders, and then puts a gryphon-sized hard hat on that says, "I got this" on it.

Before I can tell her to let me get undressed first, the overzealous little shit shifts, and we explode into her massive gryphon form. I throw up my hands in defeat.

"I fucking give up," I yell at her inside our head. *"I'm officially a nudist now; I won't fight it anymore,"* I concede.

Pigeon chuffs and then hits play on the soundtrack she's

selected for this moment. The lyrics "I came in like a wrecking ball" blast in our head as she shows me how gryphons like to get down when it comes to destruction.

I cheer my fucking head off when she rips part of the roof off as if it's the foil seal of a Pringles can. She goes to town ripping shit to shreds, and you'd think I was sitting front row at the most epic sporting event with how into it I am. I'm like a beauty pageant/soccer mom, just clapping away and telling everyone within hearing distance, "That's my baby," and pointing to the amazing things only I care about.

A feral roar tears through the night, and we look over in alarm only to find that Zeph's released the sky shadow, and that fucker is going pure Godzilla all over this place. Pigeon gives him an answering roar, and I Hercules-clap as they work as tandem forces of destruction.

Maybe Bulldozer is Pigeon's middle name.

The house crumbles one wall and board at a time, and I'm surprised by the quick work the gryphons make of turning this place into rubble. Maybe I shouldn't be shocked though; Pigeon and her mates have always ripped apart pieces of my life and what I thought I knew about the world with wild abandon. I'm beginning to understand more and more, with each day that passes, that the reality of that isn't the bad thing I once thought it was.

Zeph lifts a bed that managed to get tangled in some branches and throws it. Pigeon roars in triumph and slaps the sky shadow's butt with the tip of her tail. I choke on a laugh, because I'm pretty sure she just *good gamed* him. The sky shadow's tail flicks Pigeon right back, and she snaps at his paw before bouncing back away from him.

Alarm shoots through me, and I immediately question Pigeon's sanity. *Why the hell is she picking a fight with Zeph's gryphon?* His tail gets all sassy as though he's more amused than annoyed, and out of nowhere, he leaps for Pigeon.

I scream, shocked by the explosive attack, but Pigeon just chuffs as she dives sideways off the humongous tree. She falls like she's mimicking the rubble her and Zeph's gryphon have been tossing around, and then she spreads her wings, and we're suddenly darting around the behemoth tree trunk and soaring up into the cloudless, star-peppered night.

The sky shadow roars as Pigeon expertly dodges him, and his eyes light up with excited challenge as he dives off the tree in pursuit. I feel like Slider in *Top Gun* as I try to keep track of the bogey, but the fact that Zeph's gryphon is almost pitch black does not help with that task.

I'm waiting for him to show up inverted right above us, but Pigeon is seemingly in heaven as she finally gets the game of cat and mouse she's been begging for since we first spoke.

I squeal in anticipation, not able to contain it. *"I lost him, Pidge,"* I shout out and then immediately go quiet so we can feel the air for him.

Pigeon flashes me a *got him* two milliseconds before she dives to the left, and the sky shadow goes screaming past us, missing us by only a feather. He flips back so he can come for us again, but now it's really on. Pigeon dashes through the sky like a speeding falling star, just begging for some poor sap to make a wish.

I can practically hear the wind as it screams past us and our breakneck speed, and I love every fucking minute of it.

"Go!" I scream with glee when I can feel the sky shadow almost on our tail.

Pigeon blows my mind when she puts up the flaps and flips back going Mach *holy fucking shit*, tapping the sky shadow on the back as she evades him in some gravity defying, cat-bendy move.

I laugh so hard at the badass boop she just gave him, all because she could. A deeper chuffing noise sounds off below us, and I'm stupefied into silence.

Is Zeph's gryphon...laughing?

He grabs our paw and yanks us down out of nowhere, and I *oh shit* scream and then crack up when Pigeon releases this surprised squeal. The sky shadow rolls us onto our back, and we twirl and swoop, swirl and loop around each other in a stunning display of flying and finesse.

I watch in awe as the gryphons play and tag each other, moving seamlessly through the sky like they can anticipate each other's moves. The carefree happiness that's radiating out of Pigeon right now makes me want to cry, because she's deserved this from the beginning. This is all she's wanted from the very beginning, this simple act of trust and play. She's wanted to chase and be chased and just be free to be a gryphon.

I send her waves of warmth and love as she streaks through the night, finally letting go and just being who she was always meant to be. She was trapped inside of me for so long, and I'm overwhelmed by the beauty and rightness of her much-deserved freedom.

Pigeon dives down and nips at the sky shadow's ear, and I couldn't wipe the smile off my face if I tried, because this...Pigeon and I...is perfection. And *this* is how things should always be.

17

"**D**oes it hurt her, dad?" I ask, pulling my hand away from the little pig with the black mark like daddy's on her back. She scampers away with little piggy grunts, sniffing at the grass.

"It stings her a little, My Heart, but she's helping me teach you to protect yourself, so she doesn't mind. We'll make sure to give her extra treats and cuddles as soon as we're done," he reassures me.

"I don't want to hurt Princess, even if it is only a little," I tell him, tears welling in my eyes.

My dad's bright green gaze softens, and he gets on his knees in front of me. "I know, My Heart. I love that you want to look after her. How about we try just one more time? You focus really hard on everything I've told you, and if you do it right, then we'll never do it again," he offers me.

I study him and then Princess for a moment. "Not ever?" I ask, making sure he means it.

"Ever," he agrees.

I take a deep breath and nod once. He gets to his feet and goes to get Princess, then brings her back and sets her down in front of me again. I rest my hand on the mark dad gave her earlier and try to remember everything he said I had to do. Princess squirms a little, and I use my other hand to hold her still. Dad said I have to touch the magic if I want to stop it.

I close my eyes and focus. "Nusht fialow odreece tamod kle," I declare confidently, and I feel the magic under my hand crumble like my sandcastles do at the beach when dad and I play dragon horde and climb all over them.

Princess gives a pained squeal, and I let her go, immediately feeling bad for hurting her. Dad scoops me up, a huge smile on his face, and hugs me tightly. "Yes, My Heart, that's exactly right," he tells me proudly.

But I don't feel right, I feel sad for hurting my friend.

"Don't cry, my girl. Princess will be okay. We'll give her some special treats, and you'll see that she's just fine. Now you know how to protect yourself from harm if you ever need to," he reassures me as he wipes tears from my cheeks.

"Why would I need to?" I ask, my voice hiccupping with emotion.

"Mommy and I will do everything we can to make sure you never have to; this is just in case."

"For safety?" I ask, repeating what he said to me at the start of today's lesson.

"That's exactly right, My Heart. You touch the magic, think about what you want, and then you order the magic to do what you want it to do. You have to mean every word, just like you did today, and then you can keep yourself safe."

I give him a small smile and rest my head on his shoulder. "Can me and Princess have ice cream now?"

Dad chuckles. "Of course, should we go see if mommy and gran want some too?" he asks me in his very happy voice. I love his very happy voice. My smile grows even wider, and I scrunch up my nose.

"Let's hunt them, daddy, and then when we've caught them, we'll ask them if they want ice cream," I suggest.

He laughs his play evil laugh and then we race up the stairs.
"Don't forget Princess, dad!"

I sit up, disoriented and still trying to struggle out from under the veil of sleep. I have no idea where I am, but I can tell it's early morning from the dawning light surrounding me. My heart thumps with adrenaline as my mind wraps itself around the details of the dream.

"Holy shit," I mumble, my voice brittle and dry.

Was that really it? The key to all of this lies in a forgotten memory of Princess the pig and ice cream. I run my focus over the words that I spoke, and a tingle rips through me.

Holy fuck. That was it. My dad said I knew the words already, and he was right. Princess the pig had disappeared weeks later, and I was heartbroken yet completely forgot about all of this...until now. I run my hands over my face and look around, shock and excitement racing through me.

I'm in a tent, but it doesn't look familiar. A rough blanket scratches against my legs, and I've woken up naked enough in the last handful of months to know that's exactly what I am now. Strong arms wrap around my waist and pull me closer. My ass is suddenly being hugged like it's a beloved stuffed animal. Zeph nuzzles me, and his scratchy morning beard rubs against the soft skin of my hip. It feels like sandpaper and I squeal a little and try to pull away.

My skin warms with a blush as I take in my surroundings again. I'm naked, sitting next to an equally naked, and oddly cuddly, Zeph, in a tent with...yep, Ryn and Treno, and I can't immediately figure out how the hell I got here.

I think back on the night before. The last thing I remember is me and Pigeon racing Zeph and the sky shadow around, Pigeon eating a—I cringe at the thought—large worm-walrus looking thing, and then falling asleep in our gryphon form in one of the big trees. I pinch myself just to make sure I'm actually awake and here, but I feel it, so that must mean I somehow ended up in here naked, with my sort of mates.

I check in with my vagina, because if I got hot and heavy last night, she and I need to talk. I do a couple Kegels, but Lassie doesn't start barking like I should be worried that Timmy fell down the well again. I go full *CSI*. I'm not sore. There's no evidence of orgasms. I check my hips and waist, no hot-sex injuries of any kind. I touch my lips, nope, not sore from kissing too much.

Strangely, none of this makes me feel overly relieved. Because Zeph is hugging on my hips like I'm his favorite lovey, my lady bits are very aware of this fact, and yet here I am, untouched in any way.

Pigeon rolls her eyes at me and shoves her face back under her wing. I shoot her a glare. *"You know my confusion over this is your fault, right?"* I tell the back of her head, because she's completely ignoring me. *"I told you they were a bad match for us, but you had to go and pump me full of hormones, and now my brain is fucked up. You fucked up my brain, Pigeon. This is a good thing, and yet my brain is sending me all kinds of signals telling me that lying naked in a tent with your mates, unfucked, is the opposite of a good thing."*

Pigeon flashes me an image of my vagina and then promptly replaces that image with one of a desert, tumbleweed and all. Then she shows me a watering can watering flowers.

I stare at her incredulously. *"I do not have a dusty vagina, Pigeon,"* I snap at her, but a loud snore leaks out from under her wing. My mouth drops open, and indignation falls right out.

A sexy man-groan fills the tent out of nowhere, and I freeze. Maybe the lid for the can of worms my naked ass might have just opened is lying around on the ground some-where. And if I can just sneak out, I could possibly frisbee-throw that lid right back into place, and no one will be the wiser.

Of course, that's the moment that sleepy Zeph decides he wants to lie on his other side. The only problem with that is, his arms are wrapped around my waist, and he takes me with him WWE body slam style. I squeal in shock midair, which serves to wake everyone in the tent up immediately. Thankfully, Zeph doesn't go full Undertaker on me. But the next thing I know, my back is gently meeting the mattress we're lying on, and he's crawling on top of me protectively, growling, "What's wrong? What happened?"

Well, fuck me, this just got infinitely worse.

Pigeon takes that moment to once again flash me an image of a watering can and some now drenched flowers, leaving me no choice but to flip her off.

"What is it?" Ryn asks, shooting to his feet and scanning the tent for a threat.

Treno also pushes up out of bed, but he has one of those *Chronicles of Riddick* swoosh blades in his hand.

Zeph's weight settles on me slightly, and I ignore all the parts of my body that light up in excitement because his parts are touching them. He blinks the sleep from his eyes and looks down at me, his honeyed gaze filled with heat and then confusion.

"How'd we get back here?" he asks groggily.

"I thought you did it," I confess, and Ryn's and Treno's heads both snap over in my direction.

"What the rut?" Ryn asks, his features shifting from shocked to salacious in less than two blinks. "How in rutting Cynas did I sleep through that?" he asks no one in particular.

I try to sit up, but Zeph takes his sweet time getting off

me. I'm pretty sure he's playing some kind of game that involves seeing how many things he can rub against before I implode.

"You didn't sleep through anything. We shifted last night and woke up here. I have no idea how. We have to seriously start working with Wekun in figuring out these runes," I announce as I get to my feet and head to the entrance of the tent. "I'm just going to go get cleaned up and do exactly that," I tell them, offering them a salute as I turn to leave.

Really, Falon, a salute?

I grab for the tent flap, but I don't take another step before I'm being pulled back against another hard body sporting some serious morning wood. "What do you think you're doing?" Ryn asks incredulously.

"Ummm, leaving," I supply, matching his disbelieving tone.

"Not like that, you aren't," he scolds, and I look down to see what has him concerned.

"It's fine, I've accepted the nudist way of life," I tell him casually like that's all the reassurance he needs.

"You should only be baring yourself to your mates," he tells me on a purr that makes a lick of desire run up my spine and goose bumps rise on my arms. "Good mates do that often," he adds, fanning his fingers on my stomach and pushing me back against his *good morning*.

"Good to know, when I get some, I'll remember that," I chirp as I push away from him.

He groans. "So we're back to that again? You wake up naked and needy in our tent and still want to pretend like we mean nothing?"

"Needy?" I object, hanging on to the only part of his statement that I can disagree with.

Ryn taps the side of his nose. "Yes, very needy," he retorts.

Treno chuckles, and I don't miss the deep inhale he takes.

"Since when are all of you friends?" I ask in an effort to distract them from picking out the scent of my apparent needy vagina from the air.

"Since we gained a common enemy," Zeph states.

"And a common goal," Treno adds, his eyes fixed on me intently.

I'd *aw* at the adorable way they just finished each other's sentence, but I'm pretty sure Pigeon is awake and pumping me with hormones right now, which means I need to get the fuck out of here. I feel her chuff in amusement inside of me, and I swear I'm going to pluck out all of her feathers with tweezers just as soon as I get a chance.

"Fuck, that reminds me," I exclaim. "I think I know how to break the Vow," I tell them, and all hints of dirty thoughts and lust filled fantasies disappear from their eyes, and each of them gets very serious.

"How?" Ryn asks, stepping toward me, his features hopeful.

"Memories have been slowly coming back to me since I woke up in the Eyrie. I think most of them were blocked the way my magic was. But I remembered something my dad taught me when I was younger. It's the key," I admit, relief and exhilaration washing through me.

"Cum on a tree sprite, that's it then. We have what we need to win," Ryn crows, picking me up and swinging me around excitedly.

I can't help but giggle and hold onto him as my world swirls and blurs.

"Cree will need at least another week to get all of her fighters armed, armored, and organized," Zeph states.

"And how exactly are we planning on getting to the

Hidden without getting picked off by Lazza and his men?" Treno asks.

Ryn sets me down, and I turn in his arms. "I think Wekun can help us with that," I answer. "I'm not sure how many people he can take at one time, but he should be able to portal us to where we need to go."

The three of them all growl in unison, and Treno mumbles, "Fucking Ouphe."

I would congratulate him on his excellent use of my swear word, but using it in reference to Wekun overrides my pride.

"You three really need to let go of the Wekun hate. He's helped us every chance he could. We would have been fucked without him," I scold.

"He took you away, flower, and then tried to sever our bond. That's not helpful, that's sabotage," Treno argues.

"You three were already sabotaging everything just fine on your own, that wasn't on Wekun. He was just doing what I asked him to do. I'm not saying that you need to be besties with him, but you could be kinder. At least make an effort to be mildly respectful, because we need to figure out what all of these new marks do, and he's our best bet for accomplishing that quickly," I point out.

They don't look convinced.

"We don't have much time, and we need to be as ready as we can for when it's time to end the fighting once and for all." I look over at Zeph. "Last night was a perfect example of why we need to make sure we have some control over these abilities before we go into battle."

He looks away in thought for a moment and then fixes his intense stare back on me. "Does our learning how to use these abilities mean that we'll be keeping them?" he asks pointedly. "Are you going to try to sever our bonds again?" Zeph asks, watching me from under his lashes.

I'm surprised by the bluntness of his question, but it's Zeph, so really I shouldn't be. My face heats with a blush, and I'm not sure exactly what to say.

Do I still want that?

My thoughts and feelings are a chaotic jumble. When I asked Wekun to sever the bonds, I had no doubt that it was the best choice for everyone involved, but I can't deny that things have changed. There's no clarity in what I should or shouldn't do right now. I'm not even sure if this other Bond Weaver will even be able to help, so really all of this could be a moot point.

I sigh.

I'm glad that things aren't so awful with these three at the moment. They are making an effort, and I won't turn a blind eye to that, but I don't know what the future holds. I'm trying to accept a life here, but if I'm being honest, I was only doing that because I felt I had no choice otherwise. I know I can go home now, when all is said and done, and I can't pretend that I don't want that still. I don't know what the right move is yet.

"I think all of us should be focusing on breaking the Vow and winning this war. We can figure the rest out later," I tell him evasively.

Zeph's eyes narrow slightly, but he doesn't press for more or demand that I make a choice right then and there. He just studies me for a beat and then nods his head once.

"We have a lot to prepare for, and Falon's right, training with these runes needs to be at the top of our priority list," Ryn agrees.

I pretend like I don't hear the despondency in his tone and that its presence doesn't make my heart ache. I don't want to piss on his ice cream, but I don't know what to do. We've all shown our worst sides, and I can't pretend that I haven't seen them. What happens if things go back to that? What happens if…

I turn away from that niggling thought. I remember what my dad taught me about breaking the magic in a rune, and I know I can do that against the Vow. I won't need to die.

"Okay, let's go get our badass on," I chirp, dismissing the foreboding feeling that just crept into my chest. I give a clap and then head for the tent exit again.

"Little sparrow," Zeph calls out, his tone sensual and amused.

"Yeah?" I ask, a little breathier than I'd like.

"You're still bare," he points out, and I look down to see that, yep, I'm still naked.

"Right," I snap and finger-gun point at him, because that's something normal people do.

Everyone's mouths twitch like they're all trying to hold back a smile.

"Who has a shirt I can borrow?" I ask sheepishly.

Treno plucks his from the end of his bed and tosses it to me. I catch it and pull it on, totally not sighing at the way it smells, because that would be fucking creepy.

"Alrighty then, I'll just see you boys out on the training field later," I announce, way too cheery, and then what do I do…I fucking salute them again.

I rush out the tent, ignoring the chuckles that erupt as I do, and stare up at the brightening sky for a moment while I sigh and face palm.

Smooth, Falon. Real fucking smooth.

18

"How about now?" I ask, sounding a little constipated, but I'm concentrating so hard there's nothing I can really do about that.

"That's it!" Wekun cheers like a proud parent.

I smile and hoot out my excitement. "Finally!" I screech and do a little dance that involves some twerking followed by aggressive hip thrusting. For three days now, I've been working on this sequence of runes on my back so I can make myself disappear, and this is the first time I've actually completely done it. I've made myself fade or blend, but they've still been able to spot the outline of me, but now...I'm fucking invisible.

I look over at the guys, but instead of finding their wandering eyes as they search to locate my perfectly non-existent ass, they're all looking right at me. Ryn snickers a little, and I narrow a glare on Wekun.

"What the hell? You said I had it," I accuse.

"Well, you did, and then you...didn't," he admits on a chuckle that he immediately tries to cover up.

I groan. "So that whole 'dance like no one is watching' thing..."

"Yeah, we were all watching," he admits.

"I liked it," Ryn offers with a smile.

"As you should," I tell him, releasing the power I'm feeding into the runes on my back.

I've been kicking ass at figuring out how to work the marks on my body, which surprised the shit out of me. Honestly, I think it surprised the shit out of everybody, but apparently unlocking my marks also unlocked my inner ninja, because I'm like *super badass*.

Okay, the invisible thing is taking some time, but it's hard to get the exact right sequence of the marks. It's not at all similar to reading left to right, like I thought. I had to find which rune to start with solely by feel. I've quickly had to learn to let my Sentinel magic guide me. It's required a level of finesse and patience I'm proud of accomplishing, especially amidst the clanging of weapons as the guys sparred and learned to call on my whip swords—as Wekun calls them.

We learned that the weapons come from the garter marks around our thighs, and depending on the sequence of runes that are called, the swords can have a solid blade like a typical long sword does, or the blade can break up into connected sections to become the whip sword.

Zeph and Ryn like the solid blades best, but the whip sword is the shit, in my opinion. Especially against opponents who are bigger than me, like the guys are. It gives me way more of a lethal reach, which I suspect will come in handy when we go head-to-head with the Avowed.

The swoosh blades I discovered while fighting Cree are from Treno's marks. He calls them claw daggers, and that's what he prefers to fight with. I'm getting better with those, but I have to be really close to whoever I'm using them against, and I don't love that.

Okay, I kind of love it when I'm sparring with him, or

Zeph and Ryn, but I don't love the idea of fighting against an attacking stranger *that* up close and personal. I'm working on getting over that though, because having an aversion to killing someone is not a luxury I can afford here. I've developed a plan that I'm just going to pretend that everyone I'm fighting is Loa and hope that helps activate the rage. Then when I get my hands on Loa...she's going to wish she'd never been born.

Pigeon delivers a steady thrum of satisfaction at the direction of my thoughts, and we both get lost for a moment as we trade ideas back and forth of all the ways we're going to fuck Loa's betraying ass up.

Maybe I'm not as squeamish about killing as I thought.

I look over in time to see Zeph slip from the place he was standing and reappear behind Ryn and Treno, ready to take them both out. Ryn feels it and slips away, while Treno calls on his water ability and shoves a ball of water over Zeph's head. Zeph holds his breath and charges Treno, but Treno disappears and pops up on the other side of the clearing, where we've been training for the past four days.

I flick my wrist, and the water bubble over Zeph's head bursts. He pops up behind Treno, and their blades clang against each other as they fight to gain the upper hand.

"Cheater," Ryn whispers in my ear, slipping into existence right behind me, and then he twirls and brings his sword down in a deadly arc toward me.

A shield bursts from my arm, protecting me from Ryn's hit, and I call on a spear from Treno's rune on my shoulder blades and stab out at Ryn, forcing him to back up while his own shields activate and stop the whip of blades that I send at his other side.

I'm not ambidextrous in life in general, but I've discovered when it comes to fighting, I am. I can lead with either my right or left side and use different weapons to attack. I call it my secret sauce because it tasted so damn good when I surprised the shit out of the guys by being able to adapt like that.

Ryn is relentless in his efforts to get a hit in, and we look like Nightcrawler, minus the blue smoke, as we pop in and out of existence all over the place, striking, evading, attacking, and doing everything we can to take the other person out.

Zeph and Treno join in, which they've been doing all day...something about me needing to get used to fighting multiple attackers. I make my whip swords shift into solid blades as they close in on me, and we all become fluid motion, clangs of metal, exploding shields, and gritted teeth. I feign an opening, knowing Zeph will see it and step in to teach me a lesson. I activate my runes so I can slip through space away from them, but Zeph reaches out and grabs me by the neck to stop me.

He grins victoriously at me, which is exactly when I shove a pulse of Sentinel magic out of my center, and everyone goes flying back.

Wekun starts clapping and walking my way as the guys all get back on their feet with smiles on their faces. "That was excellent, Falon. You're an Ouphe through and through; you've taken to this like a duck to water," he observes and then blinks out of existence mid-step when someone throws a sword through the spot where he just was.

"She's not an Ouphe," Zeph growls at Wekun when he pops back into being a couple feet away from me.

Wekun rolls his eyes. "She's like three-quarters Sentinel, dude," he lobs at Zeph, annoyed.

"And we forgive her for that, but three-quarters is not *Ouphe through and through*...dude."

The ball of water I was just about to chuck at Zeph's head stops midair as I choke on a laugh instead of riding out my irritation about the "we forgive her for that" part of his comment.

Did he really just say dude?

I crack up, suddenly picturing Zeph, the king of assholes, walking around dude-ing and bro-ing people, while tossing out complex handshakes as he man-hugs strangers, and heaven forbid...smiles. I finish off my amusing little fantasy by placing him in a Hawaiian t-shirt right in the middle of the feminine products aisle at the grocery store, because that image feels like the pièce de résistance to this whole hilarious imaginary scenario.

Ryn bats my floating bubble of water away, and it ricochets off Treno's shield and slams right back into him, bursting all over his face. I pause my chuckling for exactly two milliseconds as I take in that water dripping down his face, and then I lose it even harder.

I didn't even know the water balls could do that.

I did hear Treno tell Zeph that he can kill people by pulling all the water out of their body or doing the opposite and filling their lungs from the inside out if there's a water source close enough, so really I shouldn't be surprised that we can make water balls behave like bouncy water balloons.

Ryn walks over as I'm bent at the waist, cackling like a Sanderson sister, picks me up, and wipes his wet face and hair all over my neck and chest. I squeal and try to push away from him, but he's such a strong fucker there's no way I'm getting away unless I stab him.

"That's better," he growls playfully, nipping at my neck just as someone lands in the clearing and starts to jog over to us.

I recognize one of the healer brothers, and I snicker when Treno, Ryn, and Zeph all release a low warning growl as the lighter blond brother gets closer.

I give Pigeon a look. *"That's on you, you know,"* I tell her as the possessive aggression kicks up a notch all around me.

Pigeon just fluffs her feathers and breathes deeply, like the scent of their jealousy and claim is her favorite thing to imbibe. I swear, if she had eyebrows, she'd be wagging them at me right now.

"Cree is ready to go over tactics," the large gryphon announces, the summons clear. "The Ouphe is to come as well to discuss transport," he adds, looking over at Wekun.

"He has a name," I scold the healer brother, realizing that I have no idea what *his* name is...oops. "The one that slips closest to the tent, without going inside, wins," I challenge, calling on my runes that allow me to teleport around.

"Not him," the healer brother stops us, gesturing to Treno.

Confusion prickles through me, and I let the magic I'm calling pool back into my center. "Why?"

"Because he's Avowed," the gryphon answers simply.

Incredulity flashes through me. *Is he serious?* I open my mouth to tell the gryphon off, but Ryn cuts me off.

"He's with us, and if Cree or anyone else has an issue with that, they can discuss it with us," he declares.

I just barely stop myself from adding a "yeah" like some kid backing up their friend in a neighborhood dispute.

The healer gryphon clearly doesn't like this response. He tenses and seems to debate what to do, not wanting to go against his leader, Cree, but also not overly keen to piss us off either.

"It's fine, I'll just stay and work some more," Treno announces, clearly trying to diffuse the situation. His declaration is even and casual, but I see a glint of frustration in his mismatched eyes.

"I could use some more work too," I announce, waving away the questioning looks that Ryn and Wekun give me.

"You guys go work out all the boring logistics and then come fill us in when it's all sorted."

I give the healer gryphon a pointed look. He may think that cutting Treno out of these discussions is somehow going to protect the information, but Zeph, Ryn, and Wekun are going to tell us everything anyway, so really Cree is just being an asshole.

"I can stay back too," Ryn offers.

"It's fine, you and Zeph know the Hidden and what they can do; I would have just been standing around anyway while you map everything out. And if Cree wants to see Treno as the enemy instead of a valuable resource, that's her mistake. We'll be better prepared for what we're facing than she is," I add.

Treno gives me a small smile, but I don't miss the tension still radiating from him. Ryn and Zeph give me a nod, then disappear from where they were standing. Wekun chuckles and grumbles, "Show-offs," before disappearing himself. The blond healer gryphon takes a moment to realize that he's been left behind. He then jumps into the air where his wings hurry to help him catch up.

I watch his silhouette get smaller and smaller in the distance before turning to Treno, who still looks upset.

"He's a dick, don't let it get to you," I tell him, reaching out and patting his shoulder somewhat awkwardly before dropping my hand back down to my side.

Treno looks at my hand for a moment and sort of deflates like a week-old balloon. "I'm not upset because that male is wrong, flower, I'm upset that he's right."

I pause and take a moment to sift through just what the fuck that means. *Unless he's confessing that he still sides with Lazza—which I highly doubt is the case—I got nothing.*

"Umm...come again?" I ask concerned.

Treno shakes his head disappointedly, but it's not aimed

at me. "I am Avowed, or at least I have been my whole life. Yes, I knew that the mark had been used against the Gryphons by the Ouphe, but with it also came a more powerful breed of Gryphon," he tells me, further explaining what he means by using the runes on his chest to call a spinning sphere of water to float just above his palm.

He moves his hand and guides the sphere of water around, like some street hustler who tells you to keep your eye on the ball and then guess which hand it's in.

"I believed my parents when they taught my brother and me that the Ouphe runes and magic would ultimately make us stronger and better. I've fought battles and killed because of that belief, to protect it. It's what I thought was right, and then…" he trails off, his haunted eyes focused on the water ball that's still in his hold.

Treno takes a moment to collect himself, and I want to kick myself for not realizing how much he is hurting.

"And then my brother tried to kill me with the very thing I've spent my whole life defending. It took a split second, and everything I thought I knew spilled through my fingers."

Treno releases his hold on the water, and the ball bursts, allowing the liquid to trickle past his palm, punctuating his point.

"I've been asking myself how I could be so stupid. Why didn't I open my eyes and see what Lazza really was capable of, or at least try to understand where the Hidden were coming from? I've always looked at things so black and white, but now I can't figure out why. Why couldn't the Avowed and the Hidden have lived together in harmony? Why couldn't it have been that those who want the Vow can get it and those who don't…don't?"

Treno runs his hands frustratedly through his straight white hair. He looks so lost, so pained. I hate that he's been struggling with this, clearly blaming himself for things that shouldn't rest on his shoulders.

"Why couldn't I understand that forcing what I think is right on someone who doesn't want it is wrong?"

Treno's blue and purple gaze lands on mine, and he's so fucking shattered inside, the anguish is bleeding out of his every feature like a sieve. I reach up and cup his face, my thumb caressing his cheekbone gently. I wish I could make this hurt less for him. I wish he had been born to a better family and never did anything that I know will haunt him longer than he deserves. He leans into my hand, and I feel my defenses crack just a little. Gone is the angry, spiteful Treno, and in his place is this vulnerable, adrift person.

"We all do the best we can with what we have, Treno. You see the other side now, and you'll do better. I know that doesn't change what happened. That it doesn't immediately relieve the pain, but I hope it helps you find peace in some small way."

"I don't deserve peace," he confesses quietly, his voice cracking with emotion.

My eyes prick with tears as I watch him attempt to swallow the hurt down.

"What I did to you, Falon," he starts, and I catch a tear that escapes down his cheek with the back of my fingers.

"Hey," I soothe. "What happened sucked...for both of us. I know it wasn't easy on you, Treno. The whole mate thing on top of what was happening with your brother wouldn't have been easy for anyone, but you've been figuring it out, and I'm here," I reassure him.

"Are you?" he questions, and just when I think his eyes can't fill with anymore sadness, they do. "I watch you interact with us like you're waiting for one of us to slip back into the way we were before. There's a barrier that separates you from me that was never a factor between us, and I despise myself for knowing that armor was forged in my anger and tested by my wrath."

I drop my eyes from his, not sure what to say. My natural reaction is to tell him that it's *okay*. To dismiss what was done and how I was treated, in an effort to lessen his hurt, but I can't do that. I can't pretend it was *okay*, because it wasn't. I can understand why it happened and where it all came from, but none of that makes me any more deserving of what happened.

"That," he tells me, placing a knuckle under my chin and coaxing it up so that my eyes meet his again. "*That* is what I mean, and I loathe that I created it. You should always be able to look at me, to trust me..." he trails off for a moment, and his eyes take on a faraway look.

"When you tried to sever our bond..." he starts, and I take a deep breath, readying myself for the ache I know his words are going to lure out of my chest. "I didn't know how badly I'd been hurting you until that moment. I felt you tear away from everything that I am, and I knew I'd never recover. That I would do everything in my power to fix it, because what was left of me wasn't enough anymore. I'd felt what it was like to be yours and for you to be mine, and I knew I could never go back to anything else," he tells me, the back of his fingers capturing the tear that tries to escape down my cheek.

"It would have been a half-life not worth living, flower," he confesses, stepping closer to me, his eyes pleading as he fits me against him like I'm a lock and he's the key. "Never again, flower. I know you're watching, expecting the fury and frustration to return, but I will never give you reason to arm yourself against me again."

His words throw me off. I'm not sure what to say, or if I even can, my throat is tight with emotion and hurt.

"Take this off," he tells me gently.

At first I'm confused because I think he's talking about my shirt, and quite frankly, that's pretty presumptuous, but he grabs at something a couple of inches away from the tunic that I'm wearing and pretends to heft it off my shoulders. He mimes that it's heavy as fuck and looks relieved when he drops the imaginary weight to the ground.

"And this," he adds, repeating his motion over my other shoulder. "This too," he declares, faux knocking on my chest and then pretending to undo the armor he's imagining is there.

One by one, he goes over my body, meticulously removing nonexistent armor as though I'm some great knight retiring after battle and he's my squire. I smile as he gets to his knees and pulls off my imaginary sabatons and greaves. And then all at once, I realize that the make-believe armor doesn't feel so unreal. With each motion, I can feel myself getting lighter, letting go, and just breathing freely now that the tight bands are coming off my chest.

Tears drip steadily down my face as Treno helps me take off the weight I've been carrying, and one by one drops pieces of my armor to the floor. He gets back to his feet, and looking down at me, his eyes filled with so much care and warmth, he takes off the last piece. He drops the imagined helmet, and his eyes light up.

"There you are, mate," he whispers reverently, his eyes brimming with tender affection.

Then he closes the distance slowly before his lips touch mine, and just like that, his key opens my lock.

19

The kiss starts out vulnerable and delicate. Like it's this fragile thing that could be shattered if rushed or not cared for. Treno bends my head back and devours my offered mouth, but it doesn't feel dominating or possessive, it's gentle in a *I have you, and I always will* kind of way.

I'm floored by the raw emotion I taste on both of our lips, and I tell my brain to let go of all the *what happens now*s that are floating around in my mind, waiting for me to snatch them up and fling them at Treno and then examine them myself. I tell my head to sweep away the *but what does this mean*s and shove each *there's no going back from this* next to them on the shelf.

I just got all of that armor of doubt, second-guessing, and hurt off, and I'm not putting it back on for anything.

His lips are benevolent, his tongue contrite, and even though he doesn't speak an apology into existence between us, I can feel it in the way he holds me and taste it in his kiss. My mouth and body offer absolution, and my nimble fingers make quick work of the laces that hold the neck of his shirt closed.

My needy hands skim down his torso until I find the hem of his tunic and pull it up. Our kiss breaks as he pulls my shirt off too, and then we both hurriedly move to each other's pants. Mine come away and drop to my ankles with no issue, but my tongue stalls against his expert guidance as his crotch laces become literal cock blocks.

"Fucking hell, what did you do, tie a bunch of damn sailing knots down here?" I demand, pulling from his lips so I can focus all my concentration on the ties of his pants. "Are these of Celtic origin or blessed by nuns, because this is some bullshit," I grumble when I still can't get them undone.

Treno laughs and then immediately chokes on it when I call on help in the form of a Nike swoosh blade. "Whoa!" he calls out, his hips jumping away from me, and I growl at the misbehavior.

I take a minute and assess that I did just get mad when he wouldn't let me attempt to cut him out of his pants, and Pigeon flashes me the tumbleweed desert image again. I roll my eyes but decide to put the gnarly looking black blades away.

"You'll hear no complaints from me about your eagerness, but one slip of the grip on those blades and neither one of us would be happy for a *very* long time," he tells me on a chuckle, but it soon turns into a growl when he can't get the ties of his pants undone either.

I raise one eyebrow in challenge, because I know he's thinking about calling on a blade now too. Pigeon sends me an image of her drumming her talons on a table impatiently, but I home in on the sharp claws and experience an aha moment.

Oprah was right, this shit really is life changing.

I partially shift my hand until one sharp black talon stretches out from the tip of my finger, and then I close the distance between Treno and me and carefully thread the claw up the crisscross of laces. I pull my hand toward me, shredding the ties and jerking Treno's body against mine. He gives an approving growl, and I see his gryphon rise up in his eyes, like he's riding Treno with as much excitement as Pigeon is riding me.

I release the shift of my hand, and Treno's hungry mouth claims mine as he finally shoves his pants down, and I climb him like a flight of stairs until the inside of my knees are resting on the inside of his elbows. He grabs my ass and kisses me hard as I wrap my arms around his neck. He lifts me up, and I feel him lining up just right and then dropping me down on him just the way I like it.

I moan and revel in how he feels inside of me, and his kiss morphs into a sexy grin as he pulls his lips from mine and seats himself as deeply as he can.

Fuck, I missed this!

He nips at my neck as he angles his hips back and slips out of me to the tip. "This is us, flower, always connected, never to be ripped apart again," he declares, and then he buries himself inside of me, and I cry out a resounding *yes* as I grind against him. He looks around and quickly spots whatever it is that he's looking for, because he starts walking us to the right as I hold onto his neck and work myself up and down on him.

"Yes, flower," he groans and sucks on where my neck connects with my shoulder as my thighs slap against his hips, and the beginnings of an orgasm start to tingle between my thighs.

The next thing I know, Treno is laying me down on a soft cool bed of grass and taking control of things. "Mmmmm," he hums against my ear as he kisses down my neck, over the scar across my throat, and up until his lips are skimming my opposite ear. "It doesn't get better than you on your back, opened up to me and screaming my name," he purrs in my ear, rolling his hips until he's lighting up all kinds of things inside and outside of me.

"I'm not screaming your name," I point out and then clench down as he hits an especially sweet spot.

"Yet," he challenges, and then he really gets to work.

He closes his mouth around my nipple and immediately hits me with some vibrating tongue as he sucks hard. An orgasm unfurls slowly in my belly, but just when I think it's going to take its time and crawl through me lazily until I'm squirming and even more needy, it shoots out through the rest of me and sparks a trembling cry from my lips.

Treno moves to my other breast and works in and out of me, unwaveringly relaxed, as he does everything that he can to draw out my pleasure. My orgasm starts to ebb, and I climb back down from floaty euphoria ready for more.

Treno slows his thrusts, his lips scaling my throat until they're on mine again. I can taste his passion and reverence as though I'm some prize worthy of piety and vows of allegiance. But despite what my vagina is telling me right now, I don't want to be worshipped, I just want to be respected. I want a partner, not a supplicant. I want what I myself am willing to give. Nothing more and nothing less.

I pour that into our kiss, my lips and tongue asking Treno to meet me nip for nip and stroke for stroke. I roll my hips underneath him, my body begging for him to let go and take us both to new heights. He savors my mouth for a second more and then gives me exactly what I need.

"Yes," I moan against the shell of his ear when his seductive thrusts turn serious and he starts to fuck me hard and fast the way we both love.

I suck on his neck and then bite with just enough pressure to leave imprints of my teeth on his skin. Treno does the same thing against my shoulder, and it all feels so good that I'm quickly ascending into another orgasm.

"Treno, I need..." I declare through moans and whimpers, our skin slapping together as we crash against each other and then recede like ocean waves against the shore.

"What, flower? What can I give you?" he asks, already reading my body and cries and playing both like I'm something he's mastered. Like he knows all the right strings to pluck and the sweetest rhythms to coax out of me.

"Fuck," I groan, falling into pure bliss as his cock once again starts to make my pussy sing. "I need..." I start again, so close to falling off the edge and taking him with me.

"Anything," he purrs against my mouth, pounding into me as I drink down his declaration.

"I need you," I finally cry out, and then his name is a claim and brand and a proclamation pouring out of my lips as ecstasy detonates in my every cell.

I come so fucking hard I feel every rune on my body light up, and a pulse of purple magic rockets out of me. Treno groans my name and bites my shoulder hard, shoving into me as deeply as he can go. I scream out as my already intense orgasm restarts like he just hit rewind and then play again.

Treno and all that he is clicks through me, settling in my soul, like he's as fundamental to my essence as Pigeon is. Ragged breaths clash against sweat speckled skin as we both pant and float in what just happened between us.

My mind is surprisingly calm, like not even it can question the perfectness of what we just experienced. It's as though my worry and doubt knows there's no tainting what I feel in every fiber of my being for Treno, and what I know he feels for me.

He pulls out of me and rolls to his back, both of us

working to even out our breaths. I chuckle as a case of bliss giggles bubbles up in my chest.

"Fuck, that was good," I declare, but I don't hear what he says in return because suddenly Pigeon surges through me.

I automatically give in to the frantic need I feel slamming through her as we shift, and I try to take in what around us has her demanding possession of our body. Treno is on his feet in no time, his cock still glistening with my desire as he looks around in alarm.

Then he also explodes into his gryphon, and panic pumps steadily through me. *"Pidge, what's happening?"* I demand as nothing immediately attacks us or shows itself.

Pigeon releases these weird chirps, and then the sound of a small motor starts up somewhere around us. I try to pinpoint where the sound is coming from, but when I land on Treno's gryphon, confusion surges through me.

What the hell?

Pigeon moves toward him, half body checking, half rubbing up the white gryphon's side.

"Pidge, what the hell is going on? Are we in danger?"

Out of nowhere, Pigeon snaps at Treno's gryphon and growls at him. He snarls back and rears up.

"Hey, asshole!" I shout at him, not liking the tone or understanding what the fuck is happening.

The white gryphon's claws come at us, but instead of drawing blood like I'm expecting, he grabs a hold of Pigeon and pulls her beneath him. She bellows a threat and snaps at him again, but despite the aggressive stance it seems like she's taking, I realize that there's a thrum of satisfaction humming through her and she's not actually physically fighting Treno's gryphon.

"What the..." My question dies in my mouth as Treno's gryphon mounts Pigeon from behind, and I immediately know what's happening as she arches her back with a growl.

"Pigeon, did you seriously just make me think we were being attacked when all that was really happening was you wanted to fuck Treno's gryphon?"

Pigeon ignores me completely, focusing instead on her gryphon conquest as he pins her down and lines his hips up with hers.

I cover my eyes, like somehow that's going to give them privacy. *I can't believe this is happening.* I feel like some totally creepy voyeur.

Pigeon snaps aggressively at the white gryphon again, and I'm taken aback by the hostile, violent feel of the pairing. The white gryphon bites the back of Pigeon's neck, and she feels pissed and immediately satisfied, which I find confusing as fuck.

Deep laughter rumbles through my mind, and my head snaps around, looking for the source.

Don't tell me that was the other gryphon.

"It seems they were done being patient with us," Treno tells me as our gryphons start to do their thing.

"What, how am I hearing you?" I demand, panicked.

I feel like I'm sitting in the middle of some fucked up cockpit with no means of escape while gryphons do the dirty in the background and Treno does some weird ass *National Geographic* voice-over.

"We're mates, we can push thoughts to each other like this," Treno tells me, a hint of surprise in the tone of his explanation. *"I would ask if you knew that, but it's clear that you didn't,"* he adds.

"We can hear each other all the time?" I question, my pitch a little too high and completely giving away the hysteria I feel right now.

"No, only when we push thoughts at each other purposefully. And only like this..." he trails off for a moment. *"Although I have heard of mates who could do it when they aren't shifted, but*

I've never heard you or been able to reach out mentally when we aren't," he quickly adds when I mentally clutch my chest and start to hyperventilate.

Oh wait, that's not me, that's Pigeon having a really good time.

I rein in my side-eye and try to focus on Treno's voice instead of what's happening outside of my head. It's a little too weird for me to wrap my mind around.

Fuck, is this how Pigeon feels when I'm enjoying myself?

I make a note to ask her later, as she's *very* occupied right now. Treno's words register and I pause, thinking back to the times that it seemed like Zeph could read my mind or would mysteriously react to a thought I was having. Irritation simmers inside of me as I realize that maybe Treno can't connect with me at all times, but I strongly suspect that another one of my mates can. I shake my head, and a flood of wonder hits me about what he might have heard without me knowing.

How the hell can he do that, yet I've never picked up on a stray thought from him?

Treno chuckles again, and I narrow my mental eyes at him. *"This is how it should be, flower, don't worry about it. Our gryphons need each other as much as we do. This strengthens our bond with each other and them."*

"I get that, but how do you not feel like a perv?"

A wave of pleasure crashes through me, answering the question I never thought to wonder about before, that gryphons do, in fact, have orgasms.

"It is a little...different, but we'll get used to it in time," he reassures me, and I chuckle.

There's no use denying the *in time* part of his statement or pretending that this will never happen again. I knew as soon as I accepted Treno and chose to be intimate with him, I was accepting my connection with not just him but with

Ryn and Zeph too. I wait for the worry that I've been feeling for a while in regard to my connections with Treno, Zeph, and Ryn to surface again, but surprisingly it doesn't.

I'm almost tempted to argue with the lack of concern flowing through me that there's no way to be sure they'll stay like this, but it's like my soul has no room for doubt or suspicion.

"Are you alright?" Treno asks, pulling me from my soul observations.

His question throws me off for a moment. *Am I?*

"Are you?" I slingshot back.

"Yes, our disconnect was killing me," he confesses.

Empathy washes through me, along with some other things Pigeon is experiencing. *Damn, I didn't know gryphons got down like that,* I observe, twisting my head to try and understand the angles going on.

I focus back on Treno and his thoughts. *"You know that what happened between the Avowed and the Hidden wasn't your fault, right?"* I ask, and Treno is silent for a beat too long. *"Treno, I know you're questioning everything and trying to understand why you didn't see things sooner, but you have to consider the circumstances surrounding you too before you decide that you're the only one responsible for the state of this world,"* I tell him.

A screech of joy fills my head, and I focus on Pigeon, quickly wishing I hadn't.

"Well, that's certainly one way to use a tail," Treno comments, a little stunned.

I laugh and then try to scrub the visual away, returning to what Treno and I are discussing.

"The battle about the Vow and the Gryphons started long before you were born, Treno. The Gryphons were barely even free and absolutely not at all recovered from what happened with the Ouphe when the fight for power started between your parents'

generation. You grew up in a brutal time, believing people you loved about the Vow and what it meant for you and those around you," I point out. *"I'm sorry that it took you until now to see the other side of things, but it's not like the nature of the Gryphons in general is to sit and talk things out, it's definitely much more of a 'rip someone apart first and ask questions later' kind of culture,"* I point out.

Treno chuckles a little, and the sound of it makes me feel all warm and gooey.

"I'm not saying that the self-reflection you're doing is bad or that you shouldn't feel the way that you do, but at least give yourself some credit. As soon as you saw the other side of things, you've been working to better the situation. Not everyone would do that, and you should realize what it says about you and the kind of male that you are that you're doing everything you can to be better and do better."

Treno releases a deep sigh in my mind, and I wish I could reach out and hug him right now.

"I forgot that my flower was smart, beautiful, understanding, and...wise," he tells me, and I'm relieved to hear the playful smile in his tone.

I gasp, shocked. *"How could you forget that the gate chose so wisely for you?"* I tease in mock horror.

"I truly have no excuses for such a derelict mind."

"Well, great, you get wise, smart, beautiful, and understanding for your mate, and I get derelict and forgetful," I taunt.

Treno laughs.

"Forgetful, but stunningly handsome, don't forget that part."

"True!" I concede. *"...and that cock,"* I add salaciously.

"Mmmm, and that," he agrees on a purr.

"I'd fuck the derelict out of you right now if I wasn't, you know, trapped inside my body."

Treno sighs longingly. *"By the stars, how long do you think they'll go for?"*

I shrug and shake my head, tilting it to the side as I take in what's happening. *"I mean, I thought their beaks were too sharp for what they're doing right now, so what the hell do I know about anything?"*

I mentally conjure a big fluffy recliner and plop my ass down, lifting the footrest. *"I think it's going to be a while,"* I admit as I settle in. *"But hey, plenty of time to hear all about your most embarrassing moments,"* I encourage, and then I get as excited as a kid waiting for an epic bedtime story.

"What? Why would I ever tell you that?" Treno argues.

"You already said you would, you can't take it back now."

"When did I say that?"

I tsk, disappointed. *"There's that forgetfulness again,"* I tease.

Treno barks out an incredulous laugh. *"Oh, you think you're sneaky?"*

"The sneakiest," I volley. *"Feel free to add that to your list of my incredible qualities,"* I advise, biting back a chuckle. *"Don't forget,"* I add, cracking up.

"You're going to get it, flower. Just as soon as they're done..."

"Promise?" I ask with a bawdy wag of my eyebrows. *"Until then though...tell me all your secrets,"* I demand on a faux evil laugh, with steepled fingers and happiness in my heart.

20

"Hey, I brought you...uhhh, what are you doing?" Ryn asks as he bursts unannounced into Wekun's tent.

I jump in surprise from his sudden appearance and back away from the mirror I was just making faces into because...I'm weird. I adopt a casual *what are you talking about* mien and shoot him my best innocent eyes.

"What do you mean?" I ask smoothly, not at all sounding like I just got caught doing something bizarre.

He steps further into the tent, the entrance flaps dropping closed behind him, and his eyes glitter with amusement.

Shit, he's onto me.

He walks closer, a smile twitching at the corners of his lips. "I mean, why are you looking into the glass and making that face?" he doubles down, clearly not getting the hint to just let it go.

I clear my throat and shrug nonchalantly. "What face? I was just looking in the mirror."

"Uhh, no, you were looking in the glass and doing a

creepy smile while you made your eyes bigger and then smaller and then bigger again. Are you well?"

"If someone smiled at you like that right before they killed you, would it make your blood run cold?" I ask, abandoning my efforts to pretend I'm not a freak in hopes for some honest feedback.

"No, my blood is always warm," he counters.

"No, not literally, I mean, in the sense of would you be scared? Like, if I was about to kill you and I smiled at you like that, would it terrify you, make you wet yourself, and then accept that you're going to perish in a state of soul crushing terror?" I elaborate.

"Why are you killing me?" he asks, moving to sit on the bed.

I roll my eyes. "Ryn, you're making this way more difficult than it needs to be."

"I am?" he defends. "I walk in on *you* staring into the glass with a look on your face that makes you look addled, and instead of just telling me what you're doing, you threaten to kill me and hope I die in a puddle of my own piss."

I pause. "Well, when you put it that way...but *addled* as in scary crazy or just..."

Ryn groans and throws himself back on the bed. I chuckle and move to put the mirror back where it normally sits in the corner.

"What did you bring me?" I ask, eyeing the package resting against his thigh.

"Oh no, you'll get nothing out of me until you confess whatever it was that you were doing," he taunts, grabbing the package and holding it out of reach when I make a dive for it anyway.

"Stupid fast ass gryphon reflexes," I grumble as I eye the mystery prize now being held high over my head.

I know I have no chance of getting it, because these fuckers are the size of a skyscraper, which is just completely unfair. I groan and take my turn flinging myself back on the bed in exasperation. Ryn chuckles and pulls me into him. I sigh contentedly and then side-eye myself and then Pigeon. She just looks at me like *what?*

"Well, I *was* trying to visualize breaking the Vow. I can't exactly practice on anyone here, and it's probably going to be a clutch deal, so I was attempting to prepare as much as possible," I start. "But then I began to think about Lazza and the battle that's about to go down in a couple of days. Which made me think of Loa and all the things I'm going to do to her when I see her. *That* made me wonder what I'd say to her just before I ripped her throat out, and then I suddenly needed to know what my face would look like as I said those words. Which is what you observed when you flounced in here, without knocking, I might add."

I can't read the look on Ryn's face, but it's definitely not amusement or anger or any of the things I thought I'd see when bringing up his sister and my plans for her.

"My sister is dead, Falon," he tells me, a hint of unease in his tone.

"Wait. What?" I demand, sitting up and studying his face for any hints of deception.

Ryn sits up too, obviously concerned by how upset I am. "I thought you knew. I ripped her head off before her blade was even off your throat."

"What?" I ask again, my tone high-pitched and disbelieving, like I no longer speak the same language and have no idea what he's saying. "But I wanted to kill her," I confess quietly, as all my plans for vengeance just fall out all over the floor and start to wilt.

Of all the scenarios I pictured in my head, her already being dead was never one of them. Ryn's words steal the wind from my retribution-taut sails, and I have no idea which direction to steer in now. Thoughts of killing Loa have been a driving force in how hard I've been training and working to master my runes and abilities. Yes, breaking the Vow and surviving a Gryphon war has been a factor too, but I had big plans for that bitch.

I mean, I just spent an hour perfecting my evil smile so that it would be *just right* for when Loa and I met again.

Fuck!

Ryn pulls my pissed off and distraught ass into his lap, and I'm reeling too much to object.

"Falon, I can see that you are not happy, but I woke up and Treno was yelling. I looked over to see Raquel press the knife to your neck, and then I just reacted," he tells me, his hand soothingly caressing my back while the other does the same against my thigh. "She didn't see me coming until it was too late, but you were bleeding and pulling at my life force, and all I could do was rip her apart for hurting you, for betraying us."

Ryn pauses like the pain is still fresh and lapping at him, and I hate that I can still feel the knife cut into my skin and smell Loa's disdain like it's still in the air. He brings a hand up and runs the pad of his thumb over the scar at my throat, and I close my eyes and breathe through the rush of feelings it stirs in me.

Pain, fear, sadness, and regret from the memory of what happened war with the warmth and adoration Ryn's touch tries to entice out of me.

"Zeph broke in and scooped you up. He was nearby to help extract us and the others that were going to join the Hidden. But everything went wrong when I was on my way to get you, to tell you it was time to go. I didn't know about Treno. I knew you grabbed his attention, but I've known him my whole life, and nothing has ever *kept it*. I didn't realize that you two had called to each other," he tells me, his voice suddenly softer, a touch gruffer.

"Maybe I was too focused on trying to ignore my own reactions to my mate and our unfulfilled call to pay attention to what was happening. I'll have to live with that." Ryn's thumb traces my scar again, and I realize that he blames himself for its existence. "After I killed Raquel, and Zeph had you, I grabbed Treno. He was suffering the most, we think because of your newly formed connection, and then we ran as fast as we could before we were too weak to move like you and Treno were."

His accounting of what happened pulls me back into the moment that I'm sure will haunt me until the day that I die. The feel of the metal against my throat, the warm blood pouring out of me, knowing I would be the death of the others, it's hard to sift through. I wanted to be Loa's reckoning, but Ryn got there first, and technically he bears the bigger scars from her betrayal, even if his wounds are on the inside.

"I'm sorry you went through that," I tell him, placing my hand over his on my chest as he traces my scar, his eyes filled with torment and despair. "I'm sorry she betrayed you."

Ryn closes his eyes and leans his head against mine. Just like with Treno the other day, I'm hit by the realization of what Ryn has been suffering through.

A flash of what he looked like as Lazza slowly choked him to death, and the fear that I felt when I thought he had succeeded, strikes through my mind. And then I see him grasping at the threads of our mate bond as I try to sever it, and he tries to reattach the broken bonds to his chest.

No, this... *This* will be what haunts me until the day that I die. I had my reasons, and I thought they were right at the time, but I will never get the image of his desperate tries to keep us connected out of my mind. We've all fucked up on such epic levels, and yet here I am in his lap, being comforted and trying to comfort in return.

Maybe it wasn't all for nothing.

"I thought she was dead. I never suspected for a second that somehow she survived and chose Lazza over me. She liked him as an eyas, but..."

"She was a fucking psycho. I thought she loved you and that's why she was oddly protective, but then she just watched as Lazza was killing you...I'm glad she's dead. And I'm grateful to you for protecting me."

"But I didn't," he argues.

"Yes, you did, you watched out for me in Kestrel City, made sure I was okay. I thought it was Treno, but Sice and Dri were *your* guards. You're the one who made sure Lazza didn't force the actual Vow on me." I rub the back of my neck where his friend Saner put the dead mark. "You tried to get me out of there, you rescued Treno even though he was a threat to you. You stood up for me against Zeph—"

"Not soon enough," he interrupts, as though that one thing trumps everything else.

"So you'll get better. We know he'll give you opportunities no matter what he says; asshole is in that guy's blood."

Ryn snorts and tightens his hold on me, and I breathe him in.

"And you'll stay...please," he asks me, and I lean back in shock at the foreign word whose purpose I once had to explain to him.

His knowing smile lights up his face because he knows he's got me. This hard ass just said please, regardless of how foreign the concept is to him, and if I needed more proof that things are exactly as they're supposed to be, that's it. I shake my head and chuckle.

"Please," he says again quietly, his eyes alight with

mischief and heat as he leans in, closing the distance between us. "Please," he adds again for good measure before he threads his fingers through my hair and kisses me.

The back of my neck tingles like it's reminding me of just one of the things this male has done for me, and I waste no time in fervently kissing Ryn back. Heat flickers through me as I move from simply sitting in Ryn's lap to straddling him, our kiss scorching my lips and his touch sending a blaze of need through me. He sucks on my bottom lip, eliciting a moan from me, and I grind down on his hardening length as an inferno of desire sweeps through my body.

I pull away from Ryn's lips.

Fuck, why is it suddenly so hot in here?

Ryn looks confused for a moment when my features fill with distress, and then all of a sudden, it's like someone is taking a hot poker to the back of my neck. I scream and hear a matching panicked yell from Ryn.

One second I'm in his lap, eager to reconnect and claim my place in his soul, and the next, cold wind whips my hair behind me as I look up from the purple-dirt-covered ground I just landed on, right into the aqua eyes of the enemy.

"So glad you could join us, Falon Solei Umbra, although this probably won't be as much fun for you as it will be for me," Lazza sneers, and then he hits me...hard.

I taste blood in my mouth as I lurch to the side, but I don't bother putting another foot down to steady myself. I completely pull inside of myself and give Pigeon all the room she needs to leap out and start ripping some cheap-shot-throwing motherfucker's head off.

The roar of rage that bellows out of Pigeon as we erupt into feathers, fur, talons, and wings trumps any evil smile I could ever give. Her snarl raises every hair on my now incorporeal body, and I know shit is about to go down.

Pigeon leaps for Lazza, but a brown gryphon slams into

us, keeping our razor-sharp beak from catching Lazza by only inches. Pidge screams and turns her fury on to the shit stain who's also a fan of not fighting with honor.

We rear back at the same time as our attacker, but instead of swiping at them and getting this party of pain started, another gryphon attacks us from behind. Our wing audibly snaps, and pain rips through us, as what feels like two beaks snap one of our onyx wings. Pigeon and I both scream and whirl around to deal with the attacks coming at us from all angles.

There's six gryphons immediately surrounding us, but we see more standing in the trees as though they're waiting for their turn.

"Pigeon, shift! Let me slip us out of here!" I scream at her as she spins and snaps at anything that gets too close.

We're cornered, and there's no good reason why Lazza would want us alive.

There's a part of me that shouts that this can't be it. He couldn't have stolen us away just to slaughter us in such a cowardly way, but the rest of me simply scoffs at how naive that is. Lazza doesn't care about honor or fighting fair, he cares about winning.

Pigeon doesn't listen.

She leaps at a white and tan gryphon who takes a swipe at us, and she manages to get the upper hand. She buries her beak in the gryphon's throat and tears at everything that separates this gryphon from death. It feels good to tear into something, but unfortunately, we can't kill and watch our backs at the same time.

Multiple bodies leap on us, beaks, claws, and talons ripping into us. Pigeon does this rolling maneuver, throwing the now dying gryphon away from us, the body slamming into other gryphons who are charging at us.

Snap!

Another bone in our already broken wing goes, and it hurts so fucking bad it's hard to focus on anything other than the pain.

"Pigeon, shift," I beg. *"Let me try to get us out of here."*

Pigeon flips and spins, claws, and lunges as she tries to keep attacking gryphons from mortally wounding us. She flashes me my body, and I see how fragile it is through her eyes. Someone sinks talons into our flank, and we snarl and snap for them. Tears drip down my cheeks as Pigeon is slowly brutalized. She won't shift, because she knows if one of those gryphons gets a hold of my body, we're done for *way* faster than we will be if it's her they have to work to shred apart.

Defiance thunders out of Pigeon with a roar, and as much as I want it to be a rallying cry, I know we can't defend against who knows how many fucking gryphons at one time. Helplessness rakes through me, and in its wake, rage pours in.

I've never tried to activate my runes while in our gryphon form, I don't know if it will do anything at all, but it's the only thing I can think to do other than accept our inevitable death. I focus on my core, on the well of magic that I feel there. I pull from what feels like an endless source and don't bother with finesse or figuring out which runes I can activate while in this form, I call on everything that I have.

A familiar building sensation starts in my chest, and I wait until it gets overwhelming before shoving it out of me. Instead of the magic pulsing out like I expect it to and blasting all the attacking gryphons away from us, the magic ricochets through Pigeon and starts to settle.

I watch in awe as the runes I call in my form adapt to Pigeon's form, and the next thing I know, the black swoosh blades fit the arc of our wings perfectly, turning the appendages into giant weapons. The whip swords morph into a chainmail covering Pigeon's neck and chest. The shield runes on my forearms become greaves for her front and back legs, and tasses cover our hind quarters.

Renewed fight pumps through our veins, and this time when Pigeon opens her beak and bellows out a warning, it's through a metal covering that protects the top of her beak, snakes between her eyes and fits over her ears.

In a blink, we Mighty Morphin Power Ranger-ed ourselves some gryphon armor, and these motherfuckers are about to pay the *fuck with us* toll.

21

If it were me in charge, I would have cracked my knuckles ominously and taken a moment to really build the tension and impending doom I wanted my attackers to feel. But Pigeon is a *give no fucks* kind of girl, so she just goes balls to the wall and starts cutting bitches up.

One of our wings is very badly injured, so it's more tucked against our back protectively, but the wing blades are the shit, and just one of them slicing through a crowd of honorless gryphons does a satisfactory amount of damage.

Pigeon embraces her inner rhino and charges through the gathering attackers, using her protected bits to lead the way and all her sharp bits to exact as much damage as possible. Unfortunately, that means that more gryphons get tagged in from the outskirts, and just as we take one down, another hops in to take its place.

It's a fucking flood of assholes, but we're not dead yet, so there's that.

I keep hoping that somehow Wekun will portal an army in at any moment, but the oncoming night is filling with snarls and cries, death gurgles and pain, and I have no idea how long Pigeon can keep this up.

A hurricane of air slams into us and sends me and all the gryphons around me flying. Pigeon and I try to fight against the sudden onslaught, but it seems Lazza is tired of waiting to watch us get ripped apart and wants in on the action.

I think back to when I first started training with Treno on how to use the runes he gave me that grant him an affinity for water. I learned that day that his brother, Lazza, has runes that allow him to manipulate air. I realized then, that was how he almost killed Ryn back in Kestrel and what he used to try and kill Treno—and subsequently me, Zeph and Ryn—through the Vow when we'd escaped.

Lazza's affinity for air does its best to crush Pigeon and me. Pressure pushes against us from every angle, and it feels like we're stuck in an invisible trash compactor. I try to shove magic into every inch of our gryphon form to combat it, but I'm discovering that I can activate my runes on behalf of Pigeon and protect her with them, but I can't shove magic out of her body like I can mine.

"Shift, Pidge!" I encourage again now that there isn't an attacking horde right on top of us—or at least not a visible one—and thankfully she finally agrees. But before she can fully relinquish our body back to me, Lazza's unrelenting air pressure takes its toll.

Agony splinters through me and Pigeon as multiple parts of her body break under the weight of the air that's being used against us. I feel our other wing fracture in several places, as well as our arms and legs. Pigeon's body lights up with white hot pain, and then instantaneously it shuts off as she crumples into unconsciousness inside of me.

One second I'm a bystander to Pigeon's gryphon, and in the next, she's gone. Panic ripples through me, and I release the tsunami of violet magic that's been gathering inside of me. The pressure around me cuts off, and I scream for Pigeon, terrified that I can barely feel her inside of me.

I can tell she's hurt badly, and I'm reminded of Treno's panic in Kestrel City when he found out I couldn't shift and told me that it's possible to hurt your gryphon so badly that they can't come back from it.

I wrap what I feel left of Pigeon inside of me in soft warm layers. *"Pidge, I'll be right back. Don't you fucking go anywhere, you hear me!"* I demand as I clear my cheeks of tears and swallow back the sobs that are trying to climb out of my throat. *"I love you, you rotisserie chicken, so you just stay right here. I'm going to get you some help!"*

I drop steel bars of protection around her and focus on what I need to do.

It's time to end shit once and for all.

I push to my feet and clothe myself in magic. My runes and weapons are ready to go, and I may still go down, but I know I'll be taking that power-hungry asshole with me.

"Lazza, you limp dick motherfucker, where are you?" I scream, my rage pouring out of me and coating me in a protective layer of hate and rancor.

I look through the gryphons trying to create a wall between me and where I suspect he is. "You weak ass piece of shit! Stop hiding, Syta, and face me!" I challenge, utterly pissed off, terrified, and ready to face whatever may come.

A presence closes around my throat, trying to choke me out of nowhere, but I force my purple Bond magic to climb up my throat, and the sensation immediately disappears.

Two gryphons off to my side move, and between them I spot the leader of the Avowed. His hand is buried in the hair of Saner, the green-eyed female lie detector, who Ryn had mark me with my dead Vow rune.

Well, I guess that answers how I got here. It seems that rune wasn't as dead as we thought.

Saner has very clearly been tortured. She's barely conscious and more black, purple, and bloody than her previous peachy complexion. Her green eyes look hollow, like she's no longer in possession of her body, and I can only wonder how far she had to recede inside of herself to withstand what's been done to her.

"This is your final warning, Vow traitor," Lazza snarls at her, jerking her around by her hair. Saner doesn't respond at all. "Give me control over that rune, or..." Lazza trails off, and another set of unshifted gryphons carry a male out into the middle of the field.

I'm shocked when the male is brought into Saner's lifeless line of sight and she wakes up and starts to struggle immediately. The male has been battered too, but he also seems to register that Saner is there, and he weakly battles to go to her.

I'm not sure exactly what Lazza wants from her, but I'm pretty sure it has to do with my rune, which means whatever it is, is going to be a hard pass from me.

It's clear from a mile away what's going to happen. Lazza is going to kill Saner's mate if she doesn't do what he wants, and if she does, he's probably going to kill them anyway. I don't even think about what I'm doing. As easy as breathing, I call on my runes and slip from where I'm standing in the middle of a bloody clearing and step back into existence right behind Lazza.

My heart hammers in my chest as I reach out and grab the back of his neck, everything in and around me slows, and purple magic crackles angrily across my arm as I squeeze his nape. Lazza freezes, and I can feel a wave of shock and confusion pulse out of his now tense muscles.

I call up the memory of my father coaxing me to do exactly what I'm about to, the words suddenly dancing in my head like some karaoke video with a bouncing ball over the right word of the song so you know exactly what you're supposed to sing.

"Nusht fialow odreece tamod kle," I snarl, enunciating each word of the language my father taught me, more than willing and ready to strip Lazza of the stolen power of my bloodline that he's wielded unworthily.

I can't wait to look him in the eyes as I strip everything he's ever wanted right out of his maniacal hands. Lazza screams and tries to rip out of my hold. Power builds in my chest, and I wait for the rune to crumble under my touch and end this war once and for all.

Only it doesn't.

Lazza spins and slashes out at me.

Confusion fills my head like noisy static as I watch the long dagger in Lazza's hand move closer to me millisecond by millisecond.

Chaos erupts and I try to untangle what went wrong as sudden dread pools inside of me. I've missed something. I thought I said the words perfectly, but maybe I fucked it up in some way. Was there more to that memory? The blade that's going to pierce my stomach at any moment doesn't give me enough time to work it all out.

I call on my runes for my swoosh blades and manage to get one between Lazza's blade and my body. I can't stop his momentum all together, and the dagger still cuts into my side. I keep it from hitting anything vital, but it hurts like a son of a bitch. I lift my other blade, ready to take my own swipe at him, but a fist connects with the side of my head, knocking me sideways, and I'm forced out of striking distance from the Syta of the Avowed.

I stumble and struggle to keep my feet beneath me, as the hit I just took properly rings my fucking bell. Unshifted gryphons move to surround Lazza, making it impossible for me to slip close to him and try again. My thoughts are muddled with pain, but I go over the words again and again, trying to see what I did wrong.

I shake my head to clear it, but I don't see what I missed. I touched the magic, said the words that destroyed the power in the rune. It should have worked.

"Who are you?" Lazza screams at me, his tone just a tad hysterical. I didn't break the Vow, but it's clear to see that my attempt isn't lost on him, and he's rattled as fuck.

I look down at the cut on my side; it's not gushing, so hopefully that's good. I look up and narrow my eyes at Lazza and his dumb fucking question. "I'm Falon Solei Umbra, you worthless piece of shit," I snarl at him.

I can practically see his thoughts racing as he tries to figure out what's going on. That's fine with me though, because while he's doing that, I'm activating Treno's water runes and using them to turn Lazza's guards into waterless gryphon husks.

Lazza mouths *Umbra*, and realization dawns on his face.

At the exact same time, I force his circle of protection to drop dead, and slip back to him. I don't go for his neck right away, just in case he anticipates that. Instead, I pop into existence right in front of him and slash out with a swoosh blade. He blocks me, but when he eyes the weapons I'm using, his aqua eyes darken with rage.

"So Awlon the Dark sent you back to clean up his mess?" he growls at me, trying to knock me away with a harsh blast of air as he reaches out to slash me with his other dagger-filled hand. I give him a taste of my secret sauce and block the wind with Bond magic, while blocking his blade with the hand he assumed wasn't dominant.

His eyes widen for a fraction of a second in surprise.

That's right, fucker, look...both hands.

And then karma promptly kicks me in the face for getting cocky.

Okay karma doesn't do it, but some other gryphon I don't see coming does, and as I fall to the ground, I decide it's about the same thing. I shove back to my feet, but Lazza is on me in a flash.

His fist knocks my head to the side as it connects in the exact same spot the kick just did, and black spots battle for my attention. I fight to stay on my feet, but I quickly learn that, while I have mad skills for training only a week, Lazza has been training his whole life.

He wraps his massive hand around my throat and squeezes viciously. I blast him with Bond magic and shove him away, but his eyes spark with something, and he suddenly changes the way he's looking at me. He reaches back and rubs at the back of his neck like my power pulse is doing something to him.

"I can feel your magic waking mine up," he tells me creepily, and I suddenly feel like he's looking at me the same way a person addicted to their cell phone looks at a phone charger when they're down to one percent of their battery.

"I planned to just kill you or, better yet, kill your mates in front of everyone if they showed up to try to protect you, but now I think there's a much better use for your coveted abilities."

The look in his eyes makes my skin crawl, and when he takes a step toward me, I have a spear in my hand before I even realize I've called on the runes. I stab out at him and feel the sharp end sink into his flesh.

Rage fills Lazza's face, and I ready myself for the hit I know he's going to deliver. What I don't expect is for him to explode into his gryphon. Power shoves me back as Lazza loses himself to his massive light gray gryphon. A sharp charcoal-colored beak snaps out at me, and I flinch back, just barely dodging the snapping maw. What I don't dodge is the swipe he sends my way. I go flying at least ten feet from the hit. I land on my side, blood pooling in my mouth and what feels like half my ribs screaming in protest. I've been hit in the head so many times at this point it'd be a miracle if I didn't have a concussion.

Surrounding gryphons watch the struggle lazily like this is just some everyday event. I figured they'd all jump at the chance to kick me while I'm down, but no one moves near me.

I try to push up from the purple-tinted ground, but this time I can't. Lazza's gryphon leaps for me, and I can't tell if he's going to kill me or snatch me away. I call on my whip swords, unable to stand but not willing to go down without a fight.

The air shifts oddly around me, and I prepare myself for another attack from Lazza's rune fueled air ability. A roar fills the air all around me, and then out of nowhere, an almost pure ebony-colored gryphon slams into Lazza, knocking him away from me.

Lazza's gryphon squeals and snaps at the sky shadow, but Zeph is all over him like shadows in the night.

Relief floods me, but I've learned my lesson about letting my guard down. I white knuckle hold my whip swords as I slowly and very painfully look behind me to see gryphons pouring into the dusky night sky through a portal I'm sure Wekun is responsible for.

Help is here.

I sigh and try to stay up on my one elbow, but man I'm heavy. Way heavier than the guys always make me look when they get all manhandly.

"Falon!" Ryn screams out at me, and then he's there scooping me up and quieting my pain-filled whimpers. "I have you. Fuck, what did he do to you?" he snarls, panic and fury filling his voice. "Shhhh," he tries to reassure me, and I don't even know I'm saying anything until Ryn drops his ear closer to my lips to try and hear me over the sounds of war all around us.

"It didn't work," I tell him, more whimper than words.

Ryn pulls away, his gray eyes confused and bleeding concern. "Wekun!" he bellows. "I need Vian!"

I flinch away from the booming command of his voice, not sure how he even expects Wekun to hear him. He pulls me in tighter against his chest, and I can hear him saying something, but it takes me a minute to understand what it is.

"Please, please, please, please, please," he whispers against my head, the plea spilling from his lips over and over again.

I try to lift a hand to his head to try and comfort him, but my arms suddenly don't work. *Shit, I think I'm in bad shape.*

A warm hand touches my forehead, and another pushes against my stomach. I wince but can't open my eyes to see what's going on.

Wait, when did I even close them?

A flash of heat rockets through me, and suddenly the throbbing pain that's been coursing through my whole body starts to fade. My panted breaths start to smooth out and deepen, and the anguish I was fighting through disappears, lost to the heat the hands are bathing me in.

I open my eyes and find the darker blond healer from the camp standing over me.

Fuck, that's a handy gift.

He chuckles, and I realize I must have said that out loud.

"Pigeon," I tell him, panic suddenly blazing inside of me as I try to sit up more in Ryn's arms.

Vian, the darker blond healer, furrows his brow in confusion.

"My gryphon, she's hurt," I explain, and he nods like he already knows.

"I did what I could to help her stabilize, but you'll need me and Wrye both to fix everything when this is over."

Relief slams through me at the realization that I won't lose Pidge. I figure Wrye must be his lighter blond brother, and I'm half tempted to demand that they fix her now, but we're clearly in the middle of a fucking war zone, so it will have to wait.

"Thank you," I offer Vian as the last of my throbs and aches fade.

He just looks at me funny as he pulls his hands away, and I have to stop from rolling my eyes.

I need to teach these gryphons manners. I add it to the list of shit to tackle when we're not on the brink of extinction, and try to push out of Ryn's arms to get on my feet.

He doesn't let me go.

Instead, he wraps me up in a bone-crushing hug and buries his face against my neck.

"Careful or we'll have to call Vian back," I tease, but my arms are just as tightly wrapped around his neck, and I'm breathing him in deeply as his scent and presence ground me. The citrus part of his lilac-on-a-warm-breeze smell is gone, and I inhale him deeply, loving this smell and how it makes me feel safe in ways I didn't realize until now.

I kiss Ryn quickly on the lips and then put my game face on. I look up and see gryphons flying and fighting all over. It's hard to tell which side we are and whether or not we're winning, but I scan the air for the sky shadow and Lazza, the dick who has a date with destiny.

"When this is over, I'm never letting you out of my sight again," Ryn declares, and then he also slams his Altern mask in place and starts assessing the situation.

Both of our gazes land on the fight we're looking for at almost the exact same time. I see Zeph and Treno both working together to attack Lazza high up in the air, all of them flying toward the peaks in the distance. Lazza seems like he's trying to get away, but between Treno and Zeph, he can't escape.

Just then, I spot a handful of gryphons who seem to be doing warp speed in the direction of the three battling leaders.

"He's going to make a run for it," Ryn declares, and he takes off in the direction they're flying.

"Ryn, I can't shift," I yell at his back as I rush to catch up behind him.

Ryn curses something I don't catch and turns back to me, like he's not sure what to do. A spark of something lights up his features for a split second, and then he's closing the distance between us and picking me up and flinging me onto his back.

"Then hold on, Huntress," he shouts over his shoulder, and then all of a sudden, feathers, fur, and wings explode all around me. I'm no longer holding Ryn's neck, but choke-holding his gryphon as he leaps into the air and flaps furiously to join the fight.

Well, holy fucking shit, don't mind me while I ride my gryphon mate into battle. I just hope I don't fall off!

22

I was obsessed with horses as a preteen, and then I rode one and learned *that* shit is not as easy as it looked. All the graceful equestrian riders who just appeared to be comfortably mounted on their trusty, sure-footed steed are lying liar faces. Because when I got on the back of one of those things, I bounced around so much I thought I broke my ass, and then I got bounced right off when the big beast hit the brakes but my body did not.

Riding a gryphon is a lot like riding a horse, only there's no saddle or reins to hold onto. And it's not bumpy so much as jarring in a *one wrong move and you'll fall to your death* kind of way. Oh, and you're doing all of that while sitting behind what feels like a running jet engine.

Tears streak horizontally out of my eyes from the wind whipping past me as I tighten my death grip on Ryn's gryphon's feathers in my efforts to hold on for dear life. The hurricane it feels like we're flying through shoves up my nose, and it feels like I just accidentally inhaled water, but nope it's just fast-moving air.

I've always loved speed, and I love flying, but I realize that my body just isn't as cut out for this convertible airplane ride like Pigeon's body is. Worry pools in my stomach, and I check on the other part of me. She's still wrapped up and safe, but I need to rip Lazza apart soon and get her the help she needs...and a nap. I feel like we've both earned like a month-long nap at this point.

Roars and screeches reach my ears past the sound of the wind. We must be getting close. I can't exactly see to tell, because I just so happened to not have my gryphon riding goggles on me for this little adventure. Ryn and I streak right past what sounds like one semi-truck slamming into another, and I turn to clock what the hell that was and see we just flew right past Zeph and Treno and the handful of gryphons they're fighting.

I turn back around and blink back the fresh set of wind induced tears that steadily flow out of my eyes and see Lazza not too far out in front of us. I home in on him like a sniper, tracking his every movement, and a weird sense of calm comes over me as we close the distance between us. I think he's hurt, because he's not moving very fast, and I suddenly feel like a lioness assessing injured prey.

I call on my magic and wrap myself around Ryn's neck, because we're coming in hot as fuck and I know shit's about to get a hell of a lot bumpier. Ryn doesn't release a warning growl or make any kind of vengeance-filled gryphon declaration, he moves like a Stealth Fighter I saw once at an air show when I was younger.

He slams into Lazza so hard I hear bones crack. It's like Lazza had no idea he was even there, and the next thing he knows, he's being bulldozed. Despite my koala grip on Ryn's neck, I go flying forward and off of him. It's like horseback riding all over again, only this time I won't land in a puddle of mud, I'll fall to the earth and discover what a pancake feels like.

I know Pigeon can survive that kind of experience, but I'm not sure I can.

I'm flung so hard off of Ryn that I can't even coax a scream out of my panic-tight throat. I'm just weightless, flying past the snarling that starts, and I know I need to think fast. I call on my whip swords and flick them out, hoping they find purchase somewhere and I don't start my plummet back to the ground.

I'm jerked to a stop, and I look up to see the blades of one of my whip swords wrapped around Lazza's gryphon's thigh. It cinches tighter as my weight pulls the blades deeper, and blood starts to pour out of the wound, down my weapon, and out into the sky.

Lazza and Ryn go at it, clawing and snapping and trying to shred one another. I'm hanging onto the handle of the whip sword for all that I'm worth as I'm yanked around and flung about as they battle. Ryn and Lazza break apart and then slam back together. It forces them into a dive, and I quickly go from hanging on for dear life below them to being pulled down through the sky above them like a doomed kite. I hold on with every ounce of strength I have in me, and then a crazy idea pops into my head.

I check on Pigeon out of habit because normally I have her to thank for the crazy, but she's still out, so this one is all me. I let go of the whip sword I'm clinging onto, and it disappears. I free fall toward Lazza and Ryn and where they're snapping and clawing at each other as they fall. I can't dive as fast as they can, but I know at some point they'll have to pull up, and that's where my crazy idea comes in.

I watch as Ryn tries to break away from Lazza to get to me. *"No!"* I shout at him, not sure if he can hear me in his head if I'm not in gryphon form too. *"I'm fine, just do as much damage as you can and catch me if this doesn't work,"* I shout out mentally, hoping somehow he can hear it. I extend my arms and legs like the skydivers I've seen in movies do, and it does help to stabilize my fall a bit.

The fast approaching night turns everything around me into shades of blue and purple, and I fall through wispy, barely-there clouds and know the ground is getting closer. But thankfully, it's shrouded in growing shadows and darkness, and it's hard for me to gauge how far impending pain is.

Lazza kicks off Ryn and spreads his wings. My heart leaps as his rapid descent stops, and he's lifted back up on the current, his back headed right for me.

I call on my whip swords again and aim both of them for the ends of his wings as I get closer to him. Both weapons hit their mark, and I would roar in celebration, but the wind has stolen my voice, and I know that the hard part is just about to start. I'm about to wrestle a gryphon midair which, depending on how it goes, will either be the smartest or most idiotic move I've ever made.

I slam into Lazza's back as gently as one does when they're hit by a car. It knocks the wind out of me, but thankfully I still have the wherewithal to yank on the whip swords that are wrapped about midway on both of Lazza's wings. I shove magic into my arms in hopes it will help fortify my strength, and fuck does it ever, because both of Lazza's wings snap back, and we start to flat spin down.

I gasp, trying to pull oxygen back into my chest, as Lazza roars and tries to snap at me over his shoulder. I'm too far back, thank fuck, and when he realizes he can't get to me, he twists his body so the flat spin becomes a barrel roll. He strains against my hold on his wings, trying to put them in a better position to help him navigate through the air. But the blades of the whip swords dig deeper into the muscles of his feathered appendages, and part of me hopes he struggles enough that it cuts his fucking wings off midway. He could use a taste of what his parents did to Zeph's brother.

I shove more power into my limbs to keep his wings from moving an inch and do my best to hold on as the velocity of our spin tries to fuck with my plan to ride this Syta bitch down to the ground. Each revolution threatens to rip me off of Lazza's back, and I know I can't let that happen. I can't let him get away again.

Since crazy as fuck ideas seem to be a new forte of mine, I snatch on to another one. On the next spin, when we reach the point where gravity is working in my favor again, I let go of the whip swords and dive for Lazza's gryphon's neck. I call on my swoosh blades, and instead of trying to hold onto him with my hands, I dig the blades into the sides of his throat, hoping the speed of the roll he's executing helps to decapitate him.

Warm blood leaks out of the wounds I'm pressing into his neck. It makes it hard to keep a hold of the weapons, but I grit my teeth and divert all energy into doing just that. Talons rake down my shoulder and arm as Lazza tries to rip me off him. I'm unfortunately within striking distance of his front legs again, but as he attempts to pull me around and off of him, he also helps to move the black blades in his throat. A gurgled scream rips out of his beak, and I send a mental, *"That's right, motherfucker, you're going down if I am,"* at him.

A roar sounds off behind me, but I don't pull my focus from Lazza and my efforts to inch by inch remove his head from his body as we fall like a meteor to the ground. I dig in even harder as I start to make out the details of the ground.

Just a little longer and—I'm yanked off of Lazza's back before I can even finish that thought. Strong, warm arms wrap around my waist and pluck me off like I'm a tick. I lose my hold on my weapons and cry out as I'm torn away.

I call on another swoosh blade, twisting in the arms of whoever has me so I can shove it in their neck. The sight of tan skin, onyx scruff, and wavy black hair that's being windswept away from an entirely too handsome face makes me pause.

"What are you doing, little sparrow?" Zeph asks me evenly, like it wasn't obvious.

"Saving the day," I croak back in answer, pissed that he just rained on the hero shit I was trying to pull off.

Gryphons are battling in the distance, and I can hear faint growls and cries carried over to us in the wind.

"By killing yourself?" he demands tersely.

"No, by killing *him*," I snap back, turning and looking for Lazza in the sky around us. I expect him to be trying to get away again, but I'm surprised to see he's still falling to the ground.

I don't get my hopes up that he won't somehow be able to stop his trajectory; I've seen and also survived too much to think we'll win this easily.

"Why aren't you a gryphon?" I ask, settling into Zeph's arms as his powerful black wings angle us down for a smooth gentle descent to the ground.

"Because you needed rescuing."

I scoff.

"Totally didn't. I had that handled."

"If by *handled*, you mean a feather's breadth away from being ripped off his back and shredded, then yes, little sparrow, I agree."

I roll my eyes, and he nips at my neck as I watch Lazza continue to hurtle toward the ground. I'm certain that at any moment, he's going to spread his wings and swoop back into the air, rallying impossibly like every fucking annoying villain in every movie ever. But I watch as he plunges wildly, and then with a deep boom and a plume of dirt and debris, Lazza smashes into the unforgiving ground.

I'm shocked and completely speechless. I thought for sure that wasn't going to happen. A cheer rises up through my chest, but I bite it back down. I survived two falls just like that, and if I can, he sure as fuck will. Zeph aims for the crash site, and I catch Ryn's and Treno's gryphons already landing nearby. Red-purple dirt floats heavily in the air as Zeph and I land, and I push out of his hold and immediately call on my whip swords. I keep them in their sword form, and I see out of the corner of my eye that Zeph does the same thing.

Treno shifts out of his gryphon form, but Ryn stays furry and feathered as back up. Treno moves toward us, his mismatched eyes trained on his brother's body. Worry starts to simmer in my chest. Treno knew that Lazza making it out of this alive was impossible, but knowing something and seeing it through can be very different things.

His gaze hardens, and I can't even begin to imagine the rush of emotions that must be going through him right now. He closes the distance between us in a few strides, and just when I think he's going to streak past me to either check on or maybe finish off his brother, he stops and wraps me up in a hug.

The gesture takes me by surprise, but I don't hesitate to squeeze him back, hard.

"I'm so grateful you're okay," he tells me as he presses a kiss to the top of my head. I can feel the relief that washes through him from the contact.

I can only imagine what happened after I disappeared from Ryn's lap. I'll ask them about it later, but first we need to finish this. Treno puts me down and calls on his swoosh blades. He keeps his eyes trained on the sky, like he's waiting for the stars themselves to shoot down in defense of his brother.

Looks like I'm not the only one who feels like this is suddenly too easy.

We cautiously approach the small crater that Lazza's crash to the ground created, and I see that Lazza isn't in his gryphon form anymore, but he's still just lying there. I wonder for a brief moment if this is how Zeph found me after our first meeting, and this moment feels oddly full circle.

Lazza is bruised and battered all over, but not an ounce of sympathy strikes through me as I take that in. I saw what he's done to Saner and her mate, and who the fuck knows how many other gryphons have suffered in the past from his wrath.

"Can you break the Vow with him being unconscious?" Treno asks me, and I freeze, remembering my failed attempt earlier.

"I don't know if I can at all," I confess, loathing the way it makes me feel as though I'm letting them down. "I tried earlier, I did what I thought I was supposed to do, but it didn't break. I must be missing something, but I just haven't had a moment to try and figure out what," I tell them.

"We don't have to keep him alive to break the Vow. I say cut his head off and then work on the rune later," Zeph declares, and bewilderment sifts through me.

"We don't need him to break it?" I question.

"No, he controls the Vow right now because of his bloodline, but Treno is just as capable. We can have Wekun remove the block on Treno's Vow, and you can try to destroy it that way."

"Wait. If we could do *that,* why the hell didn't we do it before?" I demand, confused. I thought Lazza was the key in all of this, not just his bloodline in general?

"Because we don't actually know for sure if that's correct," Treno interjects. "We think maybe it could work, but it's not guaranteed. We all decided that going to the source and breaking it that way was the surest option. But if you can't break it yet, I'm with Zeph; Lazza's too dangerous to keep around."

Ryn growls deeply, and I take that as his vote of agreement too.

I take a deep breath. "Let me try again, and if it doesn't work, we'll go with the gryphon way of kill first, figure the rest out later."

Zeph studies my face for a beat and then nods. Relief washes through me at his silent vote of confidence, and we start to approach Lazza's still prone body in the dirt. I feel as though I'm walking straight into quicksand as I get closer to Lazza. It's like I know it's dangerous, but I won't know how dangerous until it's probably too late and I'm being sucked under and suffocated to death.

I expect Zeph to toe him to see if he moves or if there's any indication of some other possible threat, but instead he walks over and stabs him with a sword through the shoulder. Lazza doesn't even flinch or make a peep, and as shocked as I am by the brutality of what Zeph just did, we know Lazza is completely unconscious now.

Zeph nods at me, and I tentatively make my way over to him. Lazza is face down, which makes this part easy, I guess, but now I just need to figure out what the fuck I'm missing. I kneel next to Lazza's body and reach my hand out to cover the Vow rune on the back of his neck. I take a deep breath and close my eyes and try to piece together what it is that I might be missing.

I'm touching the magic, I'm saying the words... "Nusht fialow odreece tamod kle." I'm willing the magic to break.

I wait again to see if what I just did will work this time,

but again nothing happens. Frustration slams through me, and I tighten my grip on Lazza's neck and try to figure out what the fuck is going on.

I flip through everything I can recall from Nadi to my dad and what's been said about Bonds and the Vow and how they work. Nadi said I needed to speak it into existence. My dad told me I already knew how to do this, to think back to the lessons. I sift through the lessons I can remember. The first time I used my will and got in trouble for freezing the animals. The words I used to bind them to me and force them to listen. The lesson with Princess.

I pause and retrace my mental steps.

The words I used...

I focus on the memory of the time I froze the animals. *"A word is never bad, but bad things can be done with words, and we must make sure that we keep ourselves and others from doing that."* My dad's words bounce around in my brain, and I realize something. I didn't get in trouble for using the word, I got in trouble for forcing my will on something and then using my magic to enforce it.

What if the language or the words that I've been taught have nothing to do with the magic?

I think through the lessons and the words that I was taught, but I can't recall anything that tells me that the words themselves are anything more than the language of my dad's people and that's why he was passing it down to me.

Zeph's deep voice rises up in my mind as he tells me about how the word *tamod* was used against his parents. But I can't help wondering if, even in this case, the word was inconsequential, and the will of the user was what mattered?

It would make sense that the gryphons would think the words meant more than they did. It was the language of their oppressors. It would have naturally become synony-mous with the magic that bent the Gryphons to the Ouphe will. It makes even more sense that the language of the Ouphe is practically dead. I'm sure anyone who spoke it in the presence of a gryphon was ripped apart right then and there.

The Ouphe and all that they represent has been all but destroyed, so of course the language would have been too.

It dawns on me what I've been doing wrong. I've been so focused on the words, thinking they were the key, but they were just words.

I'm the key.

My will and my magic are all that I need. Not the words. They couldn't carry my will, because they're not even mine.

I open my eyes and look up at the guys, understanding lighting up my eyes.

I know what to do.

Pain slams through my abdomen, and I gasp and look down to see Lazza shoving a dagger into my stomach. I hear the roar of my mates just as I see Lazza slowly flip over, another dagger in his other hand headed directly for my head.

I grunt against the sharp metal in my stomach and immediately get pissed with myself. I fucking knew this asshole would pull something like this, and still I kneeled down next to him and just sat here, giving his fake uncon-scious ass plenty of time to plan his next move.

Amateur move, Falon! You'd think it was my first war or something.

Lazza's dagger gets closer to my face, and I pull on my source of magic and let it overtake my entire body, including my voice.

"Stop," I order, shoving my magic and my will at Lazza like a bitch-slap of authority that will not be argued with.

He freezes mid swipe, and time picks back up as I hold a purple glowing hand up to the guys to keep them away. I have Lazza now, and I don't want to take any chances that their interference will fuck with anything.

Lazza's eyes fill with fear, and I didn't even give him my practiced smile yet. I leave his dagger in my stomach even though it hurts. I've watched enough *Grey's Anatomy* to know you don't pull shit out of you unless there's someone there to deal with the internal injuries.

Slowly I reach out for Lazza's neck again, not because I technically need to, but because it makes me feel like a dominant bitch. I blame all those years I thought I was a wolf.

"You can't," Lazza tells me between clenched teeth as I lean into him.

"This is the reclamation, Lazza. But don't worry, you won't live to see the other side of it."

I don't give him time to respond. I may have pulled a rookie move and gotten myself stabbed, but I'm not going to monologue uselessly and give anyone time to fuck with what's about to happen.

"I unbind this rune and all the magic in it. I demand that this mark cease to exist and crumble to dust, never to be used against anyone again," I order, magic pouring out of my mouth, coating the words that I'm speaking, and sinking into Lazza one spark and flicker of power at a time.

Lazza starts to pant, and I wait until his aqua gaze once again focuses on my hard lavender stare.

"So I fucking will it, so it is fucking done," I growl, and just as I feel the rune crumble to nothing under my palm, I call on a swoosh blade and shove it up through Lazza's chin until it comes out of the top of his head.

I let go of the blade and the back of Lazza's neck, and he falls away from me. Lazza's dagger in my stomach disappears, and just when I think it's all over, power slams into me like a lightning bolt. I'm hit by the magic that was in the Vow marks as they crumble to nothing on the thousands of gryphons who wore them. The magic forces its way to my center and lights me up as it tries to settle in my too small body.

I scream as it sears itself into all that I am again, and try to breathe through the pain that's pumping in my veins. I feel Pigeon wake up inside of me, and we wrap around each other as we try to withstand the tsunami of agony.

I know I promised myself I would stop letting my body shut down, but I decide exceptions to every rule are a good thing as blackness begins to overtake my consciousness. I wave it over and treat it like an old friend, surrendering freely to the oblivion being offered. The pain starts to fade, and I give the bleak darkness two enthusiastic thumbs up as it swaddles me completely, and I pass the fuck out.

23

I groan as I come to. Wherever I am is quiet, but I know it will be safe, which is an unusual feeling for me to have in this world. I stretch out, feeling oddly rejuvenated, and realize I'm dressed. For some reason, that alarms me, and I open my eyes immediately and snap up.

"What the fuck?" I grumble, my voice gravelly.

"Whoa, what happened?" Ryn demands as he rushes over and crouches down next to the cot I'm now sitting up in.

"Why am I dressed?" I ask, confused, but that just seems to make Ryn even more confused. "I never wake up dressed. It's freaking me the fuck out. Is Zeph okay? Treno? You?"

I look around, and I'm once again in a tent, but there's nothing in here except me, Ryn, and the cot I'm lying on.

Ryn's worried eyes warm, and he releases a relieved exhale. "Zeph said we should get you cleaned up, but the bath and water are still on their way. You woke up sooner than we thought you would," he explains. "Zeph and Treno are fine. They'd be here, but they had to intervene between the fighting that was still going on. They'll come back as soon as they can."

I release my own deep breath and let the tension sluff off my shoulders. "Where are we?"

"We're about a day's fly from the Eyrie. We're working on getting a temporary camp set up here while we try to smooth tensions over. Cree and her people have been bringing in and setting up tents." He gestures to our current surroundings.

I give them one last look and then focus on where Zeph and Treno are.

"Fighting, huh?" I ask, and Ryn's face grows solemn as he nods.

"Looks like getting rid of the Vow might have been the easy part. Bringing the Gryphons back together after everything both sides have been through is a whole other story," I observe, and Ryn snorts. He sighs again, and I realize how tired he looks. I reach up and run the back of my hand over the scruff on his cheek.

"Hey," I call to him as his exhausted gray eyes land on mine. "We did it."

A wide proud smile stretches slowly across Ryn's face, and he pulls my lips to his for a slow kiss before he rests his forehead against mine. "We did it," he agrees.

We stay like that for a breath, just taking the moment in.

"It almost doesn't seem real," he confesses. "I've thought of what this day would be like for so long, and now here we are, and nothing is at all like I thought it would be."

"How so?" I ask.

"For starters, I thought the fighting would stop when there wasn't a Vow left to fight over, but it's clear the wounds run deeper than magic."

I nod and run my fingers through his hair. It was so much shorter when I first saw him, and now I'm not sure which I prefer.

"It'll take time for everyone, I'm sure. Lucky for us, we

seem to live for a fucking long ass time, or at least that's the impression I got from the archives," I tell him on a chuckle. "Holy shit, it was you!" I accuse, pushing back from him as I realize something. "You put the mating book right where I would find it in the archives. That's what you were doing there."

"I gave my word to Zeph that I wouldn't tell you about the bond, but if you figured it out and came to me..." he says with a leading tone.

"But why would you agree not to tell me in the first place?" I ask, hoping to finally understand all the fucked up shit that happened between us.

Ryn hesitates, his gray eyes studying my face for a moment, and then he gives a defeated sigh. "Zeph suspected your bloodline. He wanted confirmation before completing the bond, just in case we..." His pause is weighted.

"Just in case you what?" I press.

"We had to make an impossible decision for the good of the Hidden," he admits tensely.

An impossible decision? What the hell does that mean? Like they were going to kill me or something? I joke in my mind, but as soon as I think the words and scoff in my head, I freeze.

Holy shit, that's really it.

"You know?" I accuse, as I put missing pieces together and get a good look at a shockingly clear picture.

"Know? Know what?" Ryn questions, befuddled by my reaction.

I shake my head, completely caught off guard. "You didn't want to mate with me if you were going to have to kill me," I elaborate, and the shame and silent assent I see in his eyes confirms my suspicions.

It all makes so much sense now. I was told the Hidden had been hunting down anyone who had Bond magic. I assumed they were making sure another situation like the

Vow couldn't happen again, but it's also possible that they somehow knew killing the bloodline of the original creators of the Vow would end it too.

"It wasn't as simple as that exactly; we really did suspect that you were a spy for a while, but then your potential blood ties became the larger issue. We weren't sure what to do. We didn't know about the gates or any other worlds, so we couldn't be certain that if you died, you would take the Vow with you. But we couldn't dismiss the notion either."

He takes a breath and runs a hand over his face and shakes his head, while I try to figure out my footing in all of this. They knew I was their mate and that they might have to kill me. It definitely sheds light on a lot, but I'm not sure what to think about what I'm looking at now. What if Zeph and I hadn't had that night and Ryn was able to confirm who I was faster. Would they have gone through with it? Can I even blame them for considering it, knowing what I know now?

"We didn't know you, and we'd been fighting for so long for our freedom. If you were the last of the line, it felt like this gift, and yet we were calling to each other, so it also felt like a curse all at the same time. It was as though the moon and stars were torturing us, dangling you before us and forcing an impossible decision."

He looks back at me, his eyes now beseeching.

"In the end, it didn't matter, because you and Zeph mated, and by the time I had confirmation that you were a direct Sept descendant of the Bond Makers, and possibly the last one, I had mated with you too, and everything was different."

I nod in understanding, feeling surprisingly calm. I might not have been so calm about this a couple months ago, but I've seen so much and we've all been through so much that I don't see the world the same way. I can't say, if I had been in their shoes, that I wouldn't have done the same thing. I would have been *way* less of an asshole for sure, but I would have considered killing someone for the greater good.

That thought gives me pause, and I take a moment to reflect on just how much I've changed. I loved bikes and fixing cars and other things. Beers on a Friday were a favorite pastime, and the only thing I had ever killed was spiders and a cactus someone at work gave me once. Now, pants are a cause for celebration, I have magic and gumption and three semi reformed asshole mates. I don't bat an eye at killing or doing whatever it takes to survive and thrive, and I don't feel even slightly bad or remorseful about that.

I grew up.

The flaps to the tent I'm sitting in open, and several people back in carrying what looks like a large hammered copper kid pool. Behind them file in several other people with colossal steaming buckets of water, which they pour into the pool.

It appears my bath has arrived.

The sudden presence of clean water has me slowly becoming aware of how disgusting I am. I look down at the tunic someone has put me in. It's crusted in blood and stiff with wrinkles embedded so deeply in the fabric that I doubt they will ever come out.

The bath carriers and fillers disappear back out of the tent just as fast as they came, and I don't hesitate to strip out of someone's dirty shirt and practically cannonball my stinky ass into the tub.

Ryn chuckles and then gets awkwardly quiet. He clears his throat, and I have to stop myself from smiling and teasing him for being weird. "I can go if you want some privacy," he tells me, making no effort to actually go anywhere.

I shrug as I start to remove the layers of filth and death from my skin and hair. "There's not room for two in here, otherwise I'd invite you in, but you can just hang out and watch if you want," I offer, meaning it totally innocently even though it didn't exactly sound that way.

The words *room for two* ping around in my mind for a second, and then it hits me like a kick to the face...Pigeon!

"Fucking shit!" I face palm and then dive into my center. I'm the worst body sharer in the world. I'm always forgetting about poor Pigeon. *"Pidge! Pidge, are you here? Are you okay?"* I shout at the top of my lungs, my voice frenzied as I look for her.

She holds up a wing and winces like I just flipped on the lights and she was trying to sleep. Only she flashes me an image of exactly that. *Shit. "Sorry, Pidge, I just wanted to make sure you were okay."* She waves me off and curls back up in my chest. She's better, but I can tell she's still healing. I back away quietly as she flashes me an image of a child banging on a bathroom door, chanting *mommy* over and over again.

I snort. *"If anyone is the annoying kid in this scenario, it's you, you're way needier than I am."* She rolls her eyes but makes that chuffing sound she does when she's laughing. *"Love you, Pidge,"* I lob at her, and she rolls her eyes again and flashes me a meme that says *thirsty* on it in bright neon yellow lights. *"Thirsty for your love, Pidge!"* I agree, and she chuffs again and then shoos me away.

I come back to the bath and the tent, elation pumping through me, and discover Ryn is practically in my face, his eyes filled with worry. "Are you unwell, what happened?"

"I'm an ass and completely forgot to check on Pigeon when I first woke up. She's good. Tired, but good."

Ryn visibly relaxes. "The healers spent hours working to

help her. They left completely drained. She was in bad shape."

I send another little pulse of love to Pigeon as that information sinks in. We've had too many close calls. It will be nice to just take it easy and live that lazy gryphon life we've decided to live. Well, mostly I just decided that, but I feel confident that Pidge will be on board when she wakes up.

"So you're not mad?" Ryn asks as he settles on the ground next to the kiddie pool bath. I turn to him, and water tries to slosh over the side.

"What? Mad that you and Zeph thought about killing me?" I consider it a moment. "I've thought about killing the two of you a lot, so I think we're probably pretty even on that front," I admit. "I mean, much groveling will be expected about the whole secret keeping thing," I tease, trailing off.

"I did try to tell you in my own clever way," he defends. "It's not my fault you didn't read it."

I splash water at him and drop my mouth open in faux outrage. "Oh please, blame the victim, why don't you. It's not my fault the book you chose looked all boring and factual. I prefer a different form of book porn, thank you very much."

"I have no idea what porn is, but if you can't follow the clues that are laid out, you really only have yourself to blame," he teases back.

I go to splash him again, but he grabs my hand. I try it with my other hand, but he grabs that too. I get my legs involved, but he moves behind me so if I want to get him, I have to get myself. I huff in outrage, and Ryn cracks up from behind me, thinking he's safe.

Think again, buddy.

I call on my wings and start splashing him with those. This isn't my first splash battle, and I take no mercy. Ryn does this man-squeal that almost weakens my attack because I'm laughing so hard, but I persevere. He releases my hands and tries to retreat, but he slips instead and goes down like a fucking mountain.

Oh shit.

Hurriedly, I jump out of the tub to check on him, but I hit the same slippery patch that he just did, and instead of making sure that he's okay, my feet go right out from under me, and I land hard on top of him. Ryn grunts, and I yelp, and then we both moan in pain when his hip bone tries to break my ass.

We both roll around for a second in pain, and then I start cracking up. "I can fight gryphons with practically my bare hands, but a bath and an asshole mate are what's going to do me in?" I observe, completely lost to the slaphappy attack.

There's been so much shit going on, so much never-ending bad news and attacks and doom. *I suppose I was bound to break at some point*, I observe as I grab my side and the stitch that's developing as I howl with laughter. Knowing me, I'll probably have a good cathartic cry after this, or maybe just more manic giggles, until I process all the shit that's happened.

Ryn sits up with me in his lap, and his own chuckles spill out of his mouth. He shakes his head at my mental state and brushes back the strands of wet hair that are plastered to my face. He cups my cheeks, his eyes and lips dancing with mirth, and that's when it happens: he looks at me like Moro looks at Tysa.

The adoration and love suddenly pouring out of his eyes completely shocks me, and it takes me back to nights at Tysa's house in the Eyrie and how her mate looked at her like she hung the fucking moon, and all the stars, and stitched the fabric of the sky itself by hand. I remember watching them and thinking to myself that I would never settle for anything less than the way Moro looks at Tysa.

And now here it is, only it's Ryn that I'm staring at, and he has those eyes for me.

I lean in and claim his lips, needing to taste the look on his face, to catalogue it with my tongue and every other sense I possess. I cup his cheeks. Run my fingers through his hair. I want to feel every part of him all at once, but I don't have enough hands. So I press in against him, pulling at his shirt until it's gone and I can feel his warm skin against mine.

His hands splay across my back, pressing me in even closer as he drinks me down like I'm the elixir that gives him life. The feeling is heady and overwhelming, but I'm not afraid to look it in the eye, to call it mine, to refuse to ever let it go.

We consume each other unhurriedly. We take our time trading passion and promises and desire back and forth with our mouths and hands and bodies. I've never experienced anything like it. The deep-seated need and the easy reverent exploration of each other's bodies. The ache for one another is so staggering I can't decide if I want slow devastating kisses all over my body for hours or him buried deep inside of me right now, lighting my body up with each thrust until we combust.

And the best part is, Ryn is mine, and I'm his, so I never have to truly choose just one or the other. I'm going to have a lifetime of learning his body and loving him hard and fast, or savoring the sweet slow consumption of each other. That thought settles in my soul, and something I haven't felt for a long time takes root.

I stare at the steady thrum of happiness in my chest for a moment, and a smile breaks across my face until Ryn is tasting my rapture and I'm untying his pants. He starts to push them down his thighs, but I'm suddenly impatient. I stroke him once as I line him up with me, and then I waste no time filling myself with his thick hard length.

I throw my head back and moan at the feel of him, and Ryn's passionate kisses trail down my neck and land on my breast. I pump my hips up and down his length as his hot mouth sucks on my nipples, and his hands knead my breasts and cup my throat, like he also wants to touch everything all at the same time.

As I roll my hips and ride him, our lips catch one another's here and there, and then flit away to release moans and explore each other's necks and shoulders and chests. I can't get enough of him, his kisses and his hands on my body, his cock between my thighs.

"Mine," I whisper against his ear before I nip on his lobe and suck at the spot on his neck just below his ear.

My pussy clenches around him like she's staking her own claim, and he growls low and possessively and grabs my ass as he grinds up into me. He reaches down and circles my clit with his thumb, and seconds later an orgasm strikes through me. He kisses me soundly as I grind against him and ride out my release. And then he carefully spins me on his cock so that he's still deep inside of me, but my back is to his chest instead.

He leans me back, sucking on my neck and squeezing and pinching my nipples until he has me exactly where he wants me, at the perfect angle to take over and thrust up into me hard and fast.

My moans turn into gasps and then quickly morph into cries as Ryn sets himself firmly in the driver's seat and drives his cock so deep and so fast inside of me that I'm all at once overloaded with sensations and also never want him to stop. He fucks me right into another massive orgasm as he holds onto my hips and shows me who the fuck I belong to.

He nips at my neck and drops one of his hands back

down to my clit, playing with me until I'm a mewling, writhing mess of a mate, only capable of screaming *yes* and *right there*, as he owns me body and soul.

I feel his muscles tense a second before he groans my name and bites down on my shoulder as he pumps his release into me. I'm still riding the tail end of another orgasm, and I'm half delirious as he relaxes beneath me, his hands now slowly and sensually caressing my body. We just lie like that for a while, not saying a word, but letting our hands stroke and caress and communicate everything our mouths aren't. I'm suddenly with Pigeon on the whole napping thing. I feel tired as fuck, and I wish there was a big ass bed in here instead of an inadequate looking cot.

I want a cuddle party with the guys. I want to reconnect and figure out what the next move is, between orgasms and lots of sleep.

I release a deep breath, sit up and push up off of Ryn. He slips out of me, and I turn to help him get to his feet. He kisses me slowly, and then we both clean up. We're practically dead on our feet by the time we're done, so we both zombie-walk over to the cot and then get our spoon on. Ryn's out before you can say *forking is better*, and his deep breaths on my nape soothe and relax me in ways I never knew they could.

I close my eyes and just float in the feel of his arms caging me in while his body curls protectively around me. I can't help but think about our first encounters in the Eyrie, the cleansing and air tackles, the training and evasiveness. I would have never guessed that I would be where I am right now and certainly not feeling the way that I do. But it's more than I ever hoped for, and I can't wait to see how we all grow together.

24

My stomach growls so hard I can hear it over Ryn's soft snores. I look down, almost offended by the rude demand it just gave, but more gurgles fill the quiet tent, and I accept that I need to eat. I give up on trying to fall asleep in Ryn's arms even though I feel beat. Maybe it will be easier to pass out on a full stomach.

I crawl out from under Ryn's hold and pull the blanket up around him, kissing him on the head before getting dressed in the shirt and pants sitting in a pile next to the cot. I sneak out of the tent in search of sustenance.

"Why hello there, Bond Breaker," Cree says from the side of the doorway. I grab my chest and turn to her, surprised to see her.

"You scared me," I admit on a chuckle, and she laughs too.

"No reason to be afraid, it's just me. Your mates wanted someone to keep an eye for you, and I volunteered," she explains.

"Well, that was nice of you. I'm just looking for food. Can you point me in the right direction?" I ask.

"I'd be happy to take you. Should we wait for the Altern?" Cree asks, gesturing back toward the tent.

"No, I'll bring him back something. Please tell me there's more than grot fruit," I beg as we start walking.

Cree chuckles. "Not a grot fruit lover, I see."

"If I never see those evil berries again, it will be too soon, I don't care how good a source of nutrition and vitamins they are."

Cree leads me away from the tent, toward the surrounding tree line, and I realize where we are. I registered the reddish-purple dirt before, but not what it meant. "Are we in the Amaranthine Mountains?" I ask, just to be sure.

"We are. It seems Lazza was camped out between the two tallest peaks. We set up the medical tents here, and then food is that way." She points off in the distance. "And they started setting up some residential tents over there," she says, pointing in the opposite direction.

"Are they planning on staying out here?" I ask as we weave our way through the trees in the direction of the food area she just pointed out.

"The other Ouphe-mixed gryphons and I will stay here until it can be agreed upon where a new stronghold will be, that is if both sides can learn to accept us," she tells me, a hint of hesitancy in her tone.

"What do you mean?"

"We were exiled from both sides, which is how we ended up settling near the Ouphe camp. Two unwanted races guarding each other's flanks, it made sense at the time, but now we'll see where our kind fits. We didn't want the Vow, but we were too Ouphe gifted to find a place with the Hidden. Our gifts and how we look is a threat to both sides as well as a reminder of what we've been through."

I nod, understanding what she's saying, and she continues.

"The white hair and purple eyes are a trait that only Ouphe-Gryphon mixes get. Not all who look like us have abilities, but most do, and because of that, we don't fit in either world. We're not Ouphe enough for them or Gryphon enough for the other side."

"But now we get to build a new way of life and doing things; I'm sure your people will find a place," I reassure her, but I can see in the way she studies me for a beat that she doesn't quite believe it.

"What about you, Bond Breaker, where will your place be in this new world?" she asks, and I sense a hint of something in her tone that I can't quite place. Resignation maybe, stoicism?

I take a deep breath and let it out. I haven't thought much about the *what now* or tried to picture it. I figured it will take time to sort through the aftermath of everything, to figure out how to move forward as a people and exactly what that entails. I pretty much assumed I'd be along for the ride, supporting Treno and Zeph in any way I can as they try to bring two warring sides back together.

"I'm not sure exactly. I'll be with my mates, I know that much. I used to be a mechanic in my old world, so maybe I'll figure out a way to put those skills to good use, you know, keep busy as we all figure things out."

Cree nods in thought, reaching up to pull a leaf down from a low hanging branch. She threads it between her fingers absently.

"Are you at all worried about your safety?" she asks evenly, and I'm surprised by the question.

"Do I need to be?" I ask, suddenly giving Cree the side-eye.

She smiles and holds her hands up. "I'm no threat to

you, but you are the last Bond Wielder in this land; you have to have thought about how that will make people feel."

I push a branch out of my way as we traverse through a thicker tree-filled part of the forest.

Damn, how far away is the food?

My stomach growls, the impatient sound punctuating my thoughts. Cree chuckles.

"It's not too much further. We probably should have flown, but I didn't know if you'd be up to it, and I like to walk," she explains.

I think back to what she asked and her comment about me being the last person to possess Bond magic. I suspect that isn't exactly the case, but that anyone with any kind of Bond magic is really good at hiding it. Saner comes to mind. She marked my neck with a supposed dead rune, and I didn't give much thought to it at the time, but Lazza used that rune to pull me to him, and I'd bet my left boob that she was packing more Bond magic heat than she'd ever want people to know. I wonder for a moment about how many Bond users are in hiding.

"Word that you were the one to finally break the Vow will spread, and there will be Gryphons who are grateful, but there will also be Gryphons who see you for what you are," Cree goes on, and her words call to an uneasiness in me.

"For what I am?" I question.

"Again, please know that I am not worried other than *for* you, but I think it wise to understand that the Gryphon people may not tolerate your presence. Those of us who know you will understand that you would never use your abilities against us. But there will be others who won't care about that. All they'll see is someone who *could* use their abilities against them, if they wanted to," she explains.

I trace the silhouettes of the tree trunks for a moment as

I think through what she's saying. She's not wrong. I do need to think about this and the fact that I'm not going to be everyone's favorite gryphon. Then again, who is? I want to be smart about my presence during this sensitive transition, and the guys and I need to talk about the best ways we can do that.

"I worry about the same thing for my people," Cree hurries to elaborate, probably picking up on my discomfort. "Will there ever be trust? Will the threads that unite us as Gryphons always be fragile? We're not to blame for our heritage or the Ouphe blood running through our veins, and yet I cannot blame the Gryphons for seeing a threat in me because of it either. It's a difficult path to walk, not unlike this one," she jokes as we navigate around a cluster of boulders.

Something about them looks familiar, which is a weird thing to think about a grouping of rocks. I stare at them for a beat longer, wondering where the déjà vu feeling is coming from, but when no answers appear, I let it go and focus on Cree's points.

"Honestly, I don't have the answers. I hope that with time, we can all find a way to work together, and that includes the Ouphe who are in hiding, but it won't be easy, and it won't be immediate," I confess. "I can only do what I can to make people feel safe and secure, and the rest we'll just have to deal with if or when it happens."

I spot a clearing through the trees about ten feet in front of us, and my stomach tucks a napkin into its shirt, ready to go to town. Thoughts of duda fruit and the yummy rolls from the Eyrie fill my mind, and my mouth starts to water in anticipation.

A buzzing sensation starts up on my skin, and I chuckle at how freakin' excited my body is to eat.

Cree stops just before the edge of the trees and turns to me.

"I would like to thank you, Bond Breaker, for what you've done for our people. We've been waiting for a long time for this day, and because of you and your sacrifices, a new dawn is upon us," Cree tells me as she presses her palm over her heart. Her face is split into a radiant smile, but her eyes say something else entirely.

My brow furrows as I try to pinpoint what has Cree so sad. Before I can say anything or respond in any way, she starts to move again, and we finally make our way out into the clearing, and I freeze in my tracks.

The clearing has tall unkempt grass spread across it, and in the middle is a familiar abandoned small stone cabin. It looks exactly like the clearing I was supposed to spread my gran's ashes in. The one that had the invisible gate that brought me here. I'm so stunned by the sudden presence of this place that it takes me a moment to figure out how the hell we stumbled upon it.

I turn to Cree, completely shocked, and realize she's talking. I blink the stupefaction I'm experiencing away, and her words start to resonate.

"You've done a great thing for us, and in return, I find myself obligated to do the same for you, Falon."

Her words only add to the complete confusion I'm feeling right now. Why are we here, and what does it have to do with anything she's saying?

"This won't be easy, and you may not ever understand why, but know that I'm saving your life and the lives of your mates too. You'll have to learn to let them go, because once you're through, I'm going to use my gift, and this gate will never open for you again."

"Cree, what are you—"

But I don't get to finish that question, because out of nowhere she pushes me.

I don't have time to react or to try and figure out what the hell she's talking about. I'm just flying forward toward the middle of the clearing, a shouted objection barely leaving my lips, and then the next thing I know, a crack of power slams into me. Heat and hurt shove all thoughts of anything else away, and I go flying back from the pulse of energy that just exploded all around and through me. I'm thrown against something hard, and I lose time for a moment as my body falls to the frozen ground in a battered heap.

I groan as pain bounces around my body and try to lift my head from the snow-covered ground.

Snow?

I start to shiver like the word itself reminded my body of how it's supposed to react to the cold. I push up and notice I'm in the same clearing, but it's covered in a white blanket of fresh powder. My thoughts feel foggy, like I can't make sense of why there's suddenly snow here.

"Cree?" I call out, confused. "What the fuck was that?" I ask as I push to my feet slowly.

Ow.

I rub the back of my neck and turn to look for the bitch leader of the Ouphe-mixed gryphons, but instead of finding Cree, I spot part of my motorcycle half hidden in a pile of snow and still parked in the same place I left it.

And then it hits me.

"No, no, no, no, no, no, no!" I scream as I scramble to my feet. I charge through the clearing, waiting for the telltale staticky feeling and the blast of power, but nothing happens.

Panic floods me, and I look around, trying to figure out what the fuck to do.

"Cree!" I call out, my voice breaking and my heart slowly

shattering as understanding dawns on me. "Cree, you fucking bitch, bring me back right now!" I order.

But the only thing that answers is the wind as it picks up some snow and forces it to dance around the clearing.

This can't be happening. I'm dreaming. I have to be dreaming, and this is just a nightmare.

"Pigeon, wake us up," I beg, and I feel her stir inside of me, waking up and trying to figure out what's going on. *"She sent us back, Pidge. I don't know how to get back,"* I admit, and Pigeon wakes the fuck up and fills me with fury.

"Wekun!" I scream. "Wekun, help!" I try to picture him and slip to wherever he is, but it doesn't work. Then I try Zeph, Treno, and Ryn, but when I open my eyes, I'm still sitting in the freezing snow in the middle of the wrong world.

Tears start to drip down my face. And I scream, my lament ripping out of my heart and soul. How could this happen? After everything I've been through, after everything I did to find my place, for it to all just end up like this? I shake my head, refusing to accept my circumstances.

"NO! I am not going to be fucked over by fate like this!" I shout at the wind, my enraged and tormented voice bouncing off the bare tree trunks and hopping around the clearing like destiny itself is taunting me.

"I'm going to rip your fucking head off when I get back, Cree. And I *will* get back!" I bellow, purple magic streaking over my arms and punctuating my fury. Pigeon wails and rages inside of me, and I let her out in hopes that maybe she can trigger the gate somehow. We storm around the clearing as though if we just look hard enough, we can find the way back in. But we can't.

Pigeon rips apart the stone house, chucking the roof into the trees and pulverizing the walls until the last of her energy is spent. We keen together and cling to one another as loss and desolation make us their bitch. I wanted so badly for so long to find the gate and make it back here. But I had let it go, I was finding my place, and my mates...

Agony rips me open, and I crumble in on myself. They'll think I abandoned them or that something happened to me. How long will they look? Will they know what happened? Where I am? Pigeon flashes me Wekun's face, and I nod and take a deep breath.

"You're right. Wekun can see us. He watches my Sept, he said so himself. He'll realize what happened and bring us back. It'll be okay," I reassure the both of us.

So we sit down in the snow, and we wait. He'll come. We just have to wait.

25

"No, it's called Tierit. *T-i-e-r-i-t*," I spell out, as I flip the sign on the front of the door from Open to Closed.

"Ma'am, we've looked, but we aren't finding a city or a town anywhere in Canada by that name," the secretary for the new private investigator I'm thinking of hiring tells me on the other end of the phone.

"I know you don't see it on Google Maps or any other GPS, that's why I want to hire your company so you can look for it," I explain for the seven millionth time since I started hiring PIs to help me.

I walk back over to my front desk and cross the name of this firm off of my list. If they can't figure out what I even want to hire them for, they aren't the right fit in the first place.

It's been three months.

Three months since I unfolded my snow-dusted, frozen limbs from the middle of a clearing in nowhere Alberta, Canada, and slipped back to the small town I thought I'd never see again in the Rocky Mountains of Colorado.

Three long, agonizing, heart-wrenching months.

Months filled with days sitting in a freezing clearing. Waiting. And then having to accept that Wekun wasn't coming. Months filled with hours where I ripped my gran's house to shreds, looking for clues. But no matter how hard I looked, I never discovered a map to any other gates.

I've spent months hunting and taking down every detail of what I can remember Wekun said about Sentinels and where they lived. I've gone from searching for a gate to searching for him. Maybe Cree killed him or tied up the loose end that Wekun was, in a way that keeps him from helping me or the guys, but I can't give up. I won't give up.

Someone somewhere knows, and maybe if I look in enough corners and make enough noise, they'll come see why I'm stirring up so much shit. It's clear the Sentinels want to be found about as much as the Ouphe did, but I don't care. I need to get back.

I've called every supernatural investigator I could find to help me look for any leads about people with magical marks or unusual abilities, or for anyone who knows anything about Tierit and where it could be, but so far, nothing.

"You know what? Just forget about it," I tell the secretary who's just not getting it. "Thank you for your time, but I'm going to go in a different direction."

She starts to tell me something, probably to argue that they're the right people for the job, but I hang up on her, already at my limit for stupid today. I sigh and open my laptop. I need to order parts for the Seaman car and check to see if any useful emails have come in.

I never found any useful information about the Ouphe or the Gryphons in gran's old house, but I did find a deed stating that gran bought the old Miller auto shop before she died, and she put it in my name. I wasn't ready to see it for the gift that it was when I first found it. I was too wrapped up in longing and frantically searching for a way back. But about a month ago, when I realized I couldn't solve things on my own, I went ahead and opened Griffin Automotive, partly to give me something to do other than worry and pace and feel pissed off. But really, I need to pay the bills. I'm trying to get a whole network of help going, and that shit is not cheap.

Gran's house is up for sale, which will help, and I moved into the apartment above this shop to keep expenses low, but I have no idea how long it will take to find either Wekun, Tierit, a Gate, a Sentinel, or even another Gryphon.

I rub my hands over my face and roll my neck. It feels weird to try and live a normal life day-to-day when my soul hurts so badly, but I know I need this, and not just the money part of it. It's good to keep busy and focus on something other than the fact that I'm stuck. I look down at my hands and the oil and engine grease that's settled into the cracks and nail beds. Maybe I need to get a manicure. Ms. Waters would sure love that. She always got all kinds of surly when Gran and I used to go in for manis and pedis before she died.

I chuckle at the thought and make a quick list of everything I need to order. Pigeon stretches out inside of me, and I smile.

"I'll be done soon, and then we can go flying," I tell her, and she starts doing her daily stretches. I spend all day fixing the never-ending line of cars that seem to be waiting for me. When I opened Griffin's, I didn't know the only other local mechanic's shop had just closed, and I've been busier than I ever thought I would be.

But my evenings are for Pigeon. We take off as soon as the sun starts to set and fly until the stars are kissing our back. It's been our only reprieve, and so far, so good on the not being spotted part.

The bell I keep meaning to take down above the

entryway chimes as the front door opens. *Shit.* I must have forgotten to lock it.

"Sorry, we're closed," I call out as I pull up the site I need parts from.

I look up to find tan skin, black hair, and molten brown eyes making their way to me. In another life, I would have marked this dude as a future conquest, but there's only three males who do it for me now, and I can't figure out how to get back to any of them.

"Sorry to show up after hours, but Cassie over at the motel said if I had a car that needed to be fixed, Griffin's was the best place to do it," he tells me, his voice dipped in silk and his smile captivating.

Yeah, he's definitely the kind of guy who's used to getting what he wants. I take a discreet deep breath to identify what he is. He moves like a predator, and I'd bet this shop the dude's not human. Wolf is the dominant scent, but there's hints of other things too that I don't have time to catalogue unless I want him to know I'm sniffing the shit out of him.

"You're fine, Cassie's the best, and I'm happy to help. What kind of issue are you having..." I trail off in a *fill in the blank with your name* kind of way.

"Oh sorry, Mateo Torrez, but most people call me Teo or, well, yeah...Teo is fine," he offers, getting a little tongue-tied, and it makes me wonder exactly what are the other things people call him?

"I'm Falon, it's nice to meet you, Teo. So what can I help you with?"

"Right, so my pack and I are in town for work, and we've been having issues with our cars. One won't start. I checked the battery, and that seemed fine, so I'm not sure what's wrong, and the other one makes a clunking noise when you change gears or brake. I'm hoping you all can have a look and let us know if it's anything we should be concerned about."

"Absolutely, would you like me to tow them back to the shop so I can get a thorough look? Or I can also come to the motel and just poke around and see if I can figure out what's going on," I offer, and Teo looks a little taken aback.

"Oh, you're the one who does the actual fixing?" he asks, surprised, and I try not to roll my eyes.

"Yes, this is my shop. What kind of cars are they?"

"They're both Range Rovers. Sorry, I didn't mean to go all caveman there; it's just when Cassie said go to Griffin's, I pictured someone more..." he trails off.

"Not me?"

"Yes, although as I'm saying that, I'm realizing it still sounds sexist, so I'm just going to shut the fuck up now and hope you'll still look at the cars."

I laugh and give him a kind smile. "Of course, don't even worry about it," I tell him as I push up the sleeves of my work coveralls and make a list in my head of things I should add to my toolbox for this call.

Teo's eyes fix on the markings on my forearms, and I see them widen with shock and then confusion for a fraction of a second before he takes a deep inhale so he can scent me. I'm not all that surprised by his smelling me; I mean, I did the same thing when he walked in, but it's like my marks themselves triggered something within him, and not just general curiosity.

His brown eyes move to my hands as I set them on the front desk while I wait for him to tell me what he wants to do about his cars. His shocked gaze flicks up to mine, and he opens his mouth to say something when suddenly "Who Let the Dogs Out" starts playing from his front pocket.

He takes a moment to sort of snap out of whatever

stupor he's currently in, and then he quickly reaches into his pocket for the phone.

"Fucking twins," he mumbles as he swipes to answer.

"Yeah? . . . Shit. Where?" he asks, his face going hard.

I can hear someone on the other line answer, but I can't make out what they say.

"I was just speaking with the mechanic. No, it's fine, I'll meet you guys there. Hold on one sec," he tells whoever is on the phone, and then he looks back over to me. "Sorry, a work thing has come up. Can I come back later to make arrangements?"

"Of course, just text this number," I tell him as I hand him my card.

His eyes flit back to my marks, and then he backs up and turns for the door, bringing the phone back up to his ear.

"I'm on my way now. Is the Witch there? . . . No, but something weird just happened, and I think it's something we all need to look into."

The door shuts behind him, making the bell ring again. Well, that was weird. I turn my attention back to my laptop. Maybe I'll call Cassie and see what this dude and his pack are all about.

My skin prickles, and I can practically feel Pigeon on the brink of taking over. So I quickly put my parts order in and shut everything down. I lock the front door, double-checking that I actually got it this time, and flip off all the lights. I head to the back of the shop that now houses a gryphon-sized doggy door. It's basically a metal shutter I fabricated to cover the hole an impatient little chicken wing put there a couple weeks ago. I've rigged it to go up and down like a manual garage door, so it worked out fine. But Pidge and I had a little chat about patience.

I start to strip out of my coveralls, tank top, bra, and underwear, and before I can say *Pidge is a needy bitch*, she shoves her way out of me like it's Black Friday at Walmart and the doors just opened.

"Easy dude, I just finished that," I growl at her when she uses a little too much strength to open the metal door.

She gives me a sheepish shrug, which is about as close as I'll get to an apology from her, and we're leaping for the sky and pumping our wings as hard as we can, aiming for the colors that are just starting to streak across the horizon.

We live on the outskirts of a keep-to-yourself town that's more Supe than Non. I thank my lucky stars for that; otherwise, we wouldn't be able to do this. I sit back and enjoy the view as Pidge works through her feelings with barrel rolls and corkscrew dives. She soars and races the wind and screeches out a dominant cry, claiming the sky for her own.

I try not to feel sad that there's no one to answer her like there should be. I spend my days trying not to think about the *what if*s, but when I'm trapped in my own head while Pigeon is in control, it's hard not to. I'm not sure what happens to us if we can never get back. Sure, having jeans and underwear is not something I'm in a hurry to abandon, and fuck knows the food here is a million times better. I didn't realize how much I had missed working on cars and talking to people who get my jokes or swear like I do, but this place could never feel right, because it doesn't have them in it.

Pigeon sends me an image of Zeph trying to work the coffee maker, or Treno attempting to start the microwave, and I chuckle. This world would eat them alive. They'd probably try to fight cars, altogether thinking they were wild beasts, or yell at the TV because it wouldn't obey their commands.

Pidge soars on a current, and we relax into the cool air. I can smell snow on the air and see a blanket of white clouds in the distance. Unease crawls up my spine out of nowhere, and Pigeon and I both sit up and take notice. We rise up on a cross current, quietly and attentively scanning our surroundings. Something sets the both of us off, but neither one of us spots anything.

"Is it something on the ground?" I ask, and Pidge adjusts our angle so we can scan below us. We're so high up I doubt anyone would know what to make of us even if they could pick us out. We both stay vigilant, but when a couple more minutes go by and nothing appears around us, we start to relax again.

The sun dips further down, and a chill in the air starts to nip at us as the sunset paints purple, red, and orange streaks across the sky. We start to slowly glide back in the direction of the shop to fly around the cloud-crusted mountain that's just behind the town.

I get lost in my thoughts again, making plans to try and train more, to tow Teo's cars if it snows tonight, to order fried rice and wontons for dinner, when a shadow falls over us and there's a sudden shift in the air above us. I barely have time to think *what the fuck* before something slams into us. Pigeon screeches and twists to try to get a chunk of whatever the fuck this is, but as we maneuver ourselves around in midair, our gaze settles on honey-colored eyes, and a vicious roar blasts past us.

Zeph?

Elation and confusion war for the forefront of my thoughts. Is he here? But how is he here? Did Pigeon and I get struck by lightning, and this is all just some hallucination while we fall out of the sky, a half-roasted gryphon?

Pigeon shouts a surprised screech back, which is answered by a call behind us. I tear my eyes away from the sky shadow and see a gray and white gryphon charging right for us. Exhilaration streaks through Pigeon, and the next thing I know, she drops into a dive, excitement racing through her.

"Pigeon, what are you doing?" I scream at her, panicking that she'll lose Ryn and Zeph and we'll once again never find them.

I'm still not even sure that I'm not just imagining this. Pigeon shrieks a challenge and dives with all her might. I scream at her to stop, beg her to go back, explain that this isn't the time for games, but she won't listen. I spot the clearing behind our shop and the two males standing in it, and my heart once again lurches.

Treno.

Wekun's beside him, looking up at my missile-like advancement with a smile on his face.

He found us.

Pigeon lands with a skid that leaves tracks in the dirt and turns to look up at the sky.

"Pigeon, don't you fucking dare! You are not going to have gryphon sex before I'm allowed to find out what the hell is going on," and have my own sex, I tell her, leaving the last part out.

She flashes me the seagulls from *Finding Nemo* as they squawk "mine" over and over again, and incredulity shoots through me.

"They are my mates too, Pidge, you can't just do that. I thought we were a team?"

Satisfaction blooms through her, and I feel her recede. I look at her, confused, and she flashes me a GIF of Drake clapping at a basketball game, and the caption reads, "That's what I'm talking about." She pulls all the way back inside us, and I immediately take a running leap and wrap Wekun up in a massive hug.

"I fucking knew you would find me. Thank you! Thank you so fucking much."

I feel Zeph and Ryn land, and I pull out of Wekun's hold and leap at Treno.

"Are you real?" I ask, still not believing what my eyes can see and my hands can touch. "Are you here, please tell me you're here."

Tears stream down my face. And I push out of his hold and reach for Ryn when he steps up next to us. I wrap my arms around his neck and squeeze with everything in me.

"I'm so sorry. I got hungry, and I didn't want to wake you up. Cree was there... I didn't know she was going to send me back. I didn't leave you. I would never leave you," I hurriedly tell them, pushing out of Ryn's hold and leaping for Zeph.

No one is answering me, or maybe my heart and my mind are racing too fast to hear them if they are. Zeph looks pissed, but he always looks pissed. I jump for him anyway. I know he'll catch me. That he'll listen when I explain what happened, and vow to rip Cree's head off when we get back.

Zeph wraps me up in a hug as fierce as mine and buries his head where my neck meets my shoulder, inhaling deeply.

"I was terrified I'd never see you again," I confess against his neck, my emotions a complete wreck. I'm smiling and overflowing with joy as tears drip down my cheeks and sobs sit in my chest, waiting for their time.

Zeph pulls back, but he doesn't say anything; instead, his lips crash to mine and his kiss tells me everything I need to know.

He was scared too.

He missed me.

He's happy I'm in his arms again.

And now he's going to fuck me until neither one of us can move.

Finally!

26

I pull back, reluctantly ending my kiss with Zeph, and he growls irritably, not a big fan of the move either. But I'm not about to have the hottest sex ever in the cold backyard, so it had to be done. I push out of his arms, but grab his hand, while turning to reach for Ryn and Treno. I pull them all toward the shop at once.

Wekun chuckles and shakes his head. "Don't you even want to find out what happened?" he calls at my back as I practically drag my mates inside the building.

"Later," I shout over my shoulder, and I hear him bark out a laugh as the door shuts behind us.

I lead the guys up the stairs, so many questions racing through my mind, but I'm not going to get into all of that right now. I need to feel them, all of them. I need the reality of this to be cemented in my mind and stamped all over me. I need to miss them and love on them and be entirely consumed by them, and I need to do it right fucking now. We squeeze one by one through my front door, and these massive males dwarf my apartment in a very comical way. I have vaulted ceilings, but they're all fucking giants, so that doesn't really matter.

I would laugh and bust their balls and find out how the fuck they got here in the first place, but that will happen after. I take them down the hallway, and Zeph has to turn sideways for his shoulders to fit. I pull Zeph into the room, with Ryn and Treno following, and then I pause. Because as much as I'd like to be fucking and not talking, this next part, they get a say in.

Butterflies go mental in my stomach as I look at my hot as fuck mates. They're here, and I'm never again going to let these assholes out of my sight.

"We have not talked about this, and I don't know how you feel about it, but I can't choose just one of you right now. I need the three of you. I want the three of you. You won't hurt my feelings if that's not something you are okay with. You can just wait your turn then. But if you are—" Zeph cuts me off by picking me up and sucking on my lower lip.

Well, okay then.

He kisses me senseless and then hands me to Ryn, who does the exact same thing. Desire floods my pussy as Ryn hands me to Treno, and there's no hesitation when he claims my lips and winds his tongue with mine. A strong chest pushes against my back, and Zeph growls low in my ear. "We missed you, little sparrow."

I pull away from Treno's lips and manage to gasp out, "I missed all of you, so much," before Treno claims my mouth again hungrily. I've never been more grateful for the fact that we can't shift with clothes on as they all press in against me, and I feel their hard muscles and smooth warm skin against mine.

Treno transfers his hold on me to Zeph, but his lips never leave mine as I lean back against Zeph, who snakes an arm under one knee and wraps his muscular arm across my abdomen to hold me up. He brings his other hand around to my front and starts to play with my clit as Treno sucks on my tongue. I moan into his mouth and feel Zeph's lips kissing and sucking on my shoulder and neck.

Ryn grabs my chin and angles it toward him so he can claim my lips, and Treno drops down and moves that talented mouth to my breasts. Delicious pleasure floods my senses, and I moan and writhe, my body asking for more, while Pigeon claps in the background of my mind.

Zeph stops slowly circling my clit, and everything gets infinitely hotter as he holds me up with one hand and reaches between my thighs from behind and plunges two fingers deep inside of me. My pussy squelches in appreciation as he starts finger fucking me, and I pull away from Ryn's lips so I can throw my head back and cry out.

Treno drops to his knees, and his mouth goes straight for my clit, and I know what's coming...the vibrating tongue thingy. Like they're a well-choreographed sex machine, Ryn sucks a nipple into his mouth and pinches the other hard, just as Treno starts the tongue vibrating thingy and Zeph fingers me even faster.

I turn into one giant orgasm exactly seven seconds later.

My release hits me so hard and so fast that I can't say I had an orgasm, because that bitch had me. It had me so hard I didn't know if I wanted to scream, cry, or beg for more. So I did this weird combo of all three, which was not a sexy as fuck noise, but I gave no fucks. I screamed so hard you would have thought I was serving a ball at Wimbledon.

Treno pulls Zeph's fingers out of me, and then he licks me from opening to clit like I'm an ice cream cone. And I almost come again just from watching it. I immediately want his cock down my throat so bad, because any man who can lick a woman like that deserves to come down a woman's throat, and I'm in.

So. Fucking. In.

"My turn," Ryn calls out, and Treno automatically takes

one last lick and steps back. He licks his lips like every last drop is fucking ambrosia, but I can't focus on that because the next thing I know, Zeph's fingers are back to working my pussy, and Ryn is doing the vibrating tongue thingy.

"Fuck!" I cry out. I'm so sensitive, but it also feels so fucking good.

I reach behind me and thread my fingers through Zeph's wavy black hair, and I tilt my hips just a little so he and Ryn can hit all the right spots. I explode into ecstasy again. And Zeph bites my shoulder hard as he pulls his fingers out of me and Ryn licks me up. He sucks on my clit again and then shoves his long tongue inside of me and swirls it around.

Zeph takes his slick fingers and starts circling my ass, applying pressure and lubing me up with my own release as he plays. One finger breaches me slowly, and I moan at the feel of him.

"Can you take a male here, little sparrow?" he asks me, his voice dipped in hunger and dripping need.

"If I'm wet enough, I can."

"Well, let's get you wetter then."

Like somehow Zeph just gave a command, Ryn's tongue starts to vibrate again as he licks me up and down. He's like a next level sex toy, and not to be left out, Treno starts to vibrate his tongue and then flick my nipples with it.

"Mmmm, I can feel you dripping," Zeph growls in my ear as the finger in my ass is slowly joined by another. He moves in and out of me and twirls his fingers in wider and wider circles as he takes his time and stretches me out. "Are you ready for us, little sparrow? Are you ready for your mates?" he asks me as he sucks on my neck and nips at my shoulders.

"Yes! Please!" I beg, more than ready to feel them all under and over and inside of me.

"Good, because I'm ready for you," he declares, grabbing

273

my chin until I'm leaning back far enough for him to own my mouth. His lips sear themselves to mine, and his tongue laps me up. Another orgasm crashes through me, and he happily swallows it down. Treno and Ryn step away from my flushed and well-sated body, and once again in turn, each kisses me deeply before we move to the bed.

Zeph surprises me by lying down on the bed on his back. But it's a pleasant surprise. He's the only one I haven't physically reconnected with since we all decided to take this mate thing seriously, and something about looking into his honey-hued eyes while we come feels significant. The fact that he's even here, willing to share and be part of the group that makes up our mating is huge, and I straddle his cock and slowly take him in inch by inch. I know being mated to Zeph isn't always going to be easy, but, fuck, it will be magical and exactly what I need.

Zeph leans up and kisses me as I start to ride him, and it's as though he wants to drink all my pleasure down, to savor me and treasure me in his own way. I tighten my pussy around him on purpose and then force the muscles to flutter, and he groans and lies back down, ready for when it's his turn to set the pace.

Treno moves onto the bed to my left on his knees, and I smile up at him as I work Zeph in and out of me. He bends forward to kiss me, and I have to pull away when the need to pant starts to take over.

"I'm never letting you out of my sight again, flower," he confesses, and I stare deeply into his blue and purple gaze and agree, "Never."

"You're ours," he declares, and I pant out an "always" as I lean over and grip his hard cock and lick it from base to tip, like he did me.

He groans, and I waste no time wrapping my lips around his head and pulling him deep into my throat. It takes a minute to get the rhythm of fucking Zeph and sucking on Treno at the same time, but I get there, and their answering groans to my moans spur me on.

I swallow Treno down and take him as deep as I can go, and then I go still when I feel Ryn caress down my back and then slap my ass hard. I gasp and quickly pull off Treno so I don't choke. I look behind me with a playful glare.

"She likes it—she's clamped down on me so hard I'm trying not to come."

Ryn laughs as I turn my glare to Zeph, but he just reaches up and palms my breasts as Ryn slowly works himself into my ass. I'm getting the distinct impression that group sex amongst Gryphons is not as taboo as it is amongst humans. None of them seem squeamish at all about sharing or seeing each other. In fact, they all work really well together in a very complementary way I did not see coming.

I wonder how many threesomes and foursomes these guys have been to, but I immediately dismiss that thought. I don't need to know the details, I just need to reap the benefits.

Ryn grunts as his hips push against my ass cheeks, and I suck Treno back into my mouth and wing five Pigeon for my amazing sexual prowess. Zeph and Ryn both start to fuck me at the same time. And then Treno threads his fingers through my hair and starts to fuck my mouth. I float on a cloud of bliss as each of my mates thrusts in and out of me, our bodies singing with pleasure as they slap together at different harmonious rhythms, our moans filling the room with heat and passion.

We fuck and stake our claim on each other, branding our bonds and renewing the intimacy of our connections. Vulnerability and strength, commitment and love, wrap around us as we all take what we need from each other while also giving all that we have.

I don't know how they're here, but the why has never been so clear. We were meant for each other, and this moment seals our bond forever.

Treno stills deep down my throat, the first to find his release. I swallow him down as he grinds against my mouth, and then I pull back and lick him clean, savoring his desire. He falls back on the bed on his back, and Ryn and Zeph hold nothing back as they both set an explosive pace. They feel so fucking good, and I know I'm seconds away from another orgasm that knocks through me while shouting, "Say my name, bitch" at me.

"Yes," I pant as I get closer, and Ryn buries himself deep in my ass and grunts out his release. Zeph pauses for a moment as his friend rides out his orgasm and nips at my back, and then Ryn is pulling out and collapsing onto the other side of the bed, a blissed out smile on his face.

I chuckle and then squeal as Zeph flips me over onto my back and sucks on my nipples as he starts a slow rhythm once again. I groan and spread even wider for him; he knows what I want, but he's going to toy with me. I can see it in his eyes. He splays a strong hand at the small of my back and tilts my hips up as he picks up his pace.

"Mmmm, that's a sweet spot, isn't it, little sparrow?" he purrs, and I cry out in answer.

"Are you mine, Falon?" he asks me as he starts to move even faster, and the lack of my nickname on his lips gives me pause.

I stare up into his golden honey eyes and, without doubt or hesitation, answer, "I'm yours, Zeph, and I always will be."

He smiles, and it shatters my heart into a million pieces and then puts it back together, it's so stunning.

"Good," he tells me. "Now scream my name," he orders.

It's my turn to smile now, because there's my asshole. "Make me," I growl in challenge, and then he does.

He fucks me so hard and mercilessly, exactly how he knows I love it, and I have no choice but to scream his name.

And then I scream Treno's and Ryn's too for good measure, because no motherfucker should be allowed to be *that* cocky. I smile at that thought, and my heart warms with affection. I have to keep him grounded.

* * *

"What do you mean, you just couldn't see us anymore?" I ask Wekun, reaching for my coffee that's just a little too far for me to get.

Zeph snags it off the table, takes a sip, and then hands it to me. I glare at him for the sip and then offer my lips for a peck for handing it to me. He chuckles deeply and gives me my peck but tries to steal my mug again. I hold it away, and he pretends like it's out of reach even though we know his wingspan is like the size of my living room.

"Exactly that. I was helping portal gryphons and supplies back to the Amaranthine Mountains when all of a sudden you were gone. And not just you, your whole Sept. I immediately panicked and portalled home to double-check that something hadn't happened to the threads, but I couldn't see them there either," Wekun tells me, clearly distraught.

I sip my coffee and lean back against Treno's chest in thought. The guys have stayed true to their word, they haven't even put me down, let alone let me out of their sight. We've reached a very comfortable "pee in front of each other" level in our relationship, but you won't see me complaining. Even Pigeon worked out some gryphon sexual tension last night. I'm pretty sure Ryn's gryphon is a little traumatized, but Pidge assures me he'll be begging for more in no time.

"I *did* speak with Getta in Tierit, and she mentioned that she has seen it happen to a Bond Weaver in the past and that it occurred because the threads directly affected that Bond Weaver. That's when I returned to the other world to figure out what could have made them blink out in the first place and discovered that you were missing."

"We looked everywhere for you. We were certain that maybe the Ouphe took you or a group of Gryphons acted out. We knew you were alive because we were, but there were no leads, and we spent months chasing our tails," Ryn tells me.

I ache at the thought of what it must have been like to wake up and find out I was just gone. Treno must feel my distress, because he starts to rub soothing circles on my thigh.

"It was Zeph who brought up that maybe you weren't in their world anymore," Wekun adds.

I look over at Zeph curiously, my eyebrow raised in surprise. "You always come to me in your dreams," he tells me, and goose bumps crawl up my arms. "I knew you would have been trying to get to us, and I kept searching for reasons that would explain why you couldn't. I knew there was a gate in the Amaranthine Mountains. We couldn't find it, but the thought that maybe you were not in our world wouldn't leave me."

I thread my fingers through his and squeeze his hand, my gaze filling with warmth and gratitude. He never doubted me. I was so worried that they would think I abandoned them or left without caring about what it would do to them. I wouldn't have blamed them if they did. After I tried to sever the bonds, it wouldn't have been a farfetched thought. But they never doubted, and that fact means more to me than I can say.

"So how did you three decide to come here?" I ask, looking to each of them in turn.

"That was my doing," Wekun chimes in. "I couldn't see you or feel you anymore, but I was hoping that if I brought them to this world, and you were in fact here, maybe *they* could. Our ending up here was an odd coincidence though. I was on my way to meet with friends I was hoping could help, when your mates felt you."

I close my eyes and let the gratitude I feel wash over me. "Thank you, Wekun, I don't know how I'll ever repay you, but I owe you everything," I confess as I open my eyes and fix them on his champagne-colored gaze.

"*We* owe you everything," Treno and Zeph correct at the same time, and I try not to chuckle and point out that their bromance is blossoming into a beautiful thing.

"Well, I was hoping I could ask for your help in trying to figure out what I'm being blocked from seeing. The only thing that I can think is that I'm in danger for some reason, and your Sept is tangled up in it all in some way. I know you're in a hurry to get back and strangle Cree with her own innards, but I was hoping you'd stick around for a while."

I look to the guys in an effort to gauge their reactions.

"If you need help, we are here for you," Zeph states simply.

"It's the least we could do after all that you've done for us," Treno adds.

"I like pizuus, so if we can have more of that, I'm in," Ryn teases.

I laugh. "Pizza," I correct, saying it slowly.

"I know, that's what I said," he replies, confused.

I crack up—oh man, this is going to be so much fun.

My text alert chimes, and all three of the guys stare at my phone warily. *Oh yeah, so much fucking fun.*

I open my messages to see I have a new one from an unknown number.

Hello Falon, this is Teo. I'd like to come by and make arrangements for our cars. Let me know what time works for you, and my pack and I will stop by. I think there might be some other things we should all discuss.

I read the message a second time and then shoot off a reply. I'm not sure what he thinks I'd want to discuss with his pack, but whatever, a job's a job.

Hi Teo, I'm available whenever. Text when you get to the shop and I'll meet you.

My phone chimes immediately.

We'll be there in thirty.

I get to my feet. "I have some work that needs to be done, so I'm just going to hop in the shower. Do you guys need anything? More food? Coffee?"

Ryn, Treno, and Zeph all get to their feet, and I start shaking my head. "No, you guys cannot come in this time. I need to be dry and presentable in twenty minutes," I warn them.

"I can work with that," Treno declares salaciously.

"How long is a minute again?" Ryn asks, and I bark out a laugh and hold up an angry *this is not happening* finger.

"I'm serious," I tell them, and then I leap over the back of the couch and sprint for the bathroom. If I can get the door locked and myself clean without any orgasms, it will be a miracle. Can I get an amen!

27

"Shit, I'm fucking late," I growl as I pull the wifebeater over my head and thread my arms through it. I pull on a mustard yellow slouchy sweater over it and fluff my just-dried hair.

I pretty much have an orgasm every time I use conditioner now, which really makes things difficult when I'm trying hard to get in and out of the shower quickly. It also doesn't help when your mates break down the door and proceed to try and give you more orgasms. What can I say, I'm a weak woman.

Speaking of asshole mates, they all tromp down the stairs behind me in sweats that aren't nearly long enough for their incredibly tall legs, and shirts that are way too tight. But I figure my new potential client and his pack will prefer that over them being naked, so here we are. I make my way to the front of the shop and look out the window to see eight coat-clad bodies. I look around at my front lobby area, which is currently being dwarfed by my massive gryphon mates, and decide to conduct whatever this meeting is in the two garage bays I have open. I go through the side door, a chill running up my spine at the drop in temperature from the well-insulated lobby to the garage.

"Is this a cahh?" Treno asks, rubbing a hand over the metal hood of the Seaman SUV.

I smile, remembering the first time he said *car* like he was from Boston on our little picnic back in Kestrel. It's crazy to think about how much has happened and that they're even here in my world, touching things I never thought they'd see.

"It is. We call that a Toyota Highlander," I tell him over my shoulder as I rush to press the button that opens the bay doors.

Treno, Ryn, and Zeph all seem to be distracted for a moment, feeling up Mrs. Seaman's SUV. A smile sneaks over my face, and I quickly make a list of all the other weird things I'm sure they'd be fascinated by in this world.

Snow spills in as the bay door creaks and groans in protest of being forced to work in these temperatures, and I add it to my list of things I need to look at and possibly oil. The door finally crawls high enough for Teo and his pack to slip in, and as soon as it seems the bodies have stopped slipping into the bay, I reverse its trajectory, blocking out the brittle wind that seems intent on helping us freeze to death.

"Sorry about the cold," I offer Teo. "My lobby isn't that big, and I figured a group this size might want a little more space."

I feel Zeph, Ryn, and Treno walk up behind me, and one by one the eyes widen in Teo's pack as they take in the giants behind me.

"By the stars, and I thought you were big, Knox," a male says with wavy brown hair that's pulled back in a man bun. He's good looking, and his hazel eyes seem to scan up and up and up behind me.

"Did they bottle feed them Human Growth Hormone since birth?" the hazel-eyed male asks, and the male next to him chuckles.

I realize they're twins—apparently, you put a beanie on one and it takes my brain a while to see that they look exactly alike. In addition to Teo and the twins, there's five more people: a guy with medium brown hair and bright blue eyes, a bigger dude who must be the Knox guy one of the twins was talking about. He's mixed and looking a little tense. A guy with shoulder-length blond hair and sky blue eyes. Another serious looking man with a square jaw and perfectly quaffed hair. I see a hint of a tattoo peeking out between his coat sleeve and his gloves. And last but not least, the only female in the group. She has dark hair, light green eyes, lips that people pay good money for—although you can tell her pout isn't enhanced—and a solid *fuck with me at your own risk* kind of vibe.

They're my age and all incredibly attractive, but I still don't have the foggiest clue why this wolf shifter thinks I should talk to his pack.

Teo steps forward, his brown eyes darting to the female and then back to me. "Falon, this is Bastien and Valen," he says, pointing to the twins. "Ryker and Sabin." The blond and the pretty boy with the tattoos both nod. "Siah and Knox." Blue eyes and tough guy just stand there. "And this is my mate, Vinna."

Her name sparks recognition for some reason, and I quickly try to sift through my memories for where I've heard it before. Her light green eyes are fixed on my hands like Teo's were when I first met him, and something about that is prickling through me as important.

They're all staring at me expectantly, and I abandon my memory search for politeness.

"I'm Falon, for those of you who I haven't met. This is Ryn, Treno, and Zeph," I introduce, pointing behind me.

"Are you all from here?" I think Sabin asks, or maybe his name is Ryker.

Crap.

"Uhhh, no. I grew up here, they didn't," I answer politely, and he nods once.

I get the distinct impression that I'm missing something. It's not a feeling I enjoy.

"Soo, what's up? I mean, your pack seems...great and all, but you could have just told me if you wanted your cars towed in a text, so why are all of you here?" I ask, cutting to the chase.

The female steps forward, her eyes jumping from me to my mates and back, like she's sizing them up. I take her in warily, tapping into my core on instinct, just in case this meeting somehow goes south.

"Have you ever heard of the term *Sentinel* before?" she asks me, her nostrils flaring like she's scenting the air for my answer.

It's a very wolf thing to do, but when I also take a deep breath, in an effort to figure out what's going on, I realize she's not a wolf. She has hints of a floral scent, but it has a citrusy base, the tang of caster magic, an earthy tone like the wolf shifters do, and a cool scent that smells slightly metallic that I can't quite place. I have no idea what she is. Caution weaves through me at her question.

How does this chick know that term?

Zeph releases a deep growl behind me, and everyone in the room tenses.

I narrow my eyes. "Who are you, and what do you want?" I ask evenly.

Maybe my looking around and asking about Sentinels

and the Ouphe flushed out whoever these people are, but I can't tell if they're friend or foe.

"I'm getting cold, and honestly I could really go for a taco, so if we can just speed up whatever the fuck this is, that'd be great," I add, feeling antsy, and an amused smile breaks over the female's lips.

She carefully starts pulling off her glove and then shoves the sleeve of her coat up to her elbow. She holds her hand up, palm in, and I trace the marks on her fingers with surprised eyes. She rotates her arm to the side, and I see a full line of runes that run up the outside of her forearm.

Well, damn. I didn't see that coming.

I stare at her marks on her ring finger. They stretch down past her knuckle, and she has different runes on her middle finger. My eyes snap to hers, and they're filled with intrigue and curiosity while her lips are turned up in a knowing smirk.

I breathe her in again, focusing on the undertones of what I think are jasmine and orange in her scent, and realize what that means in connection with her markings. She *is* like me. Not in the Gryphon sense, but in the Ouphe sense —or Sentinels, as they go by in this world.

Shock and excitement filter through my dumbfounded thoughts. I was looking for information about Sentinels or the Ouphe so I could figure out how to get back to my mates. But now they're here, and another Sentinel, one like me, is standing in the bay of my garage. I don't even know how to begin to process this.

What does this mean?

I pull my sweater off over my head and expose the markings on my arms and chest. Her eyes widen for a fraction of a second before she schools her features.

"She's about as marked as you, from what I can tell," one of the twins observes, and we all just sort of stare at each other for a moment as though none of us knows exactly where to go from here.

I hear footsteps clomping down the stairs in the back of the shop, and Wekun waltzes into the garage, fixing the sleeves of his sweater as he announces, "Falon, I'm going to pop over to see—"

"You!" Knox accuses aggressively, and Wekun's head snaps up in surprise at the snarl.

Wekun throws up his hands in defeat and rolls his eyes. "Always with the mate hate," he grumbles incredulously.

"Wekun?" the female asks, confused, but it's clear she knows him.

My eyes snap from Wekun back to...fuck, what was her name again...I blank for a second, and then it comes to me.

Vinna. Right. And with her and Wekun in the same place, I finally make the connection.

Oh shit, so this is Vinna? This is who he was here to check on?

"You're here!" Wekun chirps in surprise and then shakes his head in frustration. "This whole not seeing things is getting old," he grumbles and then turns happy eyes back on Vinna. "I was just going to see if you were at your hotel. Did Aydin tell you I was coming?"

Vinna's brow furrows in question for a moment and then lifts back up in understanding. She reaches into her pocket and pulls out a phone, glances at the screen quickly, and then chuckles. "Yes, he did. Sorry, I never check this thing," she confesses, and a couple of the guys around her snicker. "What's going on? Are they from Tierit?" she asks, nodding in my direction.

"No, she just learned about all of that like you did," he answers, and her eyes once again widen in shock.

Mine do too. Wekun has mentioned Vinna a couple of times in the past. I had no idea who he was talking about

286

though, and I assumed it was a friend back home. So it surprises me a little to hear that she's as new to this whole Sentinel thing as I am. Did she also wake up in a strange world, with her life fucked up beyond all recognition?

"What's going on, Wekun?" she demands, confusion and concern etching themselves into her features.

Wekun takes a deep breath, but his eyes light up with excitement. It makes me chuckle a little when Vinna suddenly regards him even more warily, as though Wekun's excitement is something that people should be cautious about.

"You two are part of the same Sept," Wekun answers and then pauses dramatically like he's waiting for her to start jumping up and down while she asks *really!*

I look from Wekun back to Vinna and decide he's barking up the wrong tree; she doesn't look like a bouncy, squealy kind of girl.

"What does that mean?" Teo asks.

"It's like a coven, only it's something that only Bond Wielders have."

"But I have a coven," Vinna declares, gesturing to the males all around her.

"No, you have Chosen, just like Falon does," Wekun corrects.

"Chosen?" I interject, confused. I haven't heard that term before.

"Your mates," Wekun quickly points out.

Oh. Okay.

"You both have Chosen, which is who you share magic and abilities with, but separate from that, you have a Sept. You all carry the same rune, which will start to work when the Sept is complete. It'll connect you to each other in a very powerful way."

"But not in a mate kind of way, right?" I ask as I try to

think back about what Wekun said about Septs before. "Because, you're hot and all," I tell Vinna, "...but that's not my thing."

"Ditto," Vinna agrees. "No offence," she offers me.

"None taken," I reply.

Wekun releases a deep breath. "Why does everything have to be about fucking?" he asks rhetorically, looking from me to Vinna.

"TGV Forevahh," she answers simply with a shrug, and all the guys with her chuckle.

Their reactions confirm what my nose has me suspecting already, and I turn to Vinna with an impressed smirk on my face. "All these guys are your mates?"

She smiles and gives them a warm look before turning back to me. "They sure are."

"Fuck, and I thought three was a handful," I mumble, looking back at my guys.

"That guy's like easily two and a half Chosen's worth," she tells me, pointing at Zeph over my shoulder. "Yeah, the grumpy looking one," Vinna confirms as I look behind me.

I snort out a laugh at her description.

"Sorry, I'm not the best with names," she confesses with a sheepish shrug.

I smile at Zeph, who just raises an unamused eyebrow at me, and wave her off. "No worries, *the grumpy looking one* is accurate."

We both chuckle, and then I feel hands on my face, coaxing me to tilt my head back. Zeph looks down at me and shakes his head. "I'll show you grumpy," he whispers in my ear, and it does all kinds of things to my body. I smile, and he plants a quick kiss on my lips before letting go of my head. I drop my chin back down, and Vinna looks perplexed as she rubs at the underside of her chin.

288

She then tilts her own head back, flashing me a peek of an identical rune under her chin.

"That's your Sept rune," Wekun tells her, answering the questions in her gaze.

"Oh," she chirps, shocked, and then her shoulders relax a little like she's relieved. "I thought it might be something else," she confesses, and all at once her guys move closer to her, like they're all magnets responding to her pull.

I watch as each of them discreetly reaches out to touch her and soothe her in some small way. I realize that they all just responded to whatever intense emotion Vinna was just feeling, and I'm completely captivated by the way they seem to ground her and calm her. She relaxes right before my eyes, simply from their presence and the small intimate things they're doing to fortify her soul.

I don't know her, although I think that's definitely going to change based on our Sept runes, but it's a beautiful thing to watch her be loved as deeply as she clearly is. Vinna gives her mates a grateful smile and leans into all of them, and I can practically see the soul-deep connections that link all of them.

"Well, now that we've gotten introductions out of the way, I'm hoping you both can help me," Wekun starts, pulling me from my observations.

Vinna stands up a little straighter, confidence pushing the vulnerability out of her light green eyes.

"We're here on a job already, but what's going on?" she asks.

"I think the two might actually be related," Wekun supplies cryptically, and it's clear Vinna doesn't know what he's saying either.

"Aydin said you're here about missing wolves, right?"

"Right," Vinna agrees.

"Well, I think the third member of your Sept might be

one of them," Wekun announces, and shock filters through both me and Vinna.

A third member of our Sept?

I'm not even sure how I feel about having a Sept to begin with, let alone *surprise, here's two members of it*. Wekun clears his throat, and I can tell just by the sound of it that he's not done dropping bombs.

"I think she's in trouble, and we need to find her...fast."

Called it.

Zeph pulls me back against him. Treno places a comforting hand on my shoulder, and Ryn reaches out and laces his fingers with mine. I look back at each of them in turn. I know we said we'd help Wekun, but I'm not sure if the development of Vinna and her mates changes anything for the guys.

Treno leans down and kisses me in answer to the question written all over my face. "Whatever you want to do, flower, we're here."

Ryn nods once and kisses me sweetly next. "Still not letting you out of our sight though," he teases as he nips my bottom lip.

I turn to Zeph, and he runs his thumb gently over my cheek as he studies me. "You know I'm always up for a good fight, little sparrow," he purrs and kisses the end of my nose. I chuckle and nod.

"Don't I know it," I snark, and he leans down and bites my shoulder, a smile on his lips.

Adoration and happiness waft through me. Pigeon does a little dance inside of me, and I giggle at her ridiculous antics. She's clearly up for more shenanigans, although that's not surprising at all.

Bliss radiates through me as I take a deep breath. It truly is a beautiful thing to be loved so deeply...I'm one lucky Ouphe-Gryphon. Or I guess I should say Sentinel-Gryphon.

Ouphon? Gryphinel? I shake my head at myself, I'll have to work on a cooler sounding name later.

My eyes land on Vinna's, she nods, and I answer with a smile.

Looks like we're going Sept hunting.

The End...

I KNOW!!! I KNOW!!!!!

You're like what the ever loving fuck, Ivy?!?! I get it. I promise I do, but fear not, I got you. The Sentinel World is building, and there are answers to the questions you have right now and soooo much more coming. Trust me, I have a plan, and it's going to be epic!!! Love you!!! Thank you for reading, reviewing, and for all of the support!!! Tackle hugs!!!

Join my Reader Group and follow me on Instagram and BookBub for updates on The Sentinel World and upcoming releases!!!

ALSO BY IVY ASHER

Book 2 coming soon

Shifter Romantic Comedy Standalone

Conveniently Convicted

Dystopian Romantic Comedy Standalone

April's Fools

IVY ASHER

Ivy Asher is addicted to chai, swearing, and laughing a lot—but not in a creepy, laughing alone kind of way. She loves the snow, books, and her family of two humans, and three fur-babies. She has worlds and characters just floating around in her head, and she's lucky enough to be surrounded by amazing people who support that kind of crazy.

Join Ivy Asher's Reader Group and follow her on Instagram and BookBub for updates on your favorite series and upcoming releases!!!

facebook.com/IvyAsherBooks

instagram.com/ivy.asher

bookbub.com/profile/ivy-asher

amazon.com/author/ivyasher